"I understand you wish to marry for love only," the duke said.

He cleared his throat. "However, it seems that our union could also be construed as for something near to that principle—your love for your soon-to-be impoverished family, my love for my niece."

Sophia turned to him. Their gazes met. "But will you make a good husband, Your Grace? Can I trust you?"

Edmund wanted to reassure her, but he was suddenly assailed by memories, by experiences he had never spoken of and by a terrible, fearful certainty that he could never be a good husband.

"Edmund," said Sophia. "I do not ask for perfection."

"I have never been a husband. But I would do my best."

"We must have parameters if we are to do this." Her gaze flashed upward. "Here is the gist of it, Your Grace. I shall marry you, but under two conditions."

He waited, holding his breath.

Jessica Nelson believes romance happens every day, and thinks the greatest, most intense romance comes from a God who woos people to Himself with passionate tenderness. When Jessica is not cleaning up after her teenagers, she can be found staring into space as she plots her next story. Or she might be daydreaming about a raspberry mocha from Starbucks. Or thinking about what kind of chocolate she should have for dinner that night. She could be thinking of any number of things, really. One thing is for certain, she is blessed with a wonderful family and a lovely life.

Books by Jessica Nelson

Love Inspired Historical

An Unlikely Duchess

JESSICA NELSON

LOVE INSPIRED
INSPIRATIONAL ROMANCE

LOVE INSPIRED®
INSPIRATIONAL ROMANCE

Recycling programs
for this product may
not exist in your area.

ISBN-13: 978-1-335-41890-6

An Unlikely Duchess

This edition published by arrangement with Harlequin Books S.A.

For questions and comments about the quality of this book, please contact us at CustomerService@Harlequin.com.

Love Inspired
22 Adelaide St. West, 41st Floor
Toronto, Ontario M5H 4E3, Canada
www.LoveInspired.com

Printed in U.S.A.

I will sing of the mercies of the Lord for ever:
with my mouth will I make known thy faithfulness
to all generations.
—*Psalm 89:1*

So much love to Curtis Hamm, Anita Howard and Ane Ryan-Walker for your help in fleshing out *An Unlikely Duchess*. This story is stronger because of your ideas, thoughts and input. Also, I'm so thankful to God and His redemptive love and faithfulness in my life.

Chapter One

Perhaps it was a foolish notion, but Sophia Seymour felt very firmly indeed that one should never marry for anything but love.

Which is why she refused to ever marry again.

She plopped a thick dollop of cream on her roll, chuckling at her mother's intermittent gasps at the other side of the kitchen table as she read aloud the engagement announcements.

"Dear hearts, listen to this." Lady Worland shivered with unsuppressed excitement, her fan swishing through the air in choppy strokes. "A duke is to take a wife."

"That's an engagement announcement?" Sophia asked, surprised.

"I've moved on to the gossip."

Every Monday morning, Sophia joined her family at their little townhome in Mayfair for breakfast. And every Monday, she learned something that she really could have gone without knowing. Family was family, though, and she would do anything for them.

Even suffer through gossip.

"Which duke, Momma?" asked Frederika, Sophia's youngest sister.

"The one called *the Beast of London*."

Sophia grimaced at the unkind moniker.

"Why is it said he's taking a wife?" Frederika pressed.

Mother squinted more closely at the paper. She refused to wear spectacles, even at home. "The speculation is due to his recent appearances at balls and the like."

"But his name is not specified?" Frederika's tone held a note of skepticism.

"The writer merely calls him a shadowy figure surrounded by lies." Eliza, the middlest, sighed deeply as she cupped her chin. "I spotted him once while riding in Hyde Park. He is utterly ferocious, with skin the color of bronze, and eyes as black as a pirate's heart."

Mother gasped. "A pirate's heart? I beg you, Eliza, do keep rein on your tongue or you'll make us a laughingstock."

"We already are," muttered Frederika.

"There are no rumors afoot yet," Sophia told her sister. Her presence in society guaranteed she would quickly find out if there were.

"Frederika's attitude and Eliza's tongue shall be the ruin of us. Mark my words." Mother harrumphed, her fan increasing speed. "To think of all I've done to keep you girls out of these papers." Mother scooped up her gossip rag, waving it in the air. "Nothing says ingratitude more than that scowl on Frederika's face."

Sophia snuck a look and almost choked on laughter. Frederika made a most fierce expression when arguing.

Her brows, thicker than fashionable, managed to form an impressive V shape above her strong nose.

"I realize we had high aspirations," Mother continued, "and that life did not proceed as we foresaw, but we must keep hope. If this reclusive and, from what I've heard, *difficult* duke can take a wife, then surely I will find each of you a husband. We are not ruined yet, ladies. And I intend to keep this family functioning in the traditional fashion. Your father will return any day to find his daughters betrothed and happy, and he shall fix everything."

At that point, her mother's voice broke a little, and a pang of sympathy rolled through Sophia.

"Even Sophia?" asked Eliza.

"I do not need fixing." Sophia shot her sister a firm look.

"Of course, you don't." Eliza's face fell. "I meant no such thing. But you are only five and twenty. Will you remarry? Will you seek to love again?"

A hard, painful lump grew in her windpipe. "Any hope I had for a husband died with Charles."

"Pish posh." Mother rapped the table with her fan, startling Sophia. "You were one of the most delightful debutantes of this decade, and you shall emerge again, a rose among thorns. Seven years a widow, and your reputation is still spotless. Even Almack's will never refuse you."

"How inspiring," Sophia muttered, half amused, half horrified. She ignored the deep ache in her chest that her mother had bruised with her vehement words.

"You were a lovely bride. I hope to be half as so." Eliza propped her face against her hands, her china-blue eyes sparkling and her cheeks a bashful pink. "When shall I have a Season?"

"Soon." Mother frowned, setting down her teacup. "Your father's office is a dreadful mess. I have contacted our solicitor and should hear from him soon as to the state of our finances." Her voice trembled then. "How I miss your father's joviality."

"He will return," Eliza ventured carefully.

If he didn't return soon, society might notice his absence and then the gossip would begin. Thus far they'd managed to keep his being missing a secret. As far as London knew, Lord Worland had remained at his country estate for business reasons.

"Of course, he shall." Frederika glared at her sister. "And of returns, let us speak of this duke. This Rennington. He is betrothed. To whom?"

"It has not been confirmed to be Rennington. And no one knows to whom." Eliza leaned forward, excitement deepening the color in her cheeks. "Ten years ago, the heir to the Duke of Rennington was murdered alongside his wife. Some said his younger brother Edmund did away with them to gain the dukedom. He is seen once or twice a year due to his duties in London, but his demeanor has been so angry and terrible that society dubbed him the Beast of London."

Mother *tsked*.

Eliza nodded. "Edmund has no family at all. His mother passed when he was young, his father never remarried, and then the duke himself died."

A knock sounded at the front door. They all paused, tension filling the air as they waited for Andrews to answer the call.

Within minutes, their butler appeared in the doorway, his cravat a crisp white to match his stately air.

"My lady, a Mr. Butterfield is here on a most important matter."

Mother shot upward, rattling the table in her haste. Sophia steadied her glass, watching her mother closely. "The solicitor. Yes, I shall see him at once. Show him to the drawing room. No, no the office. Oh!" She fluttered her fan. "The office is a dreadful mess."

"The drawing room will do." Sophia stood, touching her mother on the shoulder. "Shall I ring for tea?"

"Yes." Mother gathered herself and bustled after Andrews.

Eliza's eyes were wide. "Is he the one who can tell us the state of our finances?"

Sophia nodded, her own pulse flickering in her throat. Her family did not like to speak of their declining purses, and Sophia had tried to help with the small pittance she had been left as a widow. On her advice, her mother had sought out their solicitor for answers. Their staff were waiting for pay. Sophia had quietly noted the bare pantry and that the household was down two servants. There were some missing vases…she suspected Mother had secretly sold them.

The situation grew more serious by the day.

Frederika leaned forward toward Sophia. "Did you procure the detective from Bow Street?"

Sophia shook her head. "Not yet. Have either of you heard any news?"

"It's as though Father disappeared like mist." Eliza frowned deeply.

Before the sisters could discuss the situation more, a scream sliced through the house. They stumbled upward, rushing the door. Sophia was the first one out. She dashed down the long hall of the townhome, toward the drawing room.

She found her mother on the floor in a heap of petticoats and lace. Mr. Butterfield, the solicitor, knelt in front of her. He looked up. "Smelling salts?"

"Yes." She located the bottle Mother kept in a drawer nearby and then joined him, kneeling down and waving the salts beneath her mother's nose.

Lady Worland came to quickly. They helped her to her feet, situating her on the settee. She began dabbing at her cheeks while they looked on.

"I did not mean to startle you, my lady," said Mr. Butterfield. The poor man looked a fright, his hair askew and eyeglasses crooked.

"It is quite all right." Sophia gestured for her sisters to sit with their mother. Lady Worland had an unnatural propensity toward faints. Sophia secretly suspected Mother's corset was laced too tight, but when she proffered that suggestion, her mother had suffered a spell. "Is there anything more to be said here?"

"Not at this time. I shall be back later in the week to discuss any new findings." Mr. Butterfield, a little too eagerly, made for the door.

His words sounded ominous. Sophia was tempted to follow him and demand more information, but Mother's sobs were increasing in tempo. She took a deep breath, steeling herself against the loudness of the sound. Then she knelt in front of her mother, careful to keep her face neutral despite her mother's cries. "What is it? Please. Tell us."

Mother heaved a gaping, shuddering breath. She

pressed her lace kerchief to her eyes. "It is reprehensible that he never told me."

Sophia met her sisters' worried looks above their mother's head. Concern hollowed a pit in her stomach, whittling at the peace she'd managed to rebuild in the years since her husband died.

"Told you what?" she managed to say in a calm, unaffected voice.

"Oh, my darling. It is in writing."

"What is in writing?"

"Dear heart, firstborn of my womb. Your father had great plans for you. He was such a dreamer." She sniffled again, then met Sophia's gaze with vivid blue irises. "It's you, Sophia. You are betrothed to the Beast of London."

Edmund DeVane, Duke of Rennington, lounged in the corner of the ballroom, eyeing every young cur attempting to woo the early round of debutantes. And there were so many, looking far too young to be banking for a husband. And yet here they were, fresh-faced and ready to fulfill their expected societal roles. Just as he once had.

"If you frown any deeper, Your Grace, the lines shall be etched into the stone of your face."

Lord Boxing nudged Edmund, but he refused to give credence to his friend's laughable sentiment. *Stone of your face?*

"There you go again. Don't say I didn't warn you. No woman shall want a man who looks as though he's carved from granite. They will assume your face resembles your heart."

"You read too much Byron." Edmund studied the

crowds, little caring that his words were more growl than civil discourse. "And I am not in search of a woman."

His friend shrugged, the velvet fabric of his over-done waistcoat crinkling. The sound threatened to un-ravel Edmund's already frayed nerves. Not only did he attend this annoyance of a ball for his niece Hannah's sake, but the man he'd invited to go with him for re-connaissance dressed like a dandy. They'd been friends since university days.

At this moment, Edmund had no idea why.

"You ordered me here—" began Boxing.

"Asked."

"Ordered. I daresay, you could at least attempt polite-ness. Is it not enough that the bulk of the *ton* think you a dangerous and unstable character? Must you prance around—" Boxing cringed at the glare Edmund leveled on him. "Perhaps *prance* is not the right word. March? Yes, march about—"

"That one." Edmund pointed to a dark-haired man in earnest conversation with a woman whose back was to them. "He might do."

Edmund veered toward the couple. Boxing scram-bled to catch up to him. The throng parted easily, and he had no trouble arrowing through.

"Your Grace. You cannot choose Hannah's husband for her."

"I did not give you leave to call her by her Christian name, Boxing." Edmund threw the comment over his shoulder, intent on interrogating the young buck who could very well be his niece's future husband.

The man's head jerked up, his face of the symmet-rical sort, and what Edmund supposed a female might find pleasant. How had Hannah grown old enough to marry? How would he ever be able to let her go?

He frowned.

The man's eyes widened and before Edmund could parse a greeting, he spun and strode away.

Boxing laughed, a hearty chuckle that caused Edmund to grit his teeth. He had not brought his friend along to make fun of him, but that seemed to be his sole amusement.

"Well, now you've done it. Scared off a young chap simply looking for a dance with…why, Mrs. Seymour." Boxing bowed, and Edmund followed suit, albeit in a clumsy fashion as he had long ago stopped being polite.

"Lord Boxing." The woman, her pale pink dress billowing, dropped the most perfect curtsy Edmund had ever seen. In fact, everything about her screamed perfection.

Her hair was pulled back in a flawless chignon, a simple strand of pearls was draped about her graceful neck and her skin was the color of alabaster. His gaze roved back up to her hair for it was an unusual color that sparked a latent interest he had all but forgotten could exist. Neither brown nor blond, but light caramel woven with strands of hair so fair they were almost white.

And her eyes.

Their gazes met and he was struck by the calm ice in that cyan stare. He could not tell if her eyes were more blue or more green.

This woman looked exactly like one of Hannah's prized porcelain dolls.

"Dear Mrs. Seymour, may I introduce you to a very good friend of mine?"

"You may." Her nod was both regal and yet coolly detached.

Boxing gestured toward him. "Mrs. Sophia Seymour, may I have the pleasure of introducing you to the Most Noble Duke of Rennington, Edmund DeVane."

She bowed again, but not before he caught the slightest flicker of recognition across her face. When she straightened, there seemed to be a resolve about her, a tightening of the lips.

"Your Grace," she said, and he was struck by the husky timbre of her voice, so at odds with her fragile appearance. "How fortuitous. You are exactly who I've been looking for."

Chapter Two

Sophia could not believe this strange turn of events. Surely Providence was watching out for her family, as the very man she needed to speak to stood before her. *The Beast of London.* He was much larger than she had expected, towering above her in what some might consider an intimidating way. She wet her lips and firmed her spine. The duke had not answered a single missive she'd sent in the past two weeks. And though she did not believe the gossip about him, there was no doubt the man looked dangerous.

She was not sure she had ever seen a scowl so dark and deep on a member of the *ton.*

"Is that so, madam?"

He had an attractively deep voice, quiet yet powerful, his enunciation undulating with the unmistakable inflection of the upper class.

She smoothed her dress, lifted her chin. "Indeed. There are matters which have recently come to my attention, urgent matters. But a ball is not the place to discuss them."

His brow crinkled. "What possible business could we have? I'm certain I have never met you before."

"You are correct. We have not met." She turned to Boxing. "Thank you for the introduction, my lord. I saw your mother a fortnight ago. She is looking well. Please give her my regards."

"I shall do so." Boxing smiled at her. He was such a pleasant man. "I hope you have been well?"

Before she could respond, His Grace made a sound that could only be quantified as a growl. How very rude. She ignored him, training her attention on Lord Boxing, who had always been kind to her.

"My life is full. I have been working with several local charities. They keep me busy." She tilted her fan and gave herself air. The duke's stare seared into her. The man had few manners and might prove difficult to negotiate with. Nevertheless, she would try.

For the sake of her future.

"I must mingle now. It has been a pleasure to see you, Lord Boxing." Now was not the time for the conversation she intended to have with the duke. She offered Boxing a small curtsy and then shifted toward Rennington.

"Your Grace." She noted the glower that must be a permanent fixture on his face. He had rather messy hair as well, and was that a stain upon his cravat?

"Our conversation has not ended," said the duke.

Eliza had been right. He did indeed have eyes bordering on black. Above them, his eyebrows were unruly slashes of ebony that formed a deep shape of disapproval directed at her.

"Edmund," Boxing said quietly, but the duke held up a hand and the earl silenced.

"You said you've been in search of me. Why?"

"It is better discussed in private, Your Grace."

"And yet I do not know you."

"Our fathers were acquainted. It is for that reason we have matters to discuss." She proffered a quick, yet firm smile. The man was obviously used to getting his way, but nothing would induce her to speak in a crowded ballroom. She could only imagine what the gossips would say should they get wind that she had unknowingly been betrothed to two men at the same time.

"Good evening." She swiftly walked away. They had been introduced. It was not her intention, but it had happened. She would call on him tomorrow morning. Quietly, to keep the tongues from wagging.

"I was not finished, Mrs. Seymour."

The irksome man was at her side. His long legs had allowed him to gain on her speedily.

"Madam, please quit your infernal walking so that we may speak."

"And set the gossips aflame? I think not," she responded in a tone that usually brooked no argument. "Do cease following me."

"That prim voice will not work with me. Stop now and explain yourself."

She had reached a wall with an alcove and a plant that hid them partially from the view of others. She spun toward him, presenting the light and winsome smile she resorted to in difficult situations. "I cannot afford an ounce of impropriety to be attached to my name, Your Grace. My reputation must be protected."

He made that rude sound again, and her back stiffened. She positioned herself in such a way that the plant partially hid her profile and yet left room for a hasty retreat, should she need one.

"Do you mock me?" she asked. "Perhaps a duke has no need of a good reputation."

His lips flattened. The bottom proved fuller than the top, softening his features. She took a full look at him. The craggy cheekbones, sharp edged and harsh. The dark eyes set off by even darker, angry brows. A high forehead surrounded by wild hair. It was no wonder people referred to the man as a beast. She shivered.

"Are you in search of a husband?" he demanded.

"A good reputation is valuable, husband hunting or no."

"Is it?"

Why was he so intent on speaking with her? "Please take your leave. I am asking politely, and the polite thing to do involves turning around and walking away. It is very easy, Your Grace. One foot in front of another."

"You instruct me on the art of politeness and yet you begin a conversation without intending to finish it."

"A slip of the tongue," she said lightly. "I had no idea you'd take it as an invitation to harangue me."

"Harangue." He barked a laugh, looking surprised as he did so. Perhaps the rustiness of the sound indicated the man never laughed. What a shame.

"Yes, it is the best word to describe your uncouth behavior. And you are drawing attention. A duke conversing with the lowly widow of a lawyer. People will talk."

He raked a hand through his hair, sighing heavily. "I care not a whit for society's rules, yet I find myself constrained by them. You are *harangued*, and I apologize for my crass behavior."

She smiled, unexpectedly delighted that he'd thrown

her word back at her. His manners might be questionable, but that did not detract from his intriguing behavior. "Apology accepted. I have certain goals to attain, Your Grace, and smearing my reputation is not one of them."

He fixed her with a hard stare. She offered him a brighter smile punctuated by her own determined look. If he thought her cowed, he was wrong. She had faced far harsher storms than a stubborn duke who may or may not be a murderer.

A curious quiver worked its way through her, a tiny thrill that made her smile wobble just the slightest.

Boxing popped through the crowd then, sporting two cups of punch. "There you are, old chap. I lost you." He winked at Sophia before turning to the duke, who still looked greatly irritated. "Let's make the rounds again."

In an anticlimactic way, they left her, and she found herself sagging against the wall, her breath arrested by an overexcited thumping of the heart. She had instructed Sally to not tighten her stays overly so, but perhaps she had, for oxygen was suddenly difficult to find.

How had Rennington unsettled her so thoroughly? Perhaps his blunt manner, the intensity of his stare and stubbornness of his nature? She was used to being unbothered, unperturbed.

In control.

Though he was not handsome, there was something undeniably attractive about him. So different from her darling Charles. Thoughts of her late husband filled her memory. His soft smile. His intellectual bent. The way he laughed when reading. The gentle nature that marked his being and had made her fall in love with him. She'd been a widow for seven years, yet her heart squeezed, a painful wringing of emotion, and suddenly her eyes were burning with unspent tears.

How she hated that her pulse picked up when Rennington looked at her, when he challenged her.

She must make sure no one ever discovered the contract. The duke must agree to quietly dissolve it. Her head throbbed. What had her father done? Betrothed her to one person and yet let her marry another without a word? Why?

So many years ago, so much time had passed, yet this secret contract had existed.

Questions abounded, unanswered and disturbing. She had built a good life for herself in her widowhood. Not the life she had wanted, but the life she had been given. A life without Charles. Should news spread that she'd married Charles while a betrothal to another existed, who knew the consequences?

At the very least, vicious gossip that might not only affect her, but the future of her sisters.

She had spent much of her adulthood grieving. First Charles, whose miniature she kept always on a locket about her neck. And most recently, the strange disappearance of her father, the man who had shared her faith.

She straightened from the wall. Touched her chignon, ensuring every hair was in place. Charles would always have her heart. Indeed, it was he who had taught her the beauty of love. That was the kind of love she longed for, with a man like Charles. Kind, honest, respectable.

If Rennington refused to dissolve the contract, the life she had built for herself would be forever lost to her.

Just as Charles was.

* * *

"That is the woman you should marry. She's strong, she's regal, she's kind. She can handle a surly duke like you." Boxing clapped Edmund on the back, laughing in a way that gave Edmund a strong urge to punch his friend in the jaw. Curling his fists, he strode out of the ballroom and instructed a servant to bring his carriage around. Boxing did not follow him.

It was a fine evening, dusky and redolent with the scent of roses. The stench of the Thames so often polluting London was absent, blown to the other side of the river, he supposed. Spring was just new enough that the odor remained slight. Come summer, the height of the Season, and ladies would be holding perfumed handkerchiefs over their noses.

If it weren't for Hannah and his duties in the House of Commons, he would barely visit London. Too many memories, and a secret better left buried. But the girl wanted a Season and he couldn't blame her. It was her best chance of finding a husband and creating a better future for herself.

He stepped into his carriage, nodding to the driver to be on his way. It was a short ride to his townhome on Upper Brook Street. Hopefully the house was quiet. Hannah might not be home yet. He had instructed her chaperone to give his niece a busy Season.

Parties. Dancing. Supercilious, superficial society moving about in their ridiculous fashions and rules. How he hated them all. He remembered the looks. The gossip columns that did not quite come out and accuse him of murder, and yet nonetheless, the accusation had been there. In everyone's eyes.

One year.

No doubt Hannah would be betrothed in one year.

He would suffer through the Season and all its madness to make his niece happy. The carriage rattled to a stop and Mr. Reed, his butler, opened the front door. He stepped inside, removing his outer garments, expecting to go to sleep and rid himself of the harsh memories plaguing him.

No sooner had he started up the stairs, though, than he heard the slamming of a door. Loud thumps soon made it clear that Hannah was home. Her clattering feet punched down the staircase so fiercely the walls seemed to shudder.

"She's been crying," whispered Mr. Reed.

He glanced down at his butler. "Have Mrs. Sims prepare pastries and tea. Bring them to the parlor." His stomach clenched at the thought of dealing with Hannah, though this was certainly not the first time he had seen his niece weep. He did not think he'd ever met a girl more prone to tears than she.

Though he had many times through the years managed to muddle through her tearful moments, each instance brought the kind of irritation that made him want to return to his main estate and never emerge.

A duke could not be so fortunate, though.

Sighing, he prepared himself for the onslaught that was about to occur. Hannah barely paused at the top step before rushing down and barreling into him. Her flaming red curls rioted around her head like wildfire. He returned her hug. At times like this, she reminded him of her mother. He swallowed back sadness and grasped his niece's shoulders, gently putting her away from him. He caught her gaze, making eye contact with irises greener than an English lawn in summer. So much like her mother.

Again, that hard lump rose in his windpipe, threatening his breath. "Are these hysterics necessary?"

"If you only knew." Her hands covered her face and muffled a sob.

He guided her down to the parlor. She usually enjoyed the room as it was elegant and overdone and a trifle pompous. The tea and pastries arrived. Edmund shifted in his chair. It was an uncomfortable piece of furniture that always felt as though it might collapse beneath his weight.

Now settled, he said, "Tell me the problem. I shall fix it."

Hannah's head tilted, her eyes shiny. "You cannot fix this, Edmund."

At the dramatic proclamation, his lips quirked. "Though you may think that's true, it's not. I'm a duke. We are few and rare and we hold more power than you can imagine."

She let out a ragged little breath that reminded him of post-tantrums she'd indulged in as a young girl. Plucking a pastry from the tray, she looked at it, then set it on her plate. She stared down at her lap, and Edmund was dismayed to see a lone tear slide seamlessly down her cheek and drop onto the silk of her dress.

"Mrs. Browning has resigned her position as my chaperone. She claims that by introducing me, she is harming her own reputation."

"Resigned?"

Hannah laughed in a cynical way. "We have been given the cut direct several times. She has received no more invitations to balls this week and one of her dearest friends explained the situation to her. She was aware, of course, that your reputation is far from good. She was not aware of how deeply the *ton* holds you in disrepute. She did not know of your sobriquet."

The Beast of London.

Edmund contained the shock that rippled through him in violent waves, though the corner of his eye twitched. "*Disrepute* is a strong word. I've had several invites."

"She said people are curious about you. They want to know what really happened. But she can no longer help me. I am merely a niece and she is the wife of a baron's second son. We have not the status to overcome your reputation."

"I can't escort you."

"I know." Hannah's voice broke. "I suppose I shall end up without a proper husband."

"You don't have to marry."

She began sobbing again. He winced. That had been the wrong thing to say. He never should have allowed her to read those fanciful novels.

He patted her shoulder awkwardly. "Did Mrs. Browning have any suggestions?"

"Two." Hannah produced a lacy handkerchief, which she used to blot her tears. Once done, she set it on her lap and met his gaze. "The first is that someone of impeccable reputation must agree to introduce me about society, someone the *ton* trusts implicitly. Or, second, you must marry well, perhaps increasing your respectability. You'd probably have to marry a princess, though." Her voice cracked again, and though it did not seem to be possible, she managed to indulge in more weeping.

Edmund fought to focus on the fact that she was

upset and sad. But instead, the memory of Mrs. Seymour and her insistence on preserving her reputation staggered through his brain.

Perhaps it was true.

Perhaps reputation was more important than he realized. Had he indeed managed to ruin Hannah's chances at making a good match? His sole goal had been to raise Hannah and give her a good life. Had he failed?

A bitter sensation crept along his spine, and he frowned.

"You need not look so angry, Uncle. Simply find me a new chaperone. One of impeccable position."

The image of Mrs. Seymour's laughing mouth, her calm, sea-swept eyes, entered his mind, and his heart began an odd, little thumping rhythm. He should be alarmed. He knew he should. But instead he could only feel a titillating anticipation of potentially engaging with Mrs. Seymour again.

"Cheer up, sweet niece," he said. "I have just the paragon in mind."

Chapter Three

In the morning, Edmund awoke in a foul mood. The prior evening's decision to engage Mrs. Seymour mocked him. The better he assisted Hannah in her marriage goal, the sooner she'd leave and he'd be alone again. The realization created a swollen ache near the place where some claimed his heart no longer resided. A megrim burned behind his eyes and throbbed in his temples, worsening his temper.

He had barely stumbled out of bed and guzzled coffee in the breakfast room before Reed appeared.

The butler's hands twisted nervously. "Your Grace."

"What." Even to his own ears, his voice sounded gruff. No matter. Everything felt as if it was going wrong. He glared at his butler. The man's face paled.

"There is a…caller. Here to see you."

A hot surge flushed through Edmund, increasing the sickening stabs of pain in his head. Clenching his jaw, he eyed Reed.

The butler licked his lips.

"She is…uh, waiting."

"*She* can leave a card." Who would dare visit him

at this unearthly hour? He squinted at the clock on the far wall, trying to make out the time.

"Um, well, she is rather forward, Your Grace. She has already seated herself in the drawing room. There is an older woman with her."

Edmund stood abruptly, not bothering to hide his annoyance. "They will see me as I am, then."

Snarling, he pushed his chair back and made for the parlor. He stormed down the hall, temper giving speed to his stride. Why bother combing his hair, tying his cravat just so?

Jaw tight, he entered to find the woman who had bothered his dreams last night standing near the window. *Mrs. Seymour.* He cleared his throat and she turned to face him.

Once again he was struck by her perfect beauty.

Not only had she managed to save him the trouble of tracking her down, she looked impeccable while doing so. Radiant, even. Morning sunlight filtered through the curtains in lazy beams that cocooned her in pale, hazy light. It was almost as though she were enveloped in iridescent lace.

"Your Grace." She curtsied as if standing in front of the queen. "You have answered none of my previous correspondences."

"I rarely look at invitations or mail of a personal nature. My steward informs me of important information."

"Most assuredly, if this was not a most urgent matter, we would not have called."

Her use of *we* shifted his attention to the other woman in the room. She was older, her once blond hair shifting toward white, but despite the age, it was obvious where Mrs. Seymour had obtained her beauty.

"And you are?" he asked the woman.

Her throat worked quickly, two pale spots appeared upon her pink complexion, and her hand fluttered up to her mouth, tapping in quick, successive movements.

Mrs. Seymour stepped forward. "My mother, the Lady Worland."

He gave the lady a curt nod before bringing his focus back to Mrs. Seymour. Although he'd been planning to contact her, he didn't like that she'd shown up uninvited on his door. Even if he hadn't seen her missives, the visit bordered on rudeness.

"What do you want?" The question catapulted off his tongue in staccato beats.

"For one, you may quit yelling. I can assure you that neither of us has an issue with our hearing." She dared to smile up at him, though he was positive it was the most insincere smile he'd ever seen.

His gaze narrowed. "Perhaps only with your manners."

Mrs. Seymour chuckled then, her eyes lighting up in a most attractive way. They edged toward blue this morning, like the Thames glittering beneath an early morning sun.

"You laugh," he bit out.

The corners of her eyes crinkled and her mouth split into an extraordinary smile that was this time most certainly genuine. "The suggestion that my manners are amiss is a most amusing and strangely wonderful thought." She peered up at him, her lips creased with mirth. "And to come from you, of all people."

Jaw tight, Edmund spun away. He did not like the way her perfume, delicate and light, wove around him. Nor did he care for her cheerful disposition. He strode to a chair situated far from the widow and her mother.

For all he knew, they were both daft. And yet wasn't this the perfect scenario? Mrs. Seymour at his door, so to speak. He must be patient.

He sat, eyeing them both, his temples throbbing. At least the mother had the good sense to look nervous.

"I can only presume you did not arrive here to take humor at my expense."

"No, Your Grace." Mrs. Seymour sank gracefully onto the couch next to the older Seymour. "And thank you for sitting so far away. My ears are much relieved."

Edmund blinked.

Her mother chose that moment to speak, oblivious to the insult her daughter had just glibly delivered. "We are here on important business. You may have heard of my Sophia in passing. Though it was many years ago, she was the darling of the Season. A Diamond of the First Water, they called her." Lady Worland nodded, as if to reassure him of the widow's past success.

His gaze met Mrs. Seymour's, and for a moment lingered, for he thought he saw something beyond the laughter and perfect facade. Then she blinked and offered him a starched smile.

"And why, Lady Worland, do you think I care a whit what your daughter was called?" He tapped his fingers on the arm of his chair. "You have one minute to tell me why you're here without an invitation." He glowered, which was effective on most people who annoyed him.

He was beginning to rethink his decision to hire Mrs. Seymour as Hannah's chaperone now that she'd presumptuously barged into his home, mother in tow. What manners would she teach his niece? The headache raged on, and he felt his scowl deepening.

"Ah, yes. Certain documents have come to our attention." Mrs. Seymour's voice was entirely too positive. She lilted her consonants as though singing. "It seems that—"

"Thirty seconds."

She paused. And then said, "Very well, since you insist on brevity—"

"Ten seconds."

Nonplussed, she smoothed an invisible wrinkle in her dress. And then she met his look with a perplexing, almost sympathetic, smile.

"In short, Your Grace, we are betrothed."

"That's preposterous." The duke shot to his feet, pacing the room exactly how Sophia imagined a lion might. The man conjured the image of a wild cat, with his untamed hair and a voice that neared a roar. "What do you really want? Why are you here? Do not think I shall be nabbed into some sort of…villainy. I do not negotiate with blackmailers nor disreputable persons."

"Why, of all the terrible, horrible words you might say." Mother's face flushed crimson, and Sophia reached over to take her hand. "Do you hear this man? I do not think I could let you marry such a vile person. Oh, but whatever will we do?"

Sophia squeezed, but too late, for her mother's eyes were welling with tears. She eyed the duke, who was speaking in hushed tones to his butler. Was he going to call for the constabulary?

Perhaps the man had been taken advantage of one too many times for his lauded position. No doubt his station, along with the ugly rumors of his past, had turned him cynical and sour. She stood, patting her mother's shoulder in an unspoken command to stay where she was. She would set this to rights.

As she approached the duke, he stopped speaking to his butler, and the servant turned to leave.

"I would not go just yet," she said.

Rennington's head swung toward her. Shocked, no doubt. She suppressed a rather wicked urge to laugh.

"That's right. Keep your man here before you embarrass yourself." She paused. "Your Grace." Out of the corner of her eye, the butler chewed his cheek. Poor thing. No doubt scared witless by this ogre of a duke.

"You dare tell me my business." His voice had lowered to what she supposed he considered a dangerous level. And maybe she should be afraid, but she simply wasn't.

"I wish to spare you from a great embarrassment." She tightened her hold on her reticule, within which lay the contract. "Are you so foolish to think my mother and I would spring this on you without legal precedent? Do you think I enjoy telling a stranger that he and I are somehow encumbered by a betrothal not of our design?"

"Not of your..." He turned to the butler. "Wait in the hall." His gaze flickered past her to Lady Worland. "Do you mean to imply my father agreed to a betrothal with a baron's daughter?"

"It is all rather surprising. We found this paperwork and none of us knew anything about a betrothal made over ten years ago. We hoped to have a conversation with you. Sort it out, if you will."

"It shall be looked into."

Sophia forced her features to remain expressionless, though her stomach was a mass of tension and nerves. If word got out that she had married one man while a betrothal secretly existed with another…oh, it was just too scandalous.

"Might it not be better to dissolve the betrothal quietly?" she asked.

Rennington's eyes narrowed, the corners creasing as though in pain. "I begin to see the dilemma in which you find yourself."

"Wonderful. We must not let this get out."

"You are utterly opposed to marrying a duke?" He crossed his arms, his fingers long and splayed against his biceps. She realized then that he was hardly dressed for company. She had been so caught up in her nerves and what she ought to say that she hadn't even noticed his dishabille. Flushing, she averted her eyes.

"Think of the fortune you'd have access to," he continued. "The prestige."

At that, she laughed. "Fortune? Prestige? You are more cynical than I imagined a duke should be."

"You deny it, then. A widow, as you said, uninterested in a fortune, and yet here you are. This paper could have been burned with none the wiser. Why did you come?"

"I could not take the chance that someone else might hold a copy and bring it to light." She hoped and prayed Mr. Butterfield would not divulge the details. Solicitors, after all, were privy to all sorts of secrets and expected to keep mum. Nevertheless, she swallowed hard. "Think of my reputation. My family's. While it is true that your fortune could help my family, I have no intention of ever marrying again."

"Not a fortune seeker, yet concerned mainly with the artificial goodwill of the peerage." His mouth flattened. "I have nothing else to say to you, madam." His words were ice, slicing through her resolve in a way she was unused to.

When one went about in life without correction, without rebuke, one forgot the sting of censure. Cheeks burning, she did not move.

"And yet I still have something to say to you. And though I regret that my mother and I have so obviously interrupted your day, this is a matter that must be resolved now."

"Speak to my solicitor." He pivoted, leaving the room so quickly that Sophia stood dumbfounded.

Fuming, she pressed her lips together and glanced over at her mother. She sat as still and pale as the wax figures at Madame Tussaud's.

Gathering her skirts, Sophia marched out of the drawing room and made a quick left. The butler lingered in the hall, no doubt waiting to usher them out. She gave him her most genteel smile. "Fetch the duke."

But there was no need for such instruction.

He stepped out from a shadowed alcove, a giant mass of sizzling energy. She had gone to a rout once in which a gentleman had exhibited his electrostatic generator. He had touched some part and made his hair stand on end.

That was how Rennington now appeared. She put her hand to her mouth to hide her smile.

"Laughing again." Rather than sounding angry, he sounded confused.

She sighed, moving closer to him, noting that, though they had roused him from his morning meal, he actually smelled very nice. A bit like sandalwood and fresh soap.

"I do sincerely apologize for disturbing you so. But if we could just have a candid conversation regarding this legal document." As she spoke, she reached into her reticule and pulled out the contract. "There is already talk of your possible betrothal in certain scandal columns. Can we not resolve this quietly, without fuss or drama?"

"You are still smiling." His words dripped with disapproval, but he reached for the contract. "What talk?"

Their fingers brushed, and his skin was warmer than she expected, jolting her senses. She snatched her hand from the unanticipated contact. His butler stood nearby, and from the corner of her eyes, she saw the hem of her mother's dress peeking out from a doorframe. Eavesdropping.

Wonderful.

"The gossip alludes to the betrothal of a duke." She cleared her throat. "A duke shrouded in mystery. Easily presumed to be the same duke known as the Beast of London."

She averted her eyes, for that name brought a pang to her chest, a sad empathy for him.

"There has been nothing about who the fiancée might be. The gossip is probably caused by your resurfacing after so many years away. No doubt some see it as a sign you are in search of a bride, or perhaps have already garnered one." Sophia hesitated, then plunged on. "I am not as shallow as you suppose me to be. My father disappeared six months ago. Not once in the last seven years, not even when I married another, did he allude to any arrangement with your father."

She wet her lips, forcing herself to continue. "My family is struggling, and I can't afford to have any scandal linked to my name. I must be able to retain my social status and the benefits of widowhood in order to help them. This contract can never come to light." Drawing a deep, ragged breath, she lifted her chin, meeting the dark eyes that studied her intently. "Can you verify with your solicitor whether it is dissolvable? Perhaps we can move forward from there."

"My reputation is already in shreds. There is no moving forward on that front." He tilted his head, his tone not unkind. "I am sorry to hear of your burdens, though."

She inclined her head. "Thank you."

"Perhaps I can lessen them."

"Your Grace, if I may?" Mother's voice from behind nabbed their attentions. Sophia turned to see Mother coming toward them, her fingers twisting in her skirts. "I have more to add to the conversation."

"Is that so?"

His low, rumbling tones raked across Sophia's emotions, eliciting a small shudder. Why did she enjoy the timbre of his voice? She crossed her arms, willing the feeling to leave as she eyed her mother. What more could she say?

Lady Worland reached them and stopped, her eyes bright, her expression still somewhat fearful of the duke. "You have had a bit of difficulty, haven't you, Your Grace?"

"Nothing I can't handle," he said stiffly.

"Do you plan to let your dukedom pass on to a distant family member?" She waved a hand, losing her timidity beneath fervor. "A handsome, intelligent man like yourself the victim of gossip, slander, excluded from the very society you were born into. It's a great and terrible injustice. It simply should not be."

A stormy blackness was invading the duke's features. Sophia glanced between them. Her mother hadn't noticed his expression, caught up in whatever speech she'd mentally concocted.

"Such a sad and unnecessary state of affairs, Your Grace, and easily remedied."

"Do tell me," Rennington said in such a dry voice that Sophia was almost tempted to smirk.

"Well." Mother sniffed, shaking her shoulders in a strange little dance. "If you hadn't realized it, my sweet and happy Sophia is the epitome of reputability. She is exactly what you need, Your Grace."

His eyes flickered, and for the tiniest moment, Sophia had the distinct worry she saw interest there. Or perhaps even worse, hope. Her stomach bottomed out. Her breath fogged in her throat and it took a great deal of willpower for her to keep her expression placid. Was her mother going against Sophia's wishes? Surely not. Her fingers tightened on her reticule strings so hard she felt the braided cloth digging into her palms.

"I need nothing, madam."

"Oh, but that is simply not true. As a duke, you have a great many duties and responsibilities. The livelihood of those who depend on you is partially tied to your reputation."

Rennington scowled. "A bit overblown."

"But—" and Mother held up a finger "—not completely. And you are not getting any younger."

Sophia's eyes widened.

"Therefore, think of your future. My daughter can supply you with the two things most beneficial to you."

"Spare no detail, madam," said the duke, again in that wry tone.

"Why, the two things any respectable man is in need

of." Mother's cheeks bunched as she grinned. "A wife of sterling reputation, and a family to soften the sting of age."

Sophia barely contained her gasp.

The duke glanced at her, as if he sensed her displeasure. He returned his attention to her mother, who was preening like a chicken who'd just laid the golden egg. Sophia bit her lip in order to stifle her protest.

"As a matter of fact," he said, his eyes dark and thoughtful, "it has recently come to my attention that a wife may be just the thing, after all." And then he rolled that determined look toward Sophia, eyeing her in a way that set her nerves afire and her heart to quickening.

Surely not.

No.

Before he could speak, she clutched her mother. "We shall be going now. Thank you for looking into this, Your Grace."

Her mother sputtered but allowed Sophia to forcibly rotate her toward the front door.

"Mrs. Seymour." The words, quietly spoken, contained all the elegance and power of his station.

By conditioning, she found herself stopping and facing him.

"I shall make inquiries, but are you prepared to adhere to the contract should it be found legal?" He was peering at her, so focused she could feel the cut of his question carving into her conscience.

Everything within her shouted a firm *no*. She offered him a small tilt of her lips. "Your Grace, I wish to never marry again. I am not the wife for you."

Chapter Four

Wife, indeed.

Sophia touched an English rose with her fingertip, reveling in its velvety softness, in the wild curl of its plumage. How could her mother essentially have gone behind Sophia's back to persuade Rennington into marriage? It was beyond the pale. Even now, days later, she burned with indignation.

She straightened, observing in the garden she kept behind her townhome. Charles's family had kindly let her stay in the place after his death. It was small and quaint, located in a quiet neighborhood near enough Mayfair to be safe, but far enough to not be confused with the titled rich. Although there were two floors and a basement, the house had only enough room for a married couple and a few servants.

With her widow's dowry and the support of her late husband's family, she had fashioned for herself a peaceable life. She touched the thorny stem of another rose. The flowers traipsed through her backyard in delightful abandon. English roses, tulips and purple alliums, the latter looking like sturdy dandelions guarding the more delicate flowers.

She drew a deep breath of satisfaction and summer perfume. Finding the stone bench she and Charles had bought for their garden, she sank down to enjoy the solitude. She had finally touched base with Bow Street, but no runners wished to take on the case of finding her father, especially as her mother could only pay a small stipend for the work. Due to the financial straits her family might be in, the runners hinted he'd abandoned them.

She dared not believe such a thing. Father had been the epitome of joy and kindness. It was through him that she'd learned of God's goodness, of His faithfulness. Her heart constricted and she closed her eyes, the gentle graze of sunlight caressing her cheeks. After Charles's death, her father had comforted her. He had told her to draw near to God, to seek Him and find solace in His love.

And she had tried, but how hard it had been.

How hard it still was.

God had allowed her to lose someone so dear, so precious, that for a time, she thought she might never stop crying. The notion that her life had bottomed out, that she could not taste goodness, persisted for months. And then one morning she awoke with dry eyes. And then another morning, and another, until finally she felt hunger again, until finally she felt the urge to see a play, to sample the confections at Gunter's. And slowly she reemerged, her lifestyle changed, her goals adjusted to create a life that no longer included a husband.

A horrible pressure settled on her chest, pressing in, suffocating.

"Mrs. Seymour?" Betsy's voice intruded on the melancholy gripping Sophia.

She opened her eyes and stood. Her newest housemaid, a plucky young woman rescued from the shadowed slums of London, awaited her response.

"There's a gentleman here to see ye. A real smart gentleman. He wears Hessians."

"You," Sophia gently corrected. Betsy was an avid student, but she still slipped into the less refined English she'd grown up with. "Did you get his name?"

"I forgot, Mrs. Seymour."

"In the future, always inquire for a name."

Betsy's head bobbed, her eyes wide with curiosity and a touch of awe.

Sophia sighed. Perhaps her father-in-law. He checked in with her every so often. They shared a bond, she and Lord Windley. He had championed her work in many charities. Seeing him always brought a sharp pain, for out of all the family, Charles had resembled his father most.

"Situate him in the parlor. Then meet me in my bedroom so that I may tidy myself." She was wearing a morning dress, a dreadfully old thing that she rather liked. Time had worn it into a soft, malleable fabric.

It took more than fifteen minutes, but she was finally presentable in a rosy silk day gown that she'd been told put color in her cheeks. Should Lord Windley need her to accompany him on a mission of charity, she would be ready to leave promptly.

She thanked Betsy, and then helped her perfect her curtsy. The house was terribly silent as she ventured down the stairs to the parlor. Usually Lord Windley chatted with the maids and Tom, her manservant. He often brought the household trinkets or delicacies.

Smoothing her hair once more, she swept into the parlor. A broad-shouldered man, clothed in an exquisitely cut tailcoat, perfectly tailored pantaloons and shining Hessian boots, stood at the hearth. She paused. This was most definitely *not* Charles's father. His wildly, unruly hair brushed past the collar of his tailcoat, the blackness of the strands blending with the fabric. Her heart began an uneven pounding, and she realized her breaths had grown shallow.

The Duke of Rennington was not who she had expected to see today. Or in fact, ever again.

He heard her entry, for he turned, sweeping her with an enigmatic gaze.

"Your Grace," she said, inclining her head.

"Mrs. Seymour."

And then the dreadful man just stood there and looked at her. On a normal occasion, she found carrying a conversation easy. Some might even call her adept at drawing out reticent speakers. All with the greatest panache and manners.

But faced with his unabashed appraisal, surprised by his presence and still recovering from the sadness haunting her morning, Sophia found supreme irritation a ripe companion.

She entered the room fully, rounding the delicate couch to sit in a chair farthest from the hearth. Farthest from *him*.

Rennington cleared his throat. "I find myself in a strange predicament."

Sophia gestured to the couch. "Please, sit. I shall ring for tea."

"I don't want tea."

"There you are with those excellent manners."

"You are caustic today."

"I am in a strange predicament, as well. It is not often a duke graces me with his presence." Oh, how cutting her tone, how irritated her heart. She hated the thrill that had raced through her on seeing him. Her stomach was knotted and her nerves on edge.

"Would it help if I asked you to call me Edmund?" A tease infused his deep voice, lending to the panic beginning to spread through Sophia.

"That would be highly inappropriate, Your Grace."

"And yet isn't that who you think I am? A temperamental prig who says inappropriate things at untimely moments, haranguing reputable widows at balls?"

A grudging smile tugged at her lips. She put it back in its place, exchanging it for the distant one she often used.

"I congratulate you," she said, changing the subject.

One brow lifted, ever so slightly.

"It is evident—" and her tone proved sharp "—that you enlisted the help of your valet today. And so I congratulate you on looking the part of a duke. Now you must act the part."

"You speak more plainly than I anticipated."

"Perhaps I am only this way with you." Because he had brought himself into her home, the place she had shared with Charles. He had usurped her memories and now when she came into the parlor, she might remember the crisp tones of fresh soap and sandalwood rather than the Freshman cologne her late husband had worn. Sometimes she sprayed a tiny spurt in the room, just to recall his presence.

Yet now the room smelled like Rennington. Unique, different.

Enticing.

Sophia drew on all her powers of grace and manners, straightening her shoulders, lifting her chin, to hide the querulous feelings ratcheting through her.

"If you are only this way with me," he countered, "then I see no reason why you should not call me Edmund."

"We see much differently, Your Grace." She tacked on his title deliberately. "I am your inferior."

"It is befuddling, is it not?" His expensively clad legs stretched out before him, and he folded long fingers together. "That our fathers believed a betrothal a good idea."

"Most befuddling and clearly insane."

"Our vision is not so different, after all." He paused, and she was certain mischief glinted in his eyes. "Sophia Seymour."

She caught her gasp before it escaped her lips, settling instead on a demure tilt of her head. "Have you come here to tell me the contract has been dissolved?"

The teasing look had not left his face. She found it charming and almost wished he'd revert to his angry face. Though that was also, in an odd way, amusing. She must be cautious.

Too many of her rescued women had told her horror stories about men who behaved well and then later proved to be monsters.

"No, Mrs. Seymour. A dissolution is not the reason for this visit."

"Then whatever is, pray tell?" She spoke crisply, wearying of whatever game he thought to play with her. "I've plans for today."

"Most people know better than to speak to a duke that way."

"Most people want to become his wife."

He laughed then, and it still contained a rusty, unused note, but it was also robust. His obsidian gaze seemed to twinkle, and she found that she did not mind making him laugh. Even if she'd been happily impertinent in doing so.

When his laugh subsided, he met her eyes. "Are you being rude in order to scare me away?"

"Am I being discourteous? And here I thought I was indulging in frank conversation."

"This honesty, I presume, is what earned you the title Diamond of the First Water?"

No. It certainly hadn't, but she did not want to corroborate his skepticism toward their social circles. A particular level of artifice was a necessary evil when navigating the perils of the peerage.

"I have always tried my best to be kind and gentle, to exhibit the fruits of the spirit in all of my endeavors," she said instead.

"But not today?"

Her gaze narrowed. "Most certainly today. I am exercising a great deal of patience."

"Very well. I concede." He rested his elbows on his knees and gave her a more serious expression, more like the Rennington she'd already met. "I have done a great bit of investigation about you in the past few days, Mrs. Seymour. A baron's daughter. Impeccable character. Beloved by the stringent patronesses of Almack's. Involved in charitable works. There is not a negative report to be had. More than that, the contract is detailed enough to be legitimate, and though it was signed more than ten years ago, my father's signature is a match."

Sophia contained her cringe. The conversation was heading toward the place she feared most.

"To be frank," he said, "you are the embodiment of all that a duke's wife should be."

Edmund saw the sudden pallor she could not hide. He saw it and ignored it. The woman would be daft to refuse matrimony.

"I am an unlikely candidate for duchess," she said, "Beyond that, I have no desire to marry again."

And then she stopped talking. She wore a prim, polite expression that baffled him. What kind of woman did not wish to marry a duke? Though he had not investigated her family, she had mentioned financial straits. Surely their marriage could set things to rights. He looked for stubbornness on her features, for any sign of impoliteness, but could find none.

This woman had perfected the art of culture, class, charisma. He frowned. How did she do it? Keep that impartial, blasé look upon her patrician features?

No matter. She was exactly what Hannah needed. He'd made his inquiries and discovered that should he marry this woman, a great many doors would open for Hannah. How to persuade her, though…he was at a loss.

He drummed his fingers against the chair arm. Her parlor was fashionable without being ostentatious. He had discovered she'd married the third son of an earl who had gone into law. A studious sort, no doubt. There were a few books to be seen, but he'd guess that somewhere in this tiny home existed a library.

He watched her closely. Although he had been born

the spare, not the heir, he'd been raised to a certain kind of behavior and expectation. He knew how to command respect. He knew how to level a look so powerful that an inferior station felt the difference in class.

He was not proud of this ability, but it came with his upbringing. He sighed, for Mrs. Seymour's cheeks were extraordinarily pink although she did not say a word.

"Why do you not wish to marry?" he asked.

She folded her arms in her lap, something like relief flashing across her features.

"Marriage should be for love."

"Are you a fan of Lord Byron, then?"

"Not particularly. But I have tasted the sweetness of love and I see no reason to bind myself in matrimony to a stranger for money."

How did one refute such a statement? Hannah's face flashed before him. He had not come up to scratch with her mother. He could not, *could not*, disappoint Hannah, too. He straightened in his seat, leveling a direct stare at Mrs. Seymour.

"You fail to understand my predicament."

"How can there be an issue with dissolving the contract in a legal way? You will be free to marry whom you wish. There is no predicament."

"You fail to understand," he repeated, "because I have not fully explained my situation to you."

"Your situation?"

Again, he was amazed at her composure. Her face hardly showed her surprise, but for one delicately arched eyebrow. She would make an unlikely and yet magnificent duchess.

"Yes." He settled back in his chair, noting how comfortable it was for a man of his size. He crossed his arms. "Did you know I am raising my niece?"

"No, I did not."

"A few years after the deaths of her parents, she came to live with me."

Mrs. Seymour finally showed some emotion. Her head tilted and her mouth almost smiled. "You took in a family member?"

"You are surprised."

She chuckled, and he realized that his words had tumbled roughly out of him, sandpaper in a velvet room.

"Can you blame me?" Her soft lips curved into an even softer smile. "Your reputation precedes you. Although gossip and society columns are of no interest to me, I have heard enough to formulate a picture of whom the Duke of Rennington might be. Then I met you, and there has been nothing in your manner that would lead me to believe you protect or provide for anyone but yourself."

"A harsh answer," he said, surprised by how her truthfulness pierced him.

"Nevertheless, an honest one. But it is not the whole story of *you*, is it?"

He suddenly understood why the *ton* was so enamored of this woman. Her graceful beauty had attracted him from the moment he met her, but this look in her eyes…was it compassion? Empathy? Whatever she was feeling, it reflected like a halo upon her features.

There was a hollow space within him, one reserved for softer feelings. He rarely used it, but at this moment, a pleasant warmth invaded and he felt the oddest, most undesirable urge to empty his conscience at her feet. To explain the why of his anger. The *how* it came to be.

He wished to confess to this woman his secret. Unacceptable.

He shot to his feet, shoving a hand angrily through his hair. His fingers snagged on a tangled strand, and the sharp sting brought him to his senses. He paced the small room, little caring that her gaze followed him.

"Be it difficult or not to scrutinize the truth of my character," he said, "the situation remains that my niece, Hannah, is in need of a chaperone for her first Season. She wishes to attend balls and perhaps find love." The last word burned his tongue. "The reputation I have built for myself is impeding her goals."

"Unexpected," she mused. "You're a duke. There was no proof of any wrongdoing on your part. I have seen earls left unvilified for worse offenses."

He spun to the wall to compose himself. That white-hot rage that so often consumed him was boiling his blood, growing stronger. He was no different from his father and brother. He knew it.

"Worse than murder?" he ground out.

"Sometimes." The sound of her skirts rustled. "You have had no issues with invitations for yourself?"

"None." He stiffened, for he could smell her perfume, and the enticing aroma intimated her closeness. He turned and indeed, she stood only feet away. She was not a tall woman, and when they stood like this, he was well aware of his largeness. His strength. And the always present anger firing beneath the surface of his nerves.

Her eyes, almost green, not quite blue, searched his face.

"Hannah's chaperone has abandoned us," he said roughly, swiping a palm against his chin. "She has cited my character as an impediment to her own social status."

"I see." Sophia's lids dropped briefly, as exquisitely porcelain as the rest of her skin. They fluttered up and at this range, he could see she had long eyelashes that perfectly framed her eyes.

His mouth felt suddenly dry.

Sophia turned and walked to the parlor entrance. "There are a great many acceptable chaperones to be had. I shall send you a list of prospects."

He stalked after her. "Have you forgotten the contract?"

"Dissolve it."

"And if I don't?"

That brought her chin up. "Then I shall hire an attorney and do it myself."

A dangerous flare of heat burst within him. He advanced, backing her against the door frame. "And what if I make this betrothal public? The *ton* will know that you married another while betrothed to me. It could become a scandal. Think of your sisters. Your mother."

Her lids flickered. "You would blackmail me into marriage?"

Instant regret flared within.

"No." He backed away, jaw tight. "I spoke without thinking."

"This anger you feel is virulent. What good has it accomplished?" Her head tilted, and if he had rattled her at all, it didn't show.

Anger had carried him through the hardest moments of his life. It had kept him strong. Untouchable. But she needn't know that.

Pressing his lips together, he jerked his head toward the doorway. "Is this your way of ending my visit?"

"We have said all that needs to be said."

"I can help you. Provide a larger home. Pin money for extravagances. Whatever your heart desires."

She let out a little laugh that almost sounded sad. "Do I look like someone who wants your money?"

"You're the darling of society." Frustration flanked his words. "Superficiality adorns you in every way."

Not even a flinch, only a steady gaze that unnerved him. "Thank you for the honor you have shown me, but I must keep to my previous words—I will not marry you. If it helps you to understand at all, I love my home. I am in a comfortable situation. A widow, who can come and go with much more freedom than a wife. This is the house I shared with my husband. He was the love of my life." There was a small catch in that last sentence. "I simply cannot find it within me to leave or to change what my world has become. I shall send you a list of suitable chaperones who shall no doubt help you and Hannah."

Feeling grim, and so angry his pulse thrummed at his temples, Edmund pivoted into the hallway. Two maids huddled at the base of the steps, looking terrified. He swung the door open. He was done with this place. Done with that stubborn female.

"Your Grace," she called out.

He paused, looking over his shoulder. She had not moved from her position within the parlor entry.

"I truly empathize with your situation. I shall be praying for you."

He grunted an acceptance and left.

Prayer.

He did not know that God cared.

Chapter Five

Sophia added the last chaperone's name to her list with a flourish. Done at last. "Betsy," she called. Her maid scrambled into the bedroom. "Please give this to Tom. He needs to take a hackney over to the Duke of Rennington's house posthaste and deliver this list."

She folded the parchment neatly and handed it to Betsy. Those names would surely be enough to help Rennington.

But hours later, as she readied for an evening conversazione at a friend's house, the duke's face flashed repeatedly through her memory. The man showed so many emotions. Within the space of one visit, she had noted humor, sentimentality, sadness, frustration and then at the end, anger.

"It's not my fault," she whispered to her reflection.

"Mrs. Seymour?"

"I'm sorry, Betsy. Just thinking." She adjusted a shiny, blond curl to lay over her right shoulder. "Do you think this the best dress for tonight? It's a small literary event."

"Yes, I do." Betsy bustled over. "And wear this necklace." The ruby pendant was small but intricate and brought out the scarlet tones in her shimmering dress. Her maid's taste was exemplary.

"How are you faring, Betsy?" she asked the young woman as she fastened the necklace around Sophia's throat.

"In what?"

"In general. Do you enjoy being a lady's maid?"

"I'd rather be the wife of a duke." Betsy giggled, but it was difficult for Sophia to smile. She forced one anyway. Perhaps the entire household had overheard yesterday's conversation. She prayed they had not put two and two together regarding the nature of the contract.

Betsy stepped back, surveying her handiwork. "Perfect. Do I enjoy being a lady's maid? It's better than being a scullery maid, but it's still hard work, and unrewarding. My back hurts and my feet hurt but… I sleep at night with a full belly and a clean conscience. There's a certain pride in honest work."

Betsy had been found wasting away of fever in a back alley two years ago. She didn't speak of her past often, but the serrated scar running down her right arm spoke loudly enough. Violence had surrounded her.

"You see the best in situations," said Sophia, touching the ruby that lay cool against her skin. She had put her locket in the jewelry box for the night. "It is a gift."

"Maybe." Betsy shrugged. "I'd still rather marry a duke."

This time, Sophia chuckled. "You never know."

"Nonsense. I've got my lot in life."

"Your lot?"

"That's what I said." Betsy cocked a brow. "I never

thought I'd be even a maid, wearing fine clothes, clean and never 'ungry."

"You have a fine eye for fashion. Have you considered working in a modiste's shop?"

At that, Betsy guffawed, all proper training flying out the window as she clutched her stomach. When she finished, she wiped a tear from her cheek. "You are something, my lady. Quite something indeed."

"Always refer to me as Mrs. Seymour. I was not married to a titled man."

"Yes, madam." Betsy said promptly, as though she hadn't already been told this many times in the two months she'd worked for Sophia. The maid went to the wardrobe and pulled out a fur-trimmed emerald pelisse. "Wear this for warmth."

As Sophia shrugged into the coat, Betsy *tsked*. "Why won't you marry the duke?"

"It seems you missed part of our conversation."

"That wretched Sally was giggling. I couldn't keep her quiet."

"Good servants do not eavesdrop," Sophia told her quietly. "If you want to move up to a better position, you must endeavor discretion at all times."

"If I was you—" Betsy began, but Sophia cut her off.

"You are not. Is my hackney here yet?"

But Betsy, naughty servant, was not to be dismissed. That was one of the more challenging aspects of rehabilitating ladies of the night. They were often strong women in their own way. Survivors.

"What is the harm in accepting his proposal? Think of the women you could help? All that money at your disposal?"

Sophia paused in the smoothing of her pelisse. She

hadn't thought of how the money could be a benefit beyond the life of herself and her family. Betsy had a perspicacious spirit. What else did she see?

"May I ask you something?" Sophia faced her.

The servant's plain face and unremarkable figure had not helped her in her chosen occupation of the past. She had not even made it to courtesan, that Sophia knew. Betsy had instead lived with the basest of society. And Sophia was sure she had experienced cruelty beyond imagination.

"Of course, Mrs. Seymour." But a hesitancy had entered her pretty brown eyes. They were Betsy's most beautiful feature. A light, winsome chestnut that expressed all of her feelings.

Sophia touched her hair, feeling the sturdy curls, feeling her own hesitancy. "Perhaps I am wrong, but I believe you have a broad knowledge of certain types of characters." She paused. She must be delicate here. "What are your thoughts on His Grace?"

Betsy's wide mouth twisted to the side. "I heard the peerage gossips that he killed his brother. Servants talk."

"Do they believe that, as well?"

"No, madam." Betsy squinted, thinking hard over her next words. "He's an angry man. Short-tempered and unconcerned with manners when he's in a pique. But what I heard is he's a kind soul. He treats his staff well. Be you asking because you might become a duchess?"

"And his niece?" she asked, ignoring the question.

"The niece be a handful. She has his temper added to all the dramas of a young woman's emotions." Betsy shrugged. "But they say she's entertaining and fair to them. She's the apple of the duke's eye."

"Thank you, Betsy. Let us leave in five minutes. We shall be fashionably late, but not rudely late."

"May I tell you how perfect you look?" Betsy's fingers skimmed her own face. "Would I 'ave had that face…"

Sighing, Sophia touched her maid's shoulder. "Perfection is overrated and unrepresentative of one's true character. You have your own, exquisite Betsy beauty. Take joy in that."

They arrived to the conversazione five minutes late, just as Sophia had planned. She exited the hackney, and Betsy disappeared to the servants' quarters. The house loomed before her, brightly lit and emanating Mozart. The owner, Lord Montfort, was a good friend of Lord Windley. His wife, Caroline, was one of Sophia's dearest friends. The couple had told Sophia she might use the event to drum up support for her charitable initiatives.

The butler ushered her into the drawing room that had been rearranged to allow for the guests of the conversazione. Lady Montfort met her by the door.

"My dear Sophia." Caroline gave her a gentle hug, and then put her away to study her clothing. "Such bold colors. Your style is changing. Who is your modiste?" Caroline touched the pelisse, shaking her head. "This is striking."

"I have a new lady's maid." Sophia undid her coat and handed it to a waiting servant.

Caroline's eyes widened with admiration. "You are stunning."

Sophia let out a breathy laugh. "Silly, I am simply me. My maid has a unique taste for fashion that I am not averse to. I'm encouraging her to think about working in a modiste's shop."

Caroline linked her arm through Sophia's and they began a slow traipse about the room, which was already filling with friends eager to talk literature and innovative ideas. "Is she one of your *special* maids?"

"She is. I only employ those who are on a path of redemption and change." She patted her friend's arm as they neared some chairs. "But enough about me. Were you able to convince your husband to choose *Sense and Sensibility* over *Waverly*?"

"Sir Walter Scott won this time around. But I shall continue to pester him to expand his literary tastes."

"No *Sense and Sensibility*, then," murmured Sophia.

"He has a prejudice against women writers, I think. It is very annoying." Caroline beckoned Sophia to have a seat. "I must welcome my other friends and have them situated just so. I issued last-minute invitations which affect the seating arrangements."

Spontaneous and kind Caroline.

Sophia scanned the room, noting several people she knew and a few she recognized but for whom she couldn't recall a name. "Who have you seated next to me?"

But Caroline was already flitting away, welcoming her guests and instructing servants. A servant brought Sophia a drink, which she accepted gratefully. As the maid offered drinks to the people beside her, Sophia found herself observing the maid's expression.

Betsy's comment earlier had not stung, but neither did Sophia dismiss the fact that her maid's back and feet hurt. So often she attended these events and didn't even notice who took her coat, who brought the food. A good servant was unseen.

Yet that long-standing societal expectation rankled.

As she mused, she caught sight of Caroline heading toward her with a strange look on her face. She stood and met her near the punch.

"Not here," Caroline said in a quiet voice. She led Sophia to the pianoforte. "I would love if you could regale us with music before we begin, but I need to tell you…" She placed a hand on the pianoforte and pasted a fake smile on her face for the benefit of anyone watching. "There are rumors surfacing that your family is on the edge of ruin."

Sophia barely contained her recoil. She sat down. She placed her fingers upon the keys and ran through a warm-up sequence. Relaxing ripples of sound carried through the room.

"Thank you for telling me," she said.

Concern darkened Caroline's eyes, but she said no more and left to perform her hostess duties. Sophia concentrated on playing smoothly, on keeping serenity upon her face. Rumors? She must go to her mother promptly.

Her fingers stumbled over a note. She corrected, glancing up to see if anyone had heard the mistake.

The room buzzed with conversations and laughs. No one looked at her. A bright red head of hair moved into view.

Beside that head, the enigmatic duke watched her with an inscrutable expression.

Edmund had wondered if he might see Mrs. Seymour tonight. When she noticed his presence, he dipped his head in an unspoken greeting.

"Oh, this is so exciting." Beside him, Hannah peered

about the room. Her fingers gripped his arm in a vise tight enough to cut off blood supply.

"Why don't you find us some punch," he suggested, uncurling her fingers from their death lock.

"An excellent suggestion." She tiptoed up, planted a kiss on his cheek and bounded off.

Edmund let out a heavy sigh. He'd give anything to not be here right now. Especially with the beautiful Mrs. Seymour darting careful glances his way. The music stopped and she glided toward him.

Who had taught her to move like that? Graceful and elegant, as though guided by the hand of a queen.

"Your Grace," she said, reaching him and offering a respectable curtsy.

"Mrs. Seymour." He bowed.

"I am surprised to see you here. Are you a fan of literature?" She smiled up at him as though they hadn't just had a row a day ago.

She wore a deep green dress that shimmered when she walked. The color played against her skin like sunlight against sky. The dusky hue of her cheeks hinted at heightened emotion, but her eyes held only a casual interest.

He frowned. "I had no idea you'd be here."

Her finely drawn brow lifted, and a tiny twitch at the corner of her rosy lips betrayed amusement. "I hadn't assumed you did."

"Your friend—" he gestured toward Lady Montcroft "—invited us. My first instinct was to reject the offer, but as she is on your list of potential chaperones, and since Hannah has received very few invitations, I considered it prudent to attend."

"I am pleased you received the list." Now her eyes

sparkled with feminine pride. No doubt congratulating herself.

"It has done me no good."

"Manners, Your Grace. You may thank me before you complain."

Several guests brushed by, forcing Mrs. Seymour to move closer to him. The faintest whiff of her perfume reached his nose. He frowned more deeply.

"Thank you," he said through stiff lips. "But your list has turned out to be an empty promise."

"That is difficult to believe."

"A great many things are hard to believe, and yet they are true enough."

"Your Grace, you shall have permanent etch marks in your cheek if you keep up that expression." There was still the hint of laughter in her voice.

"Why do you find my irritation so amusing?" He waved back at Hannah, who wildly fluttered a greeting from across the room, a giant smile upon her face. "How would you feel if there was something you desired greatly but could not have?"

The oddest feeling of stillness touched him. As though his companion, the unflappable Sophia, had stopped breathing. He couldn't explain the shift in the air, yet he felt it nevertheless. He looked down at her. She offered a small smile, her face impassive.

"There are a great many desires I feel, but I manage to refrain from glowering," she answered lightly.

He had the strangest urge in that moment to hug her. For though her face showed nothing but pleasantry, a curious sheen washed across her eyes, deepening the ocean green and instilling within him the impression that he had hurt her somehow.

That thought uppermost, he took great pains to relax his mouth. He lifted the corners of his lips. "Is this better than a glower?"

She actually appeared startled. A little laugh feathered out from her lips, and she covered her mouth with an exotic fan that matched her dress. "It is probably best if you don't fake smiles."

He grinned then, surprised by her words yet not unpleased.

"Ah, *that*, Your Grace, is a very good look for your face."

Their gazes connected, strung together in a tenuous moment of understanding. And something else, something indefinable yet powerful, something that made his fingers ache to hold her close.

Unthinkable.

He pulled back, folding his arms and locating Hannah across the room. She was animated, hands gesturing. The people in her circle were dull in comparison. "The contract is in the process of being dissolved," he said, a rough bitterness coating his words. "I will not use it against you."

"Thank you." Relief was evident in her tone.

"While your list is appreciated, it has proven unproductive."

"You've contacted everyone?" She fanned herself slowly, her eyes focused forward.

"Yes."

"I'm impressed."

"Don't be. They have all rejected my most generous offers." Remembering their pitying expressions and paltry excuses, he furrowed his brow.

"Even Lady Montfort?"

"She, at least, seemed somewhat apologetic. It seems she will not be in London for the full Season this year. Family plans and other nonsense. The others…"

Mrs. Seymour continued waving her fan in slow, languorous motions. "We shall be discussing a historical novel today. Do you read?"

"Are you changing the subject?"

A slow flush of color moved up the back of her neck. He found himself noticing the beauty of her skin, the softness it promised. Her hair had been pulled into what he believed was a chignon. The varied colors, ranging from white to caramel, captivated him.

He moved closer to her. This might be a mistake, perhaps the most colossal of his life, but she was the best chance Hannah had for success.

"They are all afraid for their reputations. Perhaps they are even afraid of me. But you do not fear me." He spoke close to her ear, seeing her shiver as his quiet words swept through her. Yet she did not move away.

"I think we can help each other." Smiling, he brought his mouth closer to her ear and whispered softly, "If you'd be willing, Sophia Seymour."

Chapter Six

The duke was persistent, Sophia would give him that.

She stared out the window of her hackney as it jostled toward her mother's townhome. This morning she had awoken with a determination to find out the truth of the rumors Caroline heard. Scenery passed in a blur, as her mind was full of last night's interactions with His Grace.

Edmund, she thought carefully. Edmund DeVane, Most Noble Duke of Rennington.

All night she had tossed and turned, remembering his breath against her ear, the scent of his presence, the warmth emanating from his skin.

Sighing, she rested her chin in her palm. Though she had managed to extricate herself from the situation, she had not been able to ignore him for the rest of the night. Miss Hannah had been happily involved in the conversazione discussions and had even added thoughtful responses to several ideas articulated by older members. But the duke had retired to a corner of the room, away from their circle of chairs, and glared.

He seemed to have mastered both sullen and angry

at once. His complexion only added to the irascible complexity of his countenance. No wonder Eliza had called him a pirate.

An attractive pirate.

She banished the thought, thankful the hackney had stopped in front of her parents' home. She needed something else to think of today. Worrying about her family's prospects would take her mind off how she felt when she was around Edmund.

Rennington, she corrected herself crossly.

She entered the house, dismayed when no one met her at the door. The butler was nowhere to be seen, and neither was her family. She noted the empty space on the wall where one of her favorite paintings used to hang. Frowning, she traipsed upstairs.

Something clattered at the far end of the hall, followed by muttering and unhappy tones. Sophia strode to the farthest doorway and found her mother sitting on the chaise lounge in the library, putting items into carpetbags. Frederika and Eliza bustled about in different corners of the room.

"Whatever is going on here?" Sophia asked.

"Oh, Sophia!" Eliza was the first to see her, and her exclamation was filled with frustration. "It is horrid."

A dreadful pang of fear started a knot in Sophia's stomach. "It?"

"Your father," her mother said sharply, "has apparently left us in so much debt that we have absolutely nothing to live on. The debts have been called in."

"We are ruined," Frederika said matter-of-factly, as she was often wont to do.

"Surely not." Sophia's legs trembled. She sat in the armchair, feeling light-headed.

"Even Deerfield Cottage. Gone," said Mother.

"But where will you live? How can this be?"

"We shall sell what we have to pay as many debts as we can." Mother put an expensive-looking vase in a small bag. "Frederika, Eliza, take these items to the pawnbroker's near Drury Lane. Andrews is awaiting you with the carriage. You remember the numbers I told you to accept?"

"Yes, Mama." Eliza's face wore a pained expression that curried sadness within Sophia's heart.

"Do not let anyone see you if you want any chance for a debut."

Her sisters nodded, painfully silent, and as they sidled past Sophia, they kissed her cheek. She embraced them, and then watched them walk sedately down the hall, heads bowed. Heart constricting, she turned back to her mother.

"Surely this is not necessary."

"My dear girl, I haven't the heart nor the humor to argue with you." Mother's voice wavered. "It is possible that your father has fled to the continent in order to escape debtor's prison. He has left us here…" At that, her words faltered and she pressed her face into her hands.

Sophia rushed forward. She knelt beside her mother and rubbed circles on her back. "Father would never, ever desert us. I know that with certainty." But then again, she could never have guessed that he would have spent their fortune.

Mother sniffed, and Sophia settled beside her.

"Your father depleted our funds terribly. Both of our homes shall be sold." She sucked back a sob.

"This townhome, too?"

"Everything."

"But where will you live?"

"Once all of the debts are settled, I shall be able to ascertain the state of our finances. Perhaps we can stay with distant relatives."

"You'll stay with me," Sophia pronounced, despite the yawning pit in her stomach.

"You haven't the funds for such a thing," said her mother firmly. "And the size of your home is not conducive to housing four women."

"But Eliza's and Frederika's futures are at stake."

"Perhaps they shall marry beneath them. Just as you did."

Sophia winced. "I know I did not make an advantageous match—"

"Indeed you did not." Mother speared her with a look that sent bitter remorse through Sophia. "Marrying a lawyer, of all things. An untitled, poor third son of an earl. You could have had anyone. That viscount who kept calling, for one. And then there was the earl that singled you out several times. What a shame none of those men ever proposed."

She did her best to hide her reaction to that statement, but Mother knew her too well.

"They did, didn't they?" Mother jabbed a finger at her. "Well, now we find ourselves in a horrific situation, all because you could not find it within yourself to do your duty to your family. Imagine how different things might be had you married one of those men. Or even that sweet baron with the fortune. Do you remember him? So handsome…" Her mother sighed, a mooning expression upon her face.

"I married for love," Sophia told her mother quietly. There was a burning indignation within, a helpless anger, and a sort of bruised emotion. How unkind her mother could be. How insensitive.

"My girl—" and her mother looked at her, something akin to tenderness in her eyes "—love does not fill an empty stomach nor house a family."

Sophia stood quickly, then held out a hand to help her mother up. What could she say? How could she have known her husband would die from a short but serious illness mere months after their marriage?

"There must be something we can do," she said, ignoring the dreadful tightness in her chest and following her mother out of the library.

"There certainly is something *you* can do." Her mother shuffled ahead, shoulders back and head high. "Honor the contract your father made."

"If he wanted it honored, I would think he would have told us about it before I married Charles. Now we have a mess and I've already requested that the duke null the agreement."

Her mother whirled around, eyes flashing. "Oh, you didn't!" Her hand went to her heart. Or perhaps her lungs. Mayhap she felt a faint coming on.

"Of course, I did. Do you want all of society knowing I married one man whilst betrothed to another?" Sophia asked in a quiet yet firm voice. "This contract has created a completely different set of problems. Surely you see that?"

"Stubborn girl." Mother clutched her throat. "What shall become of us?"

For the first time that morning, Sophia feared for Lady Worland. She looped her arm through her mother's and guided her to the stairs.

But when they reached the bottom, Andrews met

them with a frown upon his austere features. The solicitor had arrived. If her family could not pay what was owed upon the townhome, they'd have to leave by month's end.

"There must be some mistake."

"There is not." Mr. Butterfield tipped his hat to them both and headed for the door. "Furthermore, as you are unable to render payment for future services, I consider my job here finished. I shall have the boxes of your husband's paperwork sent over."

And then he was gone, leaving her mother sobbing on the couch and Sophia sitting with her hands clasped politely in her lap, hardly able to breathe.

She had no choice. Allow her family to suffer or take on the suffering for them. Would God frown on a marriage made to save her family rather than to join two hearts?

Remembering the book of Esther, she did not think He would.

Yet it took quite a bit of blinking to keep a tear from sliding down her cheek. She knew what she must do.

Edmund had tried to give Mrs. Seymour time to think about what he said, but in the end, his impatient nature won out. That, and the most recent snub to Hannah at the theater. Seeing her in tears yet again tore at his resolve to give Sophia space, and patience frayed, he found himself at her home.

He paced Sophia's parlor in long, restless strides. How long did it take for a woman to throw on a day dress and present herself? He had no pressing matters this afternoon, but he wished to get Hannah involved in activities as soon as possible. The Season was commencing, but Hannah was feeling the castigation meant for him.

He paused near the window. A garden, visible from a far angle, bloomed. He allowed himself a moment to admire the verdant sight, though if those were his roses, he'd rein them in. Give them some structure.

"Your Grace." Sophia's husky voice came from the door frame.

He turned, expecting beauty, and finding it. She wore a pale blue dress trimmed in a darker blue that brought out the color in her eyes. Her regality, ever present, only confirmed that he was right to take her as his wife.

"Mrs. Seymour. I was just admiring your garden."

She joined him at the window, her perfume wrapping around him in pleasant waves that induced him to draw closer. "It is my favorite part of this home. I do so enjoy roses."

"They are too wild. Your caretaker should cut them back. Create order from the chaos."

"Perhaps I like the chaos." She glanced up at him, eyes sparkling.

A fanciful notion, but it did seem as if the afternoon sunlight made her irises glow.

"Chaos is not conducive to growth," he said.

She shrugged a delicate shoulder, the amusement in her eyes changing to speculation.

"How do you know so much about plants? Do you garden?"

"I dabble," he said gruffly. Turning away before she saw too much of him, he walked to the chair he'd sat in before. The comfortable one with the open arms and flowery embroidered cushion. He sank down and steepled his fingers.

"Oh, dear." She grinned and came toward him. "You

are wearing a very serious look, indeed. Should I be concerned?"

"I have several items of import to discuss with you."

"Worrisome."

She was laughing at him. He did not mind, he realized. In fact, his lips felt a strong urge to curve in response to her smile. She sat across from him on a worn yet attractive chaise lounge. It was placed beneath the window, and sunbeams shimmered against her dress fabric and hair.

"First," he began, "the contract is dissolved. You need not fear word of its existence. Furthermore, no evidence of an identical contract has been found in my own files nor those of my deceased father. You shall be safe from gossip mongering."

"You are too kind," Sophia murmured. He noted her clasped hands relaxed.

Happy for an unfathomable reason, he continued, "Second, Hannah has been snubbed again. I would ask you to consider how you would feel if your sisters were treated unfairly due to no fault of their own."

He did not imagine the slight flicker that crossed her face.

"Third, I was privy to an unsubstantiated rumor that I thought to clarify with you."

She had adjusted her features and if he had not been studying her so closely, he may have missed the way her eyes widened for a fraction of a second.

"This is why I have arrived today. I understand you wish to marry for—" he cleared his throat "—love. However, it seems that our union could also be construed as for something near to that principle—your love for your family, my love for Hannah."

She rose from her seat. "Will you make a good husband? Can I trust you?"

His throat worked. He wanted to speak, to reassure her, but he was suddenly assailed by memories, by experiences he had never spoken of and by a terrible, fearful certainty that he could never be a good husband. His father had utterly failed. His brother, too.

A picture of Hannah's mother filled his mind. The woman she had been before marrying Edmund's brother. Piquant and laughing, filled with joy.

"Edmund," said Sophia, breaking him from his memories. "I do not ask for perfection."

"I have never been a husband." The words tasted hollow to him. Bitter, even. "But I would do my best. I can say that I am an honest man. A fair man. Your family would be cared for, and you would lack for nothing."

He studied her profile, trying to ascertain her thoughts. She had such a straight, fine-boned nose. A strong chin and high brow. Her noble silhouette would make for a striking portrait. Worthy of a duchess.

Sighing, she left the window and resumed her seat from across him. "We must have parameters if we are to do this. Our fathers wanted us married. Do you feel as though we are honoring them by proceeding?"

"I think Hannah needs a chaperone. What our fathers wanted is of no concern to me." His words sounded cold, even to himself.

"What rumors did you hear?"

Surprised by the change in subject, Edmund cringed. "Ugly ones. Concerning your family, it is said your mother and sisters are soon to be destitute, and that your father ran away to the Continent, leaving them behind to face his debts."

She trailed her fingers along the edge of the couch, eyes downcast. "The rumors are not altogether untrue."

He leaned forward, elbows on his knees. "I am sorry to hear that."

Her gaze flashed upward. "Here is the gist of it, Your Grace. I shall marry you, but under two conditions. First, you shall hire a Bow Street Runner to find my father."

"And second?"

"We shall have a marriage in name only."

He tipped his head in acquiescence. "My thoughts exactly. I have never wished for children and I will be only too happy to let the dukedom pass from me."

"We are agreed, then." Her fingers went to her throat, playing with a delicate gold strand about her neck he had not noticed before now. A locket, rather than a jewel, hung upon the chain.

He stood. "We are agreed. I shall have my solicitors draw up the paperwork and apply for a marital license. I will post the banns."

She nodded, and he wished he did not see the sadness she was so plainly trying to hide. "You have never wanted children?" she asked.

"I am not an agreeable sort." The heavy weight of that acknowledgment lay upon his shoulders. "Better for a child to be raised by loving parents, though that is not the prevailing trend in society."

"Yes, I suppose so." She offered him a small smile. "I do have a request. My mother and sisters are losing their townhome. Their other houses in the country are being sold to pay debts."

He held up a hand. "I shall lease them a new townhome. The *ton* shall think they've simply moved. We shall have the marriage banns read immediately and rumors of your family's finances will be replaced with other gossip."

"I cannot thank you enough." Sophia inclined her head. "And when shall I begin chaperoning Miss Hannah?"

"Tonight. I was invited to a soiree. I plan to send you in my stead, with apologies, of course."

"Certainly. I believe you navigate society far better than you think you do." She rose from her place on the couch. "I shall pen a note to my family immediately. My mother is beside herself."

A pang struck Edmund. He had not thought of others' misfortunes in a very long time. There was a relief in Sophia's eyes that blossomed hope within him. He had not very often been thankful to inherit his brother's fortune, but today he was.

"Mrs. Seymour—"

"I give you leave to address me by my given name." She smiled up at him, her lips a lovely, pink bow.

"Sophia." He swallowed the jagged lump crowding his windpipe. "Inheriting the dukedom has never felt a blessing until today."

Though there was still a sadness he could not identify on her features, her smile did not leave. "Indeed. Never have I felt to be blessed in my widowhood, but today, the Lord has turned both of our pain into good."

Edmund suppressed the sudden and very unwelcome urge to pull Sophia into his arms, and to kiss her until they were both breathless. Instead, he accepted her words with a nod.

He was doing this for Hannah. It could never be anything more than a business arrangement.

Chapter Seven

Oh, why had she agreed to this arrangement? Several onerous days later, Sophia found herself in Edmund's drawing room awaiting his presence. After a few nights with his niece, she had reached multiple conclusions about the girl.

None of them tolerable.

"Sit like this, Hannah." Sophia watched the girl as she tried to gracefully sink into the delicate chair in Edmund's drawing room. "That is not badly done," she said.

Hannah immediately lounged back, dropping her head against the wall of the couch. "This is absurd. Why do we have to do this?"

"Do you want to have a successful Season?"

"You know that I do." Hannah pouted. Her hair, which had been smoothly fixed earlier in the morning, sprang out in all directions.

"And do you wish to marry a man with prospects? If so, you must prove that you can be a lady."

The girl made a sound in her throat that sounded suspiciously similar to the sound Edmund often made.

Sophia hid her smile behind her cup of tea and took a sip. "Earls do not wish to marry wild animals."

"I do not sound like an animal."

"You certainly don't sound like a human. Now, you attended finishing school?"

"That dreadful Miss Pettiham's school? It was horrid. She does not want us to show a single feeling. Why, if I so much as gasp, I am called out as uncouth."

Sophia set her cup on the table. "You have a great many feelings which you must control. Remember, self-control is a virtue. A fruit of the spirit."

"I am so dreadfully bored." Hannah sat up, cupping her cheeks with her palms. "When will Uncle Edmund arrive?"

They had been awaiting His Grace for well over an hour. He had business to attend, they'd been told. Hannah's propensity for patience rivaled her uncle's.

"It is quite simple. You may continue to insist on showing every emotion, speaking in whichever way you wish and wearing outlandish clothes, but do not expect to be successful in society. However, if you want to be accepted, if you want to have culture and manners and refinement, then you must learn what I can teach you. What do you want?"

Hannah sighed and rolled her eyes. "I do want to be successful. I truly do."

"Your first lesson is that you must never, ever roll your eyes again. It is rude." Sophia gave her a stern look.

"Very well." Hannah sat up straighter. "I can be refined, Mrs. Seymour. I truly can."

"Wonderful."

"I just don't want to change who I am to fit some whim of social norm."

"You think like your uncle. It is not a bad thing but allow yourself to consider this refinement as a pruning. You will still be a rose, gorgeous and fragrant, but with perhaps fewer thorns."

They grinned at each other and Sophia breathed an inward sigh of relief. Hannah picked up the book she'd been leafing through and Sophia turned her attentions to the window that overlooked St. George Street. The past few days with Hannah had been challenging, to say the least.

The girl was smart, though, and kind. If she could harness her emotions, she'd be welcomed by the *ton*. They might consider her unique, especially with that red hair of hers. Thus far, Sophia had managed to garner them several invitations and they had a busy week ahead.

Which was why they were awaiting Edmund. They needed permission to create a better wardrobe for Hannah.

Sophia hadn't seen him in days. After he'd left her house, she'd roamed about, feeling lost in her own home. Keeping busy with Hannah had helped mitigate some of her emotions, but she wasn't sure how she'd feel when she saw Edmund again.

Husband.

It was almost too difficult to believe she was betrothed. Soon it would be public. How would Hannah react? Sophia's own mother was thrilled but had been sworn to secrecy.

The duke chose that moment to enter the drawing room. He wore a brooding look today. His Hessians gleamed but his hair was as wild as ever, as though the business meeting had turned physical. He glanced at her but was quickly distracted when Hannah jumped up and enveloped him in a hug.

"Finally," she said, sweeping her arm around the room. "We have been waiting forever."

"An overstatement," said Edmund. His gaze centered on Sophia, and the intensity of that dark look caused a shiver to ripple through her.

He patted Hannah's shoulder and joined her on the couch. That left Sophia across from them, the focal point of the duke's attention.

"I thought you two were riding in Hyde Park this morning."

"Your Grace, Hannah's wardrobe is…" How did she say it without insulting Hannah's taste in clothing?

Both Hannah and Edmund were staring at her, unsmiling. Sophia found her own mouth attempting to quirk upward. They were rather amusing, those two. They did not see their similarities, nor how their temperaments impeded their goals.

She tried again. "A lady of excellent breeding must present herself in a certain fashion. Especially in her debut year. Hannah's wardrobe, though expensive, is a bit…" She made a delicate throat clear, but they were both staring at her as if she'd lost her mind. She sighed. "Her clothing is not in keeping with what one expects of a duke's niece."

"But I picked those fabrics myself," burst out Hannah. "And the modiste loved my ideas. My dresses are in the height of fashion."

Sophia bit her lip to keep from smiling. The bright oranges and turquoises Hannah preferred were not in any height of fashion, in any country, even if the cuts of the dresses were sublime. "Your modiste, no doubt, was dutifully impressed by your uncle's title. Perhaps she did not possess the fortitude to deny your demands."

Edmund drummed his fingers against the couch arm. "I spent a fortune on her clothes."

"We shall keep some, but she is a debutante. Her gowns are too colorful, too forceful, and some of them are quite unbecoming."

Hannah snorted. "You expect me to look like a pasty girl out of the schoolroom."

"You *are* out of the schoolroom," Edmund reminded her, and if Sophia wasn't mistaken, she noted a sudden twinkle in his eye.

So Edmund had a soft spot for Hannah. Observing them together warmed Sophia.

"You shall never be pasty," she said to Hannah.

Hannah squinted at her, forehead furrowed and mouth scrunched.

"Also, you should master the art of not concocting odd facial expressions, or you shall give yourself wrinkles," Sophia told her. "No husband wants a bride with lines all about her face from too much scowling."

They both gaped at her. No doubt they were never spoken to in such a way. She didn't care to be so plainspoken, but desperate times called for desperate measures.

"If I am to be your chaperone," she said serenely, "then you must trust my judgment. I do not wish to link my reputation to a girl who does not care about hers."

"Hannah, will you excuse us?" Edmund interlaced his fingers, brows lowered.

"Very well." Hannah stood, tossing her hair. "I sup-

pose I shall donate all those dresses you deem so ugly."
She flounced out of the room.

"Your niece has been spoiled," Sophia said without
preamble.

Edmund's head cocked to the side. "A whole new
wardrobe? That seems to define spoiling."

"Hannah has not been accepted by her peers. Her
clothes and manner make it clear that she is not suitable for certain…circles."

"Who says?" He shoved a hand through his hair, raking it around into a mess.

"The lack of invitations says."

"Absurd."

"Is this what Hannah wants? To be on the marriage
mart, to make a good match?"

"You know it is."

"Then she must grow up and accept that success requires sacrifice."

Edmund leaned back, stretching out his legs and eyeing her with something akin to annoyance. His fingers
remained joined, an argument against his relaxed posture. "You place a great emphasis on reputation and
facade."

"Is that not why you've chosen me? We could avoid
marriage and I could simply chaperone her."

He made a sound in the back of his throat. "Then
who would care for your family?"

Perhaps he did not intend it to be so, but the comment carried barbs that jabbed right into the vicinity of
her heart. Had she married more *advantageously*, as her
mother had put it, she would be able to support her family. She refused to allow any emotion to cross her face.

Instead, she said, "Your point is taken. May I have your permission to amend her wardrobe?"

"That will not solve the issue of her manners, though."

"I'm afraid, Your Grace, that you may be the biggest influence on her behavior. Perhaps if you attend a few events with us, she will cease her bias against people she doesn't even know."

"But I know them." He sat up, irritation shouting through the sharp angles of his form. "If it were up to me, she'd never marry. She would never become a shell of a person."

Sophia dipped her head to hide how his words stung. She played with her locket, thinking of Charles and his gentle way of speaking. How different from this man before her. And yet, Edmund's straightforwardness, while uncomfortable, gave her freedom to speak plainly herself.

Gathering her breath, she met his jutting jaw and flashing eyes with a calm serenity she most certainly did not feel. "All people wear a mask, you included, to hide and to protect what lies within. You accuse others of inauthenticity, yet you while away at a country estate, refusing to interact with society. I do not believe comportment, decorum and good manners equal a facade. They are simply the outermost layer of a human. Consider how your manner and words make others feel. That is the crux of the matter, I think, that you would rather pummel everyone with your fickle emotions and then take no responsibility for the consequences of that bombardment."

Edmund had unleashed a side of Mrs. Seymour he had not thought existed.

Though the remnants of irritation still pulsed through his blood, another emotion was rising. That of curiosity. Perhaps he'd always been curious about Mrs. Seymour and her ability to contain her every feeling, bottling herself into a perfect porcelain product for the *haut ton*'s appetite.

This impassioned response increased his curiosity. What secret thoughts did she have but never express? What ideas ran through her mind that no one else knew about? He watched her hands flowing through the air as she spoke. Fluid and graceful.

"Have you heard a word I said?" she demanded, and there was such a picture of indignation upon her face that Edmund surprised himself with a bark of laughter.

Sophia's mouth made a small pink O.

"Forgive me," he said. "I should not laugh at your concerns."

Color stained her cheeks.

"I heard all that you said, Mrs. Seymour. I'll admit—" he stroked his chin "—your accusations have surprised me."

She had the presence to blush more deeply.

"Has my riotous temper always caused you to feel so vehemently? I do recall at our first ball that you felt harangued."

He had never seen someone turn so red. Not even Hannah, and she had an enormous capacity for flushed cheeks.

"I'll confess, these last few days have been trying," she hedged.

"Hannah is wearing on your nerves?"

She blinked, and he felt an indefinable tug in his chest. If anything, his newly betrothed lady inspired some sort of feeling within. He supposed that was a good thing. He knew many a husband who disliked their wives.

"Our betrothal has me on edge," she answered.

"I am not immune to the feeling."

"No?"

He laughed again, but this time it was harsher, less from amusement and more from a frightening scorn that lurked within. "I am nearing my twenty-ninth year, Mrs. Seymour. Do you not think if I wished for a wife, I would have found one by now?"

"With all due respect, Your Grace, you would need to overcome your reputation first."

"That is exactly my point. I have taken no pains to reassure society as to my husbandly qualities. Our arrangement, though unexpected, is conducive to our life-styles and interests."

"That is true. I suppose my circumstance could be much worse."

"It is not outside the realm of possibility that you keep your home," he said quietly.

"That is far too kind of you." Her lips pressed together ever so circumspectly. "I do not feel I deserve such an offer."

"Why? Do you regret your outburst?" he asked.

She could not meet his eyes, staring instead at some space beyond his right shoulder. "It was not well done of me."

"I rather enjoyed your lapse in perfection."

When she didn't respond, he battled the urge to go to her, to touch her slender jaw and turn her face toward him. "Why are you so opposed to showing any type of feeling? Would you have me believe that you have no deeper emotions, that you are a superficial woman of means?"

"We both know I have no means to speak of. Regarding emotions, they are best kept from the helm." Now she met his gaze, her eyes suspiciously bright.

Was she trying not to cry? Edmund had the most uncomfortable notion that he had caused this and now he must fix it. "Buy whatever you need for Hannah. I have plenty of money."

She rendered a conciliatory nod.

"And," he added, hoping to make her smile, "I have procured a Runner. He is following up on your father's whereabouts as we speak. Soon we shall find him."

Happily, her expression lightened. "That is wonderful news. Thank you so much."

Now he felt awkward, though he could not explain why. "Perhaps you have a point about how I treat others. There are reasons…but I suppose they are not excuses. I shall speak with Hannah. She is not spoiled. She's impetuous and strong-willed."

"Much like you." Now the original Sophia had returned, sweetly cool, her face softened with understanding amusement.

"Say it isn't so." He cringed. "And do you really believe it best that I attend a social event with her?"

"Yes. Lady Valeria is hosting a ball tonight. It's sure to be a crush. Why don't you come and set the example for to Hannah on how one's station influences one's behavior?"

He groaned. "You are torturing me."

"Nonsense," Sophia said lightly, leaning over and rapping his knee with her fan. "You shall be the talk of the *ton*. I shall introduce Hannah to several ladies of importance and screen her dance partners. You shall let people know you expect Hannah to be treated with all the significance of your title."

"Isn't my title *Beast*?"

Her head tilted. She regarded him with a tender smirk. "Only if you so choose."

Chapter Eight

The ball was every bit the crush Sophia had anticipated. She meandered among the guests, exchanging pleasantries and looking for Edmund and Hannah. She had not heard their names called yet, and gathered they must not have arrived.

She scanned the room yet again, disarmed by the nervous patter of her heart.

"Mrs. Seymour, how well you look." Lady Britton appeared beside her. She gave a sincere smile, and Sophia returned it.

"As do you. How goes your charity with the orphans?"

"We have been busy, needless to say. The poor souls. Half their mothers are in Newgate prison and the fathers are nowhere to be found. I wish I could take in every child, but we are doing our best to administer at least one hot meal a day and to provide clean clothes."

"I understand your challenge," Sophia said. "We are in a difficult situation, are we not? Blessed beyond measure with financial stability and yet still unable to fully fund our causes."

She and Lady Britton had long served together in helping London's impoverished, though their courses had veered into separate paths.

"How are your ladies?" asked Lady Britton.

"The results of Lord Windley's good works have been most astounding."

"Indeed?" Surprise registered upon the lady's handsome features.

"Yes, it seems at first difficult to pull the young women from their chosen professions, but when offered respite, good food and the promise of respectable income, most are open to leaving prostitution. There are some who return to their old lives, but many find hope in a different way of living." Sophia thought of dear Betsy, who had dressed her tonight and accompanied her as a lady's maid. "My current maid has the most astounding gift of fashion."

Lady Britton looked through her eyepiece at Sophia. "You are indeed the picture of style tonight. I would have never thought of pairing that fan with your dress, and yet it is riveting. The colors bring out your complexion. Is this the work of your maid?"

"Yes. I did question her choice as well as the color of the dress."

"Well, I think that hue of rose is fabulous on you. It's light enough to hearken back to your spectacular debut, but dark enough to indicate your status."

"My widowhood, you mean." Sophia felt emotion tug at her mouth. She maintained her composure, but perhaps Lady Britton, who was as close a friend as a lady of her station could be, touched her shoulder.

"I did not mean to dredge up memories, my dear." The lady's gaze was compassionate. "I find it heartening how you've thrown yourself into good works. Who would guess such talent from a maid? And if not for your charities, wasted in the streets."

"The Lord hears the call of His own," murmured Sophia. She had to believe that despite her losses, He heard the cries of her heart. Especially for the vulnerable women wandering London's slums, destroying their futures and those of their children.

A sudden hush filled the room. Even the music stopped. As the Most Honorable Duke of Rennington was announced, along with his niece, Miss Hannah DeVane, murmurs created a steady buzz. Sophia could not see them at the entrance of the ballroom, but she supposed now was the time to start her duty as not only chaperone, but redeemer of reputation.

"I have heard the duke is in search of a wife," Lady Britton whispered to Sophia from behind her fan.

"I have heard he is betrothed," replied Sophia nonchalantly.

She grinned, leaving a dumbfounded aristocrat behind her. She made her way toward Hannah and Edmund. The music drummed up again, a perky quadrille that quelled the dregs of gossip as people searched for their partners.

As she skirted the ballroom, several women greeted her. She mentioned to each that she'd be chaperoning Miss Hannah and would bring her around for introductions.

She threaded through another group and spotted Edmund near the refreshments. Her heart thudded into her throat.

Magnificent did not begin to describe his presence. Never could she have guessed the power of proper attire upon his form. He had combed his hair, yet it still fell in wild abandon.

His tailcoat was cut to perfection. His boots, shiny and unmarked. She came closer, seeing that for tonight, even his cravat was exquisitely tied. Beside him, Hannah had the presence of mind to wear a frothy white gown. The plethora of sequins and frills festooning her dress glittered beneath the lights of the ballroom. She looked radiant.

Sophia reached them in short order, noting the look of welcome upon Edmund's face.

"Mrs. Seymour." He bowed and she curtsied.

"Your Grace, I am here to take Hannah about the room. There are several people to introduce her to."

"Shall I accompany you?"

Sophia's first instinct was to say no. He was too large, too compelling. Her senses felt overwhelmed by his nearness. She smelled sandalwood and the press of the ball pushed them closer than she liked. She looked up at him, prepared to tell him to mingle with his friends, but a peculiar look lit his dark eyes. Almost akin to nervousness.

Compassion welled within.

"Yes, join us. Hannah shall get the maximum amount of introductions and fill her dance card in no time."

His eyes glittered as he peered down at her. Heart pattering, she fanned her neck, which had grown exceedingly warm.

She did not move away, although she knew she should. Hannah stood in front of them, watching the dancing and sipping at her punch. Every so often she'd raise up on her toes to see someone better. Her oblivious rapture gave Sophia a contented feeling.

Edmund let out a long, heavy sigh. "This is excruciating. I do not even know who to talk to first."

"Why don't we see if Lord Boxing is here? Isn't he a friend of yours? Has he met Hannah?"

"He is not suitable."

Sophia chuckled at the cantankerous remark. "If you are like most fathers, no man shall measure up. Let us find her someone to love."

"You and love. Why are you so determined about such an ephemeral emotion? A good marriage requires stability and finances, not feelings. Emotions do not put food on the table."

How much he sounded like her mother. She lifted a shoulder, watching the joy on Hannah's face and the interplay amongst the dancers. "Love feeds the soul."

Beside her, Edmund made a wheezing sound. She turned and found him *laughing*.

"You are impossible, Your Grace."

"You did not answer my question," he said when he was done making fun of her. "What inspires your devotion to the cause of love?"

"Experience has taught me that a marriage built on the foundation of love tends to be more agreeable."

"We should define love then, for I agree a mutual respect, even a friendship, could create a marriage conducive to peace and harmony."

A young man stopped in front of them, standing close enough to peek at Hannah every so often, but as they had not been introduced, he could only give her covert looks. Hannah was not immune to his attentions. She glanced at him and smiled.

Sophia felt rather than saw the duke's head snap up. She put out her arm just as he surged forward and managed to stop him from ruining Hannah's first ball. "Your Grace," she whispered, "let us do this properly."

She looked up at him and almost laughed at the scowl marking his features. The duke could emote, she would give him that. The young man looked behind him, as though sensing Edmund's annoyance, and a startled expression flitted across his face. He disappeared into the throng.

Hannah spun around and pointed her finger at her uncle. "You."

Oh, dear. This could turn out disastrous. Seeking damage control, Sophia quickly moved between them.

"Hannah," she said quietly, hoping the people standing near them would not hear. "You must at this very moment control both your expression and your temper. It is one thing for a duke to have a reputation as irascible and rude. It is quite another for a debutante. If you create a scene, I assure you, your Season will be a dismal failure."

Hannah's eyes widened. Her cheeks lost color. "But—"

"Whatever you say, be quiet and be discreet." Sophia smiled as though having an ordinary conversation. "And trust me when I tell you that we are being watched at this very moment. Our every expression noted and stored away for future fodder. Do try to smile, dear."

Hannah's lips curved in what looked more like a grimace.

"Show some teeth," Sophia prompted.

She bared them, and Edmund started laughing.

"This is not funny," Hannah gritted out. "That man was going to ask me for a dance. I know it."

"He has not been introduced to you," said Sophia.

"Because Uncle Edmund scared him away." Hannah's mouth relaxed and though her eyes were darting angry glares toward her uncle, she managed to look somewhat civil.

Sophia took her arm, steering her toward the direction the young man had disappeared to. "There is an easy way to fix this. We shall find him in the crowd and I'll see if anyone I know is acquainted with him. We shall ask for an introduction." She gave Edmund a pointed look.

He had the grace to appear dutifully abashed. He inclined his head, and she released a relieved sigh. This wouldn't work without his cooperation. Thankfully he spent the rest of the evening following them about, mostly scowling, but trying at times to smile.

The young men they encountered avoided meeting the eyes of the duke but somehow both Hannah and Sophia ended up with full dance cards. Edmund stayed out of the dancing, preferring to glower from a distance.

Sometime after midnight, Sophia left Hannah chatting a few feet away to check on His Grace. He stood near potted plants, his hands clasped behind his back, his legs set apart in a stubborn stance.

"Now that you've put in an appearance, you should go home." She tapped his shoulder with her fan. "I have this well in hand."

Edmund's mouth pressed together. "I really do not think Hannah should be left alone in that circle. Look at those young bucks. Fortune hunters, all of them."

Sophia laughed. "Nonsense. Hannah is beautiful and entertaining. She is also new. They are all champing at the bit to get to know her. Isn't this what you wanted?"

"No."

"You may not wish to lose Hannah, but you do hope her to be successful, correct?"

He gave a grudging nod, but tightness tugged the corner of his eyes.

"Go home, Edmund. You haven't danced, you've barely eaten. Let me do what you have—" She almost said "hired" but caught herself. "What you expect me to do."

Edmund did not want to leave the ball. Did Sophia really suppose he would leave Hannah with these gaping, slack-jawed boys?

His hands balled at his sides as his body began to heat with frustration. Anger was a hard ball in his chest. Hannah may not be the little girl bereaved by the loss of her parents anymore, but she was still *his* little girl. Innocent, expressive, unprepared for the cynical world he once inhabited.

"And what happens," he said gruffly to Sophia, who stood looking over the ballroom with a beatific smile, "when they abandon her. When someone new arrives on the scene. Someone prettier. More witty. What happens when she becomes the focus of their scorn and disapproval? No, I shall stay right here and if anyone dare cut her, they shall deal with my wrath."

"Your wrath? Really, Your Grace, there is no cause for melodrama. This is the normal course of things."

He growled. At that, Sophia turned and looked up at him. Beauty shone from her tonight and every curl had its place.

"You truly must stop with that silly noise. And fix your expression. Don't you want Hannah to find a good man? All the good ones shall be scared away and only the foolish ones remaining if you continue with your ridiculous faces."

"My face is not ridiculous."

"Your expressions are. Do try to control your emotions or the gossip columns shall be filled with your facial antics and Hannah will most assuredly suffer for it."

He tried very hard to curve his lips, but he couldn't quite force them into a smile. "None of them are good enough for her."

"How can you possibly know such a thing? Do you recognize any of them? Are you personally acquainted with their characters? And yet you sit in judgment." She delivered the words in a gentle tone.

He rolled back his shoulders in an effort to release the stress of seeing his little girl grown into a woman. Hannah laughed, tossing her head back, at something the towhead beside her said. The circle she stood with consisted of several men and women, mostly young, and it was obvious she was enjoying herself immensely.

He inhaled deeply. Sophia's perfume rose to greet him, and for a moment, he forgot his anger. He saw only her, felt only her, the strength and beauty of her presence.

Stubborn female that she was, she had made this happen. Hannah's face shone with joy and all the knots that had tied Edmund's stomach for weeks began to unravel.

Sophia used her fan languorously, her head tilted to the side as she watched his niece. He had not ever wanted to marry. He had actively avoided such a shackle. But now…could there be a better person to attach his name to?

"Edmund," murmured Sophia, casting a playful look his way, "you are staring at me again."

"I am thinking."

"About what an amazing chaperone I am? About how Hannah shall fall in love and live happily ever after?"

He laughed. "Hardly. I'm attempting to find the wicked in you. No one can be perfect."

She swiveled to face him, her eyes large and earnest. Perhaps even a little sad. "I assure you, I am very far from perfection."

"I know it." He winked at her, surprised by the responding flush in her cheeks. "I will discover all your secrets."

"Speaking of discovery, any word on my father?"

"You shall be the first to know when there is."

"Then this arrangement we have made is probably for the best." She played with the chain around her neck.

"No ruby tonight?"

"You noticed?"

"I notice everything." *About you.* But he could not utter such a thing. She might misconstrue his meaning, begin to expect more from their partnership than he ever intended to give. Money, he had plenty of. Affection, he could offer, if he so chose. *If* she earned such a thing, over time.

But his heart…no, that had turned to stone long ago.

He trusted no one, especially a woman whose crowning achievement was in earning the blessings of a society that had betrayed him.

A society from which he must keep his deepest secret.

Chapter Nine

"Oh, Sophia, look at them all." Hannah spun about her bedroom, touching each new dress with reverent fingers. Only a week later, and their modiste had delivered an entirely new wardrobe. Edmund's money and station ensured prompt service.

"I shall admit that you were right and I was wrong. These are splendidly fashionable," Hannah gushed.

"They are much more suited to your complexion." Sophia inspected the clothes draped across the bed. They had been delivered this morning and Hannah had sent a note for Sophia to come see them. When she'd arrived, it was to find an exuberant Hannah trying on each dress. Even her lady's maid seemed to be enjoying the process, giggling with Hannah as she shrugged out of the current concoction.

"Thank you so much." Without warning, Hannah pulled Sophia into a hug. The girl was a little shorter than Sophia, but she was surprised by her strength.

"You're welcome." A surprising lump caught in Sophia's throat. "You remind me of my sisters. I shall have to introduce you sometime."

"I would dearly love that. How old are they?" Hannah showed her back to the maid, who began removing the new day dress.

Sophia sat in a chair located in the corner of the room. "Frederika is fifteen and Eliza is eighteen."

"Eliza has not had her Come Out yet?"

"She shall, soon, I hope. Our father has gone for a while. When he returns, life shall resume." She dared not think about if he was dead somewhere. The thought had bothered her for months, but after the initial panic of him missing the first month, she and her sisters had decided to presume him alive somewhere. He would explain himself.

He had to.

Hannah gasped, pulling Sophia from the fearful thoughts plaguing her. She held up a velvet lined, powder blue riding habit. "Oh, this is darling. What is the weather like today?"

"It was sunny when I arrived." She had been up early, unable to sleep, thinking of Edmund and his behavior at the ball. He was so protective of Hannah. It was quite endearing. And then he had winked at her... almost as if flirting.

Which was incredibly silly, of course. They were to be wed. It made sense he'd want to be on good terms with her, and she with him. Looking beyond the perfection, he'd said.

Her face felt warm as she remembered his words, and the way it seemed he truly wished to see her, to see beyond the visible.

Hannah walked over and dropped a pile of letters into Sophia's lap. "These are invitations. I was apparently a grand success at Lady Valeria's, due to your impeccable advice." Her green eyes sparkled with merriment. "We shall go riding this afternoon in Hyde Park. Invite your sisters."

Sophia started to protest but Hannah held up a hand in an imperious manner. "It shall do no good to argue with me. I fancy a ride today, and I shall show off my outfit. Have you any plans this afternoon?"

"I had thought to do some charity work—"

"You shall ride in the park with me as my chaperone. Write to your sisters at once. Or better yet, let us take Uncle Edmund's carriage. Do you suppose I could convince him to buy a phaeton and let me drive it?" Hannah giggled at the thought.

Hours later, they found themselves in Hyde Park, riding complacent mares and showing off Hannah's new riding habit. While warm, the afternoon sun was not unbearable. Frederika had declined the invitation to ride, having been caught up in some sort of experiment with her science society. Eliza had accompanied them, and she and Hannah got along famously.

They rode ahead of Sophia, their heads bent as they giggled together. There were several other riders in the park, as well as curricles and fancy phaetons. Some ladies were taking a promenade, their gowns like flowers in a field.

Sophia smiled, thinking of her own first Season. Such a whirlwind of dances, soirees and theater. And then Charles. The surprisingly quiet lawyer who won her heart with gentle glances and intelligent conversation. Perhaps she had not made the best match, but they had been in love and that was all they had needed.

She watched the girls, noting their ladylike horsemanship.

"Mrs. Seymour." Edmund pulled up beside her, riding an impressive bay thoroughbred with a lively gait. "My staff informed me you two had gone for a ride. I thought I'd join you."

Sophia tried to ignore the sudden skip her heart made. "But of course. I did not realize you enjoy riding."

"What do you think I do all day in the country?"

"Read? Bake? Count your shillings, one by one."

He raised his brow at her, looking both amused and affronted.

"Hannah is enjoying herself," he said, instead. "It is a beautiful day for a ride."

Indeed, the grass gleamed verdant and a refreshing breeze ever so often brushed one's face. A few wispy clouds traversed the sky in slow abandon.

"I do not get out enough," Sophia confessed. "Hannah insisted on the park today."

"She is a force to be reckoned with."

They rode in companionable silence. Sophia waved to several peers, and she was happy to see that many of the women they passed had also acknowledged Hannah and Eliza.

"What sort of hobbies do you enjoy?" asked Edmund.

The question surprised her. Such an ordinary inquiry, but it struck her as out of the ordinary. To take interest in her personally…but perhaps she should get used to it. They were to be married, after all. Hadn't he said he wanted to know more about her?

"I like roses. Despite your disapproval of their chaos, I find great enjoyment in watering them and tending to the garden," she answered.

"You will not like my roses, then."

"Whyever not? Do they have a peculiar stench?"

He laughed. "I shall let you decide."

"Very cryptic, Your Grace." She patted the mare's neck, enjoying the feel of her soft coat beneath her fingertips. "I am not much of a horsewoman, but I do like animals."

"Do you have any pets?"

"No, and I'm not sure why." She squinted against the sun. A pet would have brought great comfort after her husband's death. Acquiring one had never occurred to her.

"We have a few hounds at my estate," he said. "A mastiff, as well. They are great beasts but gentle with family."

"Oh, my. A mastiff." Her hand went to her heart. "They are quite large."

"They're fearsome protectors."

"Really?" She guided her mare to follow the girls, who had veered off onto a sun-dappled path that, if she remembered correctly, wound toward the Serpentine. "That is a helpful piece of information to know. I am involved with a charity in which mastiffs might serve well. Do you breed your dogs?"

She glanced at him, noting he looked close to handsome despite a general disarray about his person. Even more, he rode in a relaxed way, as if the openness of nature induced him to contentment.

"I could breed them," he mused. "I hadn't thought of doing so, nor have I a reason. What type of charity requires a guard dog?"

"The kind that protects ladies of the night."

His expression almost made her smile.

"You're serious?" Nothing she had said could have surprised Edmund more. Sophia Seymour, Diamond of the First Water, Notable Chaperone, sullying her hands with the lower classes? He knew she was kind. That was obvious. But what of her station and place in society?

"Now you are surprised by me. How the tables have turned." A rueful smile crossed her face.

She looked resplendent today, he grudgingly noted. The deep blue of her habit accentuated her creamy complexion and brought out the blue in her eyes. The warm weather rosied her lips, a visual he tried not to dwell on.

"I understand now your pique when I was surprised you took in Hannah," she continued. "How uncomfortable to be unfairly judged. Am I right in assuming that you supposed me too perfect to associate with those not of my social equal?"

The heat of shame coursed through Edmund. His horse, sensing tension, tried to break into a canter. He tightened the reins, weighing his words carefully. "I did not think you involved yourself in charity."

"All ladies are to be charitable. A lesson Hannah should learn soon."

"Do you actually associate with these women?"

"If by associate, you mean talk to, then yes." She sent him a prim look. "I also teach etiquette classes and find employment for those who wish to leave that lifestyle."

Admiration grew within Edmund. "How have I never heard of this?"

"We both know how."

Because he had shunned society. Cheeky woman. He grinned. "And how would mastiffs fit into this charity work of yours?"

"We've a few houses where we keep boarders. These are, of course, the women who have left their lives on the streets or as courtesans to learn a new trade or skill.

As you may guess, we can only afford so much, and our houses are not always in the best of neighborhoods."

The girls ahead reached the river and dismounted, tethering their horses' reins to a post. Sophia made no move to dismount. She stared across the river, as though deep in thought. He pulled his horse forward, situating himself beside her.

The Serpentine glittered beneath the sunlight.

"Have there been issues, then?"

She blinked, focusing back to him. How pretty she was, he realized again. She had stayed a widow for how long? He tried to do the math but realized he had no clue as to her age.

"Yes, plenty of issues. The problem is that we don't like to keep a man at the houses where our ladies live, but sometimes men from their past show up. Only a fortnight ago, one tried to force his way in, and he gave the women quite the scare. As you might imagine, it takes more than a bit to terrify these women."

"A mastiff would discourage that kind of behavior."

"Yes." She smiled brightly, the whites of her teeth gleaming in the afternoon bloom. "And the women would have a puppy to love, to care for. We all need to have someone, don't we?"

"Yes." How right she was. There had been that cold, dead place inside of him when his brother and Hannah's mother died, and he had been sure it would never thaw. It had when Hannah had come to live with him, but much like a frostbite, first the dullness, then burning as his nerves came back to life. As his new reality superimposed upon his naive ideals.

Hannah and the other girl skipped rocks at the river's

edge. Her hair was fairly glowing. She looked like her mother, but for her hair color.

Sophia watched the girls for a moment. "Does Hannah favor her mother?"

"She is the spitting image." His throat felt parched, dried of all feeling.

"I cannot imagine a life without my mother. She must miss her terribly."

Edmund took in Sophia's profile. "She doesn't speak of her often. Naomi was a bright soul, but a bit like a butterfly. She did not pay Hannah much mind."

"How sad. My mother is so involved with her daughters…"

"I didn't think anything of it at the time. I was only twelve when my brother, who was much older than me, married. And Naomi only a few years my senior. Hannah was often left at their country estate with my old nanny."

Sophia glanced at him. "Is that where you live when not in London?"

"No. I prefer to live at Rennington, my estate near Devonshire."

"Devonshire?" Her voice rose in a pleasant way. "I have heard that region is lovely."

"I have other holdings, as well. When we are married, you may choose any of my houses to make your home. Or, as I have suggested already, you may keep your current townhome and stay in town."

He didn't know where she wished to live after their marriage and the last time he'd mentioned her home, she'd been noncommittal. A surprising curiosity bothered him. He wanted to know what she preferred.

As usual, her expression revealed nothing but polite acceptance.

"And where does Hannah stay?"

"She lived with me until I sent her to finishing school."

"How did that come about?"

He shrugged. "After her parents' deaths, she stayed with an aunt, but the woman was a poor relation. About two years later, she brought Hannah to me and asked that I see to her education and future."

"Could you have refused?"

He held her gaze. "Yes."

Three riders came upon them, thankfully interrupting the conversation. He did not like to think of those days when darkness had been his comfort and anger his nourishment.

Sophia knew the lady and made introductions. He made no effort to smile and the woman and the two gentlemen accompanying her, sons he found out, did not try to engage him in conversation. His horse stomped a hoof and Edmund backed out of the little circle to give the stallion space. Hannah and the other girl rode over, and more introductions were made.

He listened with half an ear and breathed a sigh of relief when the trio left.

"Let's go to Gunter's for ices," Hannah declared, wheeling her horse toward the direction of the park's exit.

"You just want to see if Mr. Aimsley will be there," teased the other girl.

Edmund's gaze narrowed. Who was this young woman, anyway? Sophia had not had a chance to introduce them yet.

She came to that conclusion just as he did.

"Your Grace, allow me to introduce my younger sister, Miss Eliza Hawkins. She is not out yet but we hope when Father returns…"

"I see." Edmund gave Miss Hawkins a stiff nod. She resembled Sophia, though darker in complexion. A spattering of freckles danced across her nose and her hair lacked the whiteness of Sophia's.

"It is a pleasure to meet you," said Eliza. "Truly an honor."

He lifted a brow, glancing at Sophia, but the lady's polite smile didn't even budge.

"Did you know he's called the Beast of London?" Hannah giggled, covering her mouth in a paltry attempt to stifle her mirth.

A scowl tugged at his lips. He felt his mood darkening by the moment. And here he'd thought he might enjoy an outing with the ladies.

"Oh, yes." Eliza nodded perkily. "I know a great deal about your uncle."

Sophia shushed them, her eyes darting up to meet his, an apology within.

"Now, about Mr. Aimsley. Do you think he shall like lemon ices? I think he was rather romantic the way he made sheep's eyes at you." Miss Hawkins laughed.

Sheep's eyes? The girls started forward, jabbering about the man, and Edmund's jaw clenched.

"Come now," said Sophia, edging her horse near to his. "There's no need to look like a pirate on the prowl. They are just two women laughing about a handsome man."

"Who is this Aimsley?"

Talking ceased and both girls turned to look at him. He had shouted the words, he realized.

A grimace cut across Sophia's face. "I do not know if my hearing shall recover from that volume."

"I apologize," he said, teeth grinding. "Now, who is Aimsley?"

Sophia laughed. To his annoyance, he liked the clear sound. Like a bell on a cold day, her laughter warmed him.

"One of the two brothers who were just introduced to you," she said. "They are both Mr. Aimsley, though one is a Peter and one is a Paul."

He tried to remember their faces and failed.

"Take deep breaths, Your Grace. They are both suitable candidates for marriage. The elder will inherit the earldom and the younger has plans to purchase a commission."

"To be an officer?"

They moved out into the open park again, crossing dappled grass.

"Yes, an honorable profession."

He made a disapproving sound in his throat.

"I see where Hannah gets her habit of making animal noises."

Edmund glared at Sophia. She ignored him.

"Does it bother you when people call you a beast?" The question was gently asked.

He glanced at her, but she was staring ahead, steering her horse to follow the girls as they rode presumably toward sweet confections and annoying society.

"No," he answered truthfully. "I care not a whit what people think."

"Then why are you so angry?"

"I dislike people." He swept a hand in front of him, gesturing to the crowds that surrounded them. "Hyde Park on a sunny day proves a popular place to see and be seen. That is their sole purpose in being here."

"For shame, Edmund." Her tone held light censure. "You know very little of who is here today, and you cannot presume their motives. Certainly we go to the park for superficial reasons, but we also go for companionship and social connections. I enjoy seeing old friends and acquaintances, catching up on their news and admiring the finery of my peers. It is as though seeing a rainbow of colors. Is it wrong to appreciate beauty?"

Now she looked at him, and her features were the perfect orchestra of symmetry. Patrician nose, gently curved lips and eyes the color of the Celtic sea beneath a clear sky.

He swallowed hard, ruing the dryness of his mouth and the sudden uptick in his pulse. "No. It is not wrong."

"That's settled, then." She pulled to the left, following the girls. "I have an idea. Are you involved in any type of charity?"

"I am a duke. Of course I support charities."

"But are you involved? Do you see or know the people you help?"

"I prefer to be alone."

She made a *tsking* noise that was not unattractive. "You shall accompany me tomorrow. I have plans with Lord Windley to visit one of the houses I told you about and I will be conducting a small seminar on etiquette."

He side-eyed her. A smirk edged her face.

"Also, I believe it would be a worthwhile endeavor to hold a ball."

He snorted. "No."

"Oh, Edmund, don't be a stodgy old bear."

Taken aback, he laughed. Her smirk widened and if he wasn't mistaken, the blue in her eyes sparkled. "This is the perfect opportunity to repair your reputation and to increase Hannah's visibility. She can easily make a smart match if introduced to the right kind of people."

"I don't want the people I despise flooding my house with their chatter and gossip. I shall attend your etiquette class, but only because I want to make sure my future wife is involved with people who are on the up-and-up."

Sighing, she nudged her heels into her horse's flanks. "I shall change your mind."

"Never," he said, but she was already racing ahead of him, catching up to the ladies.

Her laugh carried behind her, and he had the feeling that if he wasn't careful, this lady was going to get all that she wanted, at an expense more costly than he wanted to pay.

Chapter Ten

A month later, somehow a ball was being held in his house.

His home, a spacious townhome worthy of a duke, and held by his family for two generations, had been transformed. People from all over London were arriving. He had heard Sophia explaining they would invite gentlemen as well as landed gentry. She wanted this to be a crush.

What he wanted was to crush his head against the wall. In a moment of weakness, he had bent beneath the force of two willful souls and agreed to allow a party.

A *party*. But alas, that word proved to be subjective when interpreted by ambitious females, and its synonym became *torture*.

He bowed to the next guests in line as the master of ceremonies announced them. Sophia had insisted he greet people.

He loathed this more than words could say. His face hurt from smiling. A tic pulled at the corner of his eye. At the small of his back a cramp insisted on spasming every time he straightened from a bow.

Gritting his teeth, he waited for the next arrivals.

Lord and Lady Graham appeared in front of him. A frigid anger took hold. He remembered them well. They had aged since he'd seen them last, their wrinkles deeper, their girths wider. He refused to bow.

The lady exchanged a look with her husband, her chin wiggling at the movement.

"You deign to visit my home? Attend my ball?" Even to his own ears, his voice sounded gravelly and hard. Their gossip had been particularly vicious. They had gone so far as to bar their son, a friend from Eton, from having an acquaintance with him.

"Lord and Lady Graham. I am so pleased you could attend." Sophia appeared out of nowhere. She whisked to his side and curtsied. They returned pleasantries, not meeting Edmund's glare. "Please, help yourself to refreshments. Supper will be served later this evening." She pointed to the left and they scrambled away.

Edmund's fingers twitched. His jaw ached with the force of his anger.

Sophia placed her hand on his shoulder, ever so lightly. "Come, Your Grace. Let us walk about the room for a moment."

The orchestra swirled a happy tune that did nothing to drown out the pulsing beat of blood in his temples. Everywhere he looked, he saw traitors. Gossipers. People who had found joy in repeating the news of the murder of his family and his subsequent gain of the title. Who had shown him sympathy?

No one.

His brother had not been popular with the *ton*, but Edmund at one point had enjoyed society. He had looked forward to social events, to friends. He had been accepted.

He walked beside Sophia on wooden legs, feeling the eyes of his guests boring into his back. Although he had attended other balls this Season to find Hannah a husband, there had been a certain anonymity in doing so. Not many recognized him after so many years out of society. But tonight, everyone would know his face. And if they hadn't heard of his past, they'd soon learn because the story would be gleefully passed around like warmed up tea. A little bitter, but still palatable.

"This has been a colossal mistake," he said through numb lips.

"Do not lose your nerve now," came her saucy reply.

"I am not losing my nerve, but I will lose my temper if this provocation continues."

Thankfully she guided him to the portico before he erupted. Hands clenched, he went straight to the rail, hardly seeing the lights strung from the trees and dotting his property like colorful stars. They were on the second floor of his townhome. He looked down at the garden area. Guests meandered the paths, their conversations muted and happy.

Sophia came to his side, the soft sweep of her dress brushing his feet. Before he'd become so irritated, when he had emerged from his rooms and found her directing the servants into their duties, he had been astonished by her appearance.

Dry mouthed and gut punched.

Her dress, a shimmering pale green, brought out the color in her cheeks and the brightness of her eyes. He had never seen anyone look so lovely. He had almost told her so.

"Edmund, you are clutching the rail so tightly your

knuckles are white." Sophia's finger skimmed across his forefinger.

He looked down at her, and her eyes were luminous beneath the moonlight. Her skin shone pearlescent and her lips were gently parted, an unfurled rose. Unnamed emotion gripped his chest, making it difficult to think clearly.

Her finger slid down, hooking beneath his finger. By reflex, he let her slip through, thinking she was removing his hold. But no, she left her finger there. Warm and tiny, vulnerable to his own strength. Forcing him to relax his grasp lest he hurt her somehow.

His throat closed.

He wanted to speak, but an odd paralysis had hold of his vocal cords. Her finger beneath his moved ever so slowly, as though she was reassuring him with her touch. It was not a hug nor a kiss, but a caress. Someone would have to be close to see the movement, the small breach of etiquette and social mores.

"See," she teased in a quiet voice. "I can break the rules."

He found his voice. "That's because no one sees you."

She lifted her shoulder in a shrug. "Perhaps. Perhaps not."

The heaviness knotting him eased at her words. An unraveling began until he finally felt he could breathe. "I'm angry."

"So your face says."

He grunted.

"I do not want to return to my own ball. Which," he added, "I thought was to be a small dinner party."

"We had the best of intentions, Your Grace."

"Don't 'Your Grace' me." He shut his eyes for a moment to block out the lanterns in his garden, to simply smell the night air, the scents of jasmine and rose and Sophia.

"They are not all terrible people." Her voice filtered over. "What happened?"

"Ask anyone in there." He did not care for the bitterness in his tone yet could not stop the sour coat to his words.

"I am asking you."

He yearned to tell her, to tell someone…but especially Sophia. Her finger had stopped moving beneath his, but she had kept it there, like a miniature anchor that grounded him to the reality of the present.

This wasn't ten years ago. He wasn't a bright-eyed, hopeful eighteen-year-old looking to create a new life away from his family. And maybe that added to the guilt. He had wanted to get away from his father and brother. He had wanted a different life, apart from them.

And then they had died, and he got what he wanted, but never in the way he expected.

"While supervising the decorations in the garden, I noticed your roses," she said randomly.

A wry smile tugged at his mouth. "And did you feel an overwhelming urge to move them?"

She laughed then, a real laugh that thawed the chill in his bones. "I did, indeed. But then I had the horrifying notion that should I touch one of those meticulous stems, should I so much as clip a thorn, you might come storming down, thunderous that I had dared disturb the perfection of your designs."

"Your horrifying notion would be correct."

"I do so enjoy being right."

Such a strong satisfaction laced her words that he couldn't help but grin.

"Tell me, Edmund, do I remind you of your roses?"

His brain cast about for what she might mean by that question. Was she asking if she was pretty? Did she smell good? Or maybe she meant that he thought her prickly? He searched for a suitable response, panic licking at his blood.

"What I mean is," she said, catching his pause and moving past it, "is my orderly living reminiscent of your garden?"

Relief scattered through him. His finger moved lightly over hers, just a quick skim that he caught and stopped. But he still didn't know exactly what she was getting at. "Elaborate."

"Your roses are carefully cultivated. They are organized and in their proper spots. There are no weeds. No wildness. Is that your preference?"

He moved his hand away from her finger, suddenly alarmed by her words. Excellence was why he had chosen her, wasn't it? Despite the ridiculous contract, it was her pristine reputation that had swayed his opinion.

"Yes," he said, and watched as her hand, delicate in the glow of faux light, dropped to her side.

Perfection was for jewelry.

That's what Sophia repeated to herself the following afternoon as she stood near her bedroom window, watching sunlight glint off the diamonds encrusting the ring on her finger. She tilted her hand in the light so the jewels reflected rainbows on the wooden floor.

Could a marriage thrive on friendship alone? It was not a romantic notion of marriage, to be sure. But she felt as though her parents had always had that bantering, friendly camaraderie and then with Charles, she'd had it, as well. Perhaps not bantering, as she had not fallen in love with him for his comedic slant. He had been quietly funny, though, and she had appreciated the trait. As for him, he had seen past her calm nature, into the introspective parts that were unwelcome in a world of gowns, gossip and tea.

The ring, far more valuable than she had expected him to be able to afford, had symbolized perfection. She remembered the day Charles gave it to her, and even now, in the remembering, her chest clinched tightly. He had held her hand, slipped the ring on her finger and told her the only impeccability he expected was from his diamonds.

She well remembered the joy of that day, of knowing she was accepted for herself.

Sorrow banded across her chest in tight circles. She had not only lost her best friend, but the man who'd seen her for who she was.

She pulled the wedding ring off her finger and cushioned it carefully in her top drawer. Last night had been sleepless, and exhaustion pulled at her limbs, but she had too much to accomplish today. She looked around the room she had once shared with her husband, practicing saying goodbye in her mind.

Edmund had said she could keep this home. He wanted nothing more from their marriage than Hannah's happiness and perhaps his own peace of mind. It was time for her to leave, though. To let the past rest.

After last night on the balcony…her skin tingled thinking of his finger over hers. How the woundedness in his gaze had snagged her attention in the ballroom, how the raw suffering in his features had propelled her to lead him outside, away from the press of society.

Away from whatever tormented him.

She didn't know why she had done such a thing. And then allowing herself to actually touch him. Perhaps it was not entirely scandalous, but it was certainly something that would be talked about if seen. A widow and an angry hermit, hobnobbing on the balcony. A tiny smile pulled at her lips. What drew her to him? She wished she knew. He was difficult. Complex. A turbulent sea where Charles had been a peaceful pond, still and deep. Both good men, she sensed, and yet so different.

Rubbing her thumb across the empty skin of her ring finger, she turned away from the dresser. She could be the perfect wife for Edmund. In return, he'd take care of her family and financially back the charities close to her heart. She would live out her days serving others and be content.

But the memory of their skin touching circled her thoughts.

"Mrs. Seymour." Betsy appeared in the doorway. "His Grace and his niece have called. He asked to see the library."

"Is that where you put them?"

Betsy nodded and left before Sophia could remind her to never show someone to the home library without permission. She glanced once more at herself in the looking glass, and then descended to the second floor, to the library where countless hours had been spent curled with a book.

Her first thought was that Edmund was too big for such a small space. He was pacing, his hands locked behind his back, a scowl stitched across his face. Her second was that seeing him made the circling thoughts in her head increase. Her gaze dropped to his hands, remembering their large strength.

"Your Grace." She inclined her head.

"Sophia." Her name rushed from him, tightly strung. "Hannah is receiving requests to be called upon."

Her brow lifted. She looked to Hannah, who sat in a ladylike fashion upon the settee. "This is problematic?"

"Uncle Edmund has turned them all away, and then he dragged me here because he's irritable and old and obviously doesn't understand the nature of courtship."

A faint flush suffused the jagged planes of his face. "I understand that these suitors are not acceptable."

"They are not rich enough," Hannah supplied, a sardonic twist to her words.

"They lack pedigree," he growled. Tension fairly crackled off him.

No wonder he had earned the nickname Beast. Sophia imagined the anger he had exhibited years ago surpassed anything she was seeing now. There was a certain charm to his irritation, though, to the way his jacket held too many creases because he kept plucking at it, to the way his heavy-lidded glare fit with his swarthy skin.

She weighed both the situation and the glares Hannah and Edmund skewered at each other. Sighing, she went to the other couch and patted the cushion beside her. "Come, sit. You look like a pirate about to die from apoplexy."

Edmund stopped pacing, his brows drawing together. "A pirate?"

"Would you prefer beast?"

His lips pursed. "I like neither, but pirate is particularly fanciful and unlike you."

"My sister's words, but I can't help but now see the resemblance," she said pertly.

Could a man's face darken much more? She bit back her smile, little knowing why teasing him gave her such a delightful thrill.

She tapped the seat again. "Let us have a conversation that does not require my eyes to follow your restlessly roving self across the room."

"I don't wish to sit."

Stubborn man. She lifted a shoulder and faced Hannah. "Dear girl, tell me of your suitors."

Hannah broke into a grin, eyes gleaming. After twenty minutes of her excited prattling, Edmund finally decided to sit. His large body took up a great deal of the couch. If Edmund looked like a pirate, he certainly did not smell like one. Sandalwood floated between them, and she did not move as far away from him as she should.

"They are all fortune hunters and title seekers." He crossed his arms, as if daring Sophia to disagree.

"And is that not what Hannah is, as well?"

A shocked gasp from the other settee told Sophia that her words had hit a mark. She looked at the girl. "I was blessed to find a man I loved to marry. He was good and kind and though not wealthy, he had a stable career and was able to provide for me. When you asked your uncle for a Season, what was your goal?"

"To secure my future."

"Exactly. Because should anything happen to Edmund—" she gave him a pointed look, "—you would be at the mercy of other relatives for the rest of your life. Therefore, you were smart enough to realize that a good marriage will ensure your quality of life. My observation is that your title means nothing to you, Edmund."

"I was not raised to believe I'd have it," he admitted. Such a grudging, sulky tone.

"You cannot let these suitors upset you so. They are doing what they need to in order to better their lives. Hannah will do the same, but we will carefully screen her choices."

Edmund grimaced and reached into his pocket. "Here." He dropped a pile of calling cards and invitations onto her lap. "Look through these and decipher who deserves Hannah."

"Manners, Your Grace."

"Please," he growled.

"Have you answered any of this correspondence?" His heavy glare told her the answer to that. She looked to Hannah. "Have you responded to these?"

Hannah wrinkled her nose. "I gave instructions that everyone be told I'm not receiving callers today."

"Very well. I doubt these men will call again, so no need to waste your time sifting through these. We no longer want this earl." She picked the card up by its corner, dangling it in front of Edmund's nose. She opened her fingers and the card drifted down to his lap. Returning to the pile he'd dumped in hers, she found another and plucked it out. "Or this baron, known for his great fortune and a general degree of kindness."

Smiling, she plopped the card next to the other still sitting on Edmund's thigh.

"You are being very tiresome, Mrs. Seymour. What point do you wish to make?"

"Catching a husband is serious business. I think you two should quit treating this as though it is a game." Ack, she sounded like her mother. Fighting a grimace, she gave Hannah a stern look. "You have a privilege so many would wish for. You are loved and you are secure. Do not throw that away."

Hannah let out a long, drawn-out sigh. "You're always so serious. And here I thought you popular for your wit." She stood and meandered over to a bookshelf in a seemingly idle stride.

That comment annoyed Sophia more than she let on. Biting back a retort, she looked to Edmund and smiled serenely. "We will accept most of these invitations and Hannah will entertain callers. It is a necessity to suss out the acceptable from the unacceptable."

He dropped his head in his hands.

Her irritation eased, partially because his unabashed emotional expression amused her, but also because she felt a pang of sympathy for him. She almost touched his leg, intent on comforting him. At the last second, she snatched her hand back.

"If it makes you feel better, male guardians usually leave it up to the women to do the sifting. We shall let you know if we have need of your assistance."

He lifted his head. "I know this is all necessary, but I hate it. Hannah marrying? I remember the day she came to live with me."

Sophia threaded through the invitations, hoping not to look too interested in what he had to say. Hannah flounced back to the couch and plopped down.

"I was terrified," Hannah said, laughing. "Now I know what a softhearted lout you are."

Both Sophia and Edmund shared a grimace, then realized they were sharing it, and quickly looked back to Hannah.

"How did the arrangement come to pass?" asked Sophia, her cheeks burning at the slightly nosy question. An uncomfortable urge to understand more of the duke and his niece flooded her, and the knowledge that she longed to know them in a deeper way suddenly terrified her.

Chapter Eleven

Edmund heard something like strain in Sophia's voice, and wondered at it. He openly stared at her, noting the high color in her cheeks and how she very casually looked at invitations after asking Hannah about the past.

He leaned back on the couch, letting his long legs stretch. This morning's bout with irritation had exhausted him on all counts. Just thinking about Hannah leaving tore at his insides. He had known this day would come. He just hadn't realized it would be so painful. She sat across from him, a bright smile in her eyes, dreaming of her future. One he didn't know if he'd be a part of.

But he was so tired of being angry. Going to Sophia's etiquette class had opened his eyes last month. He'd met her former father-in-law and saw their charity in action. Years of condemning others, of loathing the hypocrisy and cruelty of the *ton*, was slowly fading with every new interaction. Perhaps it had been easier to hide away, to pretend everyone was to blame when in reality, he had blamed himself the most for what had happened.

But then there was Hannah. She was strong and happy. She had gotten the best traits from both of her parents, and none of the worst. The maid brought in tea and biscuits and set them on a small table beside Hannah's couch.

"Thank you, Betsy," said Sophia. The maid nodded and left.

"I'm not certain how it was decided where I'd live." Hannah's brow furrowed. "I was young when my parents died."

"A proper little hellion," put in Edmund.

"I'm sorry," murmured Sophia, standing up and walking over to the table where the tea sat.

"I barely knew them." Hannah held out a cup and Sophia poured.

"Tea?" she asked him.

He nodded, admiring the gracefulness of her movements. She would teach Hannah more than finishing school ever had. Hannah sipped from her cup and Sophia returned beside him, bringing both a cup of tea and a fresh round of perfume that he tried not to look overly appreciative of.

Hannah side-eyed him.

"Uncle Edmund talks to me of my parents sometimes, especially when I was younger and more inquisitive." She lowered the teacup to her lap. "I do believe he may have been half in love with my mother."

Sophia had the grace to contain her gasp, though Edmund felt her startlement in the slight recoil she made.

"I was not in love with her," Edmund clarified. "I was bowled over by her. My brother was twenty years my senior but he married a girl only six years older than I."

"That much difference?" asked Sophia.

"I was a surprise for my parents, and having me killed my mother."

Sophia shot him a sympathetic frown, which he shrugged off with a wry smile. "She was older and she did manage to live a few years after my birth. But I was a boy of twelve when William brought Naomi home for the holidays. She was eighteen when they married. She'd made a successful debut and snagged herself an heir to the dukedom."

As usual, Hannah was a rapt listener to the story of her parents. What surprised him was Sophia's attention. She stared at him in wide-eyed silence.

He cocked his head. "You've never heard this before?"

"I do not dabble in gossip." Color burnished her cheekbones. "I am also only twenty-five. This would have happened when I was barely in the schoolroom."

"Yes, but the scandalous nature of their deaths happened when you were fifteen."

"Edmund's quite young," put in Hannah. "Only around twenty-one when I came to live with him. I believe I gave my aunt, my mother's sister, a bit of the runaround. She decided I was too much for her." Hannah spoke, but Edmund could not stop looking at Sophia.

"Did you think me older?" he asked her.

"You have the air of an older, wiser man."

He laughed because she looked so mortified, and she tried so hard to save him from the truth. "I am irascible, you mean."

She recovered gracefully, tipping her head. "I said what I mean."

"Uncle raised me well, except when he sent me to that ridiculous girls' school," interrupted Hannah. "I always had governesses. Once I had a young and beautiful governess."

Edmund finally looked at his niece. What was she

getting at? It was rude to interrupt and Hannah wasn't usually one to hog the attentions of a room. She was up to something. Mischievous minx. He well knew that stubborn jut to her chin.

"Young and beautiful?" Sophia's voice held amusement. "Do tell."

"I kept hoping and praying Uncle Edmund would fall in love with her, but he never did, and then that boring reverend snatched her up, right beneath our noses." Hannah's brows rose. "I suppose she is living out her dreams now, in a little parsonage full of children and flowers. If only she had tried harder for Uncle, but perhaps it wouldn't work. I do not believe he has ever felt the pangs of true love."

A dramatic sigh ensued, and Edmund coughed to cover his laugh.

"Pangs, are they? Speaking of…" Sophia held up a calling card. "There are two of these in your pile, Hannah. This gentleman called twice in one day."

"Oooh!" Hannah leaned forward. "Who is it?"

"A Mr. Paul Aimsley. Isn't he one of those handsome brothers?"

Hannah wiggled on the settee, clapping her hands together. "I must tell Eliza."

"There will be plenty more of these callers," Sophia reminded his niece, much to his annoyance. "Do not get hung up on one in particular. Now, Rennington, where are the vouchers to Almack's? Hannah must be invited to their balls if she is to be considered to be of good breeding."

"Almack's? The social club home to stale biscuits and weak lemonade?"

"They probably haven't heard the banns," put in Hannah, a mischievous smile spreading across her face.

Edmund frowned. She'd obviously noted the announcement from the pulpit last Sunday. He hadn't gone to church that day, but now he wished he would have told Hannah about his impending marriage himself. Though his irrepressible niece did not look as though her feelings were hurt.

"Naturally, all the cavorting about you two have been doing has caused tongues to wag," Hannah continued with a smirk, and Sophia flushed. "It's a good thing you two are getting married, although I'm not sure when you planned to tell me. I should have been the first to know."

"You're right," Edmund said slowly. "I didn't know how you'd feel."

"I feel ecstatic." Hannah jumped up and gave each of them a hug, almost spilling his tea with her exuberance. "But do not keep things from me again. You can only imagine how disconcerting it was to hear and have to pretend I already knew."

"I apologize." Edmund tipped his head humbly.

"I shall accept."

"Is Almack's really necessary?" he asked.

"To ensure Hannah's proper place? Yes." Sophia had evidently regained her composure. "If you do not care about proper places and entrance to the most selective of events, then no."

How he hated proper places and selective events and the Almack's of the world. Why couldn't they just live and enjoy their lives without worrying about social order.

Hannah's face fell, for she was watching him with

anticipation. He hefted out a sigh. "Very well. I shall inquire as to the location of our missing vouchers."

That earned him the smile he wanted, but more surprising was how Sophia's approving grin captured him and tied knots in his stomach. Had he been wanting to earn her smile, as well?

A muscle clenched in his jaw. That couldn't be. He was in this for Hannah's sake and maybe even his own. It had not been lost on him that this agreement benefited him by freeing him from mothers eager to marry off their daughters. It freed him from social obligations as Sophia could surely handle their social life on her own. After Hannah married, he would return to Rennington and live out his days happy and alone.

He waited to feel satisfaction, but it didn't come.

"I have decided to move here after our wedding." A few days later, Sophia regarded Edmund soberly from her place near the window. She had arrived this afternoon unexpectedly and when Reed told him of her presence, his heart had done a strange little flop.

"My home belongs to Charles's family," she continued, her tone subdued, her body stiff, hands still against her dress. He could not tell if she was sad or not, and that bothered him. "They will be able to use it themselves or sell it."

He eyed her thoughtfully. "Would you prefer to live in town?"

"Yes." She paused, and her fingers still did not move. No nervous plucking at her skirt, no telltale movements to betray any emotion at all. "I should like to live here. You have several bedrooms. Perhaps there is one not in use."

"I'll only come to London to attend to parliament matters. Once we've completed our nuptials a little over a fortnight from now, I shall instruct the servants to move my things out of the master bedroom, and yours in."

"Thank you." Her head dipped.

"On another note, I'm happy to tell you I spoke with Lord Windley while you were teaching etiquette last month."

"Oh?" Surprise brightened her eyes.

"He agrees mastiffs would increase the protection for the women your charity is helping. Three are to be delivered later this week. I have also donated him a small home to house more women."

"I know not what to say."

"I will not object to fervent admiration."

Her eyebrows rose, and a tiny smile tilted the corners of her lips. "Very well. You have earned my unending fervent admiration."

"As is proper," he said, though heat filled his face. Of course, he'd been teasing, and so had she, but nevertheless he noted a look in her eyes that seemed different. He cleared his throat. "Are you attending the play tonight?"

"Yes, I plan to introduce Hannah to Mr. Raleigh, a gentleman from the States who is known for his charitable works and wealth."

Edmund grunted. "She is not a prize sow."

A trace of smile flirted with Sophia's lips. "I believe she thinks herself the greatest prize sow of the *ton*."

It took every ounce of his self-control to contain his laugh. What did one say to the truth?

"Your Grace, you truly must take a deep breath and enjoy this time in her life. Very few women marry their first Season out. She shall have many balls and theaters and dance partners. Allow her the wonder of looking for love."

"Love." He scowled at the ridiculous notion.

And so it was, later that evening, that he found himself calling for Hannah to hurry up as the show they were to attend started within an hour. Sophia had left the house earlier and had now come back to attend theater with them. He trained his eyes on the staircase, determined not to stare at Sophia.

"Your Grace." A young woman bobbed down the stairs, color in her cheeks. Based on her dress, he thought she might be Hannah's lady's maid, but he really couldn't remember.

"What," he barked.

Sophia elbowed him.

"Yes," he asked more carefully, noting the maid looked like she might faint from fright.

"Miss Hannah is not feeling well." A stutter broke her words. "She is st-staying home."

Edmund rolled his eyes and started for the stairs. A hand on his arm stopped him.

"If I may?" Sophia asked.

He nodded, because looking at her tied his tongue. She had outdone herself tonight, dressing in bold colors that accentuated the beauty of her complexion and the brightness of her eyes. He found it difficult not to gawp, and he felt like a young buck full of nervous tension, which was truly ludicrous. Pushing visions of Sophia from his mind, he focused on his upcoming plans to help Lord Windley while Sophia went to attend to Hannah.

It had been so long since he'd allowed himself to interact with others in the *ton*. How easy to cast them all in the same mold, yet Lord Windley was different. He had met with the man again to discuss ways Edmund could support his organization. The members of Windley's charity truly cared about helping women trapped within a soul-emptying profession. It was one thing for Edmund to have given to charities throughout the years without a second thought as to where the money was going.

Quite another to see the money put to use. To meet the people helped. To be involved. The past few weeks had challenged assumptions he'd clung to for years. The weight of his anger, his bitterness, faded every day beneath the knowledge that perhaps people were not as terrible as he believed.

Not everyone lied. Not everyone served their own selfish needs to the harm of others.

He wanted to believe that. For the first time since his brother and sister-in-law died, he longed to hope for good in humanity. He heard footsteps. Sophia glided down the stairs, her posture as regal as always, her pearlescent throat encircled by sapphires.

He forced his gaze to her face, hating the dryness of his mouth, the paralysis of his vocal cords. Sophia spoke first.

"Hannah does not look well."

The lady's maid had disappeared. His butler waited by the door, ready to do anything Edmund instructed. His first thought was to send the coach back to the stables. Without Hannah, there was no need to go out. He could spend the evening in his study, enjoying the quietude. Or perhaps he'd call up Lord Boxing. See if he'd like to join him at White's for a game of whist.

"How sick is she?" Edmund asked.

"I believe…" Sophia's cheeks filled with color. "That it is a monthly issue and shall resolve itself."

"Shall I send for a coach to take you home?"

Her head tilted to the side. She peered up at him through thick-fringed lashes, her full lips curved. "I can call for a hackney, but I shall still be attending the theater. There are people to see. Friends whom I have not spoken to recently."

It had never occurred to him that she might still go. He frowned.

"Come now." She laughed then, a quiet ladylike tinkle that wasn't a chuckle but something infinitely more feminine. "You certainly do not need to go nor worry about my whereabouts. I assure you, I am the soul of propriety."

Normally he believed that, but tonight there was something bright and sparkling in her eyes, something he could not label but which told him there might be more to Mrs. Sophia Seymour than just propriety.

His fingers flexed at his side. In a flash, his imagination conjured images of Sophia laughing, swirling around in her gown, and other men talking to her. Making her laugh.

Wasn't the purpose of their arrangement that people see them together, that the stuffy patronesses of Almack's know his niece was good enough, proper enough, to dance at their functions? He hadn't attended the theater in years, but tonight he would go. He'd share his box with Sophia and invite others to join them.

While he did not enjoy social outings, for this particular instance, he would make an exception.

"We are engaged," he said through stiff lips. "I will go with you."

Chapter Twelve

The world, otherwise known as the *haut monde*, now knew of their engagement.

Sophia covertly eyed Edmund while smiling benignly at her friends' chatter. The play had ended and they were discussing attending a small party nearby. Lady Montfort knew the family and said she had a standing invitation to bring friends.

Sophia did not doubt it, as Caroline was even more social than she. They'd invited Caroline and her friend Lady Oster to Edmund's spacious theater box, and it had been a pleasant experience. Caroline nudged Sophia at intermission, when Edmund had left the box to greet someone, and demanded to know details of their pending nuptials. Though she was put out that Sophia hadn't told her about the engagement, she understood the desire for privacy.

Telling Caroline the truth of the arrangement had been tempting, but she did not know Lady Oster well and had no wish to feed the gossips. Then Edmund had returned, removing the privacy to speak.

"Shall we be off?" Caroline held out her arm for

Sophia. "You are more than welcome to attend, Your Grace. The hosts would be honored."

Sophia shook her head. "You really need not join us, Rennington. I know how you hate these affairs and I am sure you are tired."

She would certainly feel better if he went home. Sitting beside him the last few hours had been difficult in a way she'd found hard to comprehend. There was a certain intimacy to his closeness, in hearing his quiet chuckles during the entertaining parts of the play, that made her fidget. For seven long years she had floated along in society, blissfully ignoring potential suitors in favor of cuddling with her warm memories of Charles.

But tonight, and if she were honest, many other times recently, the recollection of her late husband was growing hazier, and it was getting harder and harder to bring him to mind when she was near Edmund.

"Tired?" Edmund interrupted her musings. He turned to the ladies and held up his hands in a supplicating manner. "The lady calls me tired. Do I seem so old to the rest of you?"

He grinned at Sophia, and she plastered a calm look upon her face but her insides were roiling. Was Edmund flirting with her? Irritable and frowning Edmund she found amusing. But this version, relaxed and smiling, was a little more challenging to interpret. That twinkle in his eyes set her off-kilter.

She moistened her lips, searching for a response, when Caroline laughed and placed her hand on Sophia's shoulder.

"No one could look at you and call you old, Your Grace." She patted Sophia's shoulder. "Our darling Sophia hasn't attended a party with a man in tow in many long years. She simply assumed you would not wish to go. A plainly wrong assumption."

Caroline's hand slipped away, and Sophia's cheeks burned as she took in her friend's mischievous smile. She turned to Edmund, meeting his gaze with a calmness that pleased her.

"Indeed, I'd be most pleased if you attend." How the words found their way past her lips was an unpleasant mystery.

The presence of ducal power clung to his personality, and now she realized that others saw the same eminence, and perhaps even felt a grudging awe. The man was a duke, after all, and a young one. She was not one to feel intimidated by another's station, but at this moment, a certain daunting undertone permeated the theater box. She knew her friends felt it, too.

"You shall ride with me," he said, the darkness of his eyes fixed upon her, and he held no brook to his tone.

She might have to get through the awkwardness of being with him longer this night, but she did not need to ride alone with him again. Her backbone was just as strong as Edmund's will.

She flashed him a serene smile, knowing it would irritate him. "You are so kind, but I have already accepted a ride with Lady Montfort and Lady Oster. We shall meet you there. You will give him directions?" she inquired of Caroline, ignoring the heat of Edmund's glare.

"It is quite all right if you'd like to ride with your fiancé," stuttered Caroline. "Did you not ride with him here?"

Sophia kept her expression placid. She had indeed ridden with him in his elaborate and fancy phaeton.

"She did, it is true. And such torture it was, being

stuck with a man of my advanced, and perhaps I shall go so far as to say decrepit, age." Edmund winked, breaking the tension in the air, and the ladies giggled.

How dare he charm her friends. She lifted her chin. "I was looking forward to catching up with Lady Oster and Lady Montfort, but if you are in need of company, I'd be happy to oblige you. Your Grace," she added, knowing full well her tone displayed polite ennui.

"Far be it from me to steal you away from these lovely ladies. I shall meet you there," he said, leaving Sophia dumbfounded.

As he strode away, threading through the crowds and leaving the ladies alone in the box, she attempted to pull herself together.

"That was…interesting." Caroline's brows drew together. "I do not recall the duke ever being so congenial."

"I find him charming," said Lady Oster. "Utterly charming. Well done, Sophia."

"Thank you," she murmured, wondering at the change in Edmund. How did she reconcile the version she had become acquainted with in the past month to the charmer who had suddenly appeared this evening?

And which Edmund would he be at tonight's rout?

Edmund felt like a different man this evening.

Alive, vital and intrigued. Something had revived in him this evening. A lone part of himself, long lost, but now rising from the proverbial grave.

He scoured the ballroom for Sophia, receiving curious yet not unkind looks from his fellow partygoers. He had thought the rout to be a small affair but this was more in line with a ball, and a crush at that.

Normally he'd be grinding his teeth and counting the minutes until he could leave, but tonight was different. Tonight he almost felt like the old Edmund. Or rather, the young one. The naive eighteen-year-old who'd left Eton with stars in his eyes. Who had attended balls and waltzed. He had made friends in society his first year out of school, and he had been planning his grand tour, and then in the space of one morning, it was all gone. His brother. His friends. His confidence in the goodness of humanity.

Everything.

People had eyed him with suspicion. The brother he wanted to look up to, the one who had failed him as dismally as his father, was dead. The sister-in-law whom he'd wanted to protect, dead.

And life had changed for the worse.

But now, tonight, with Sophia and her friends, the aching wound within had stopped pulsating. For hours at a time, he forgot that he was angry, annoyed, disenchanted. Having Sophia beside him had felt like something close to contentment.

From the moment he'd met her, she had intrigued him. She was proving that people were not always who he assumed them to be, and if some were worse than expected, a great many were better.

And so he kneaded his palms, tugged at his waistcoat, awaiting the lady who made his future feel a little more interesting.

He couldn't deny the thrill he experienced when he was around Sophia. At times she seemed determined to put him in his place, to thwart him, and for once, he had thwarted her. He grinned, thinking of tonight's little disagreement. She might play society's game of superficiality to perfection, but inside of her lived an independent, feisty woman whom he wanted to know better.

Hannah deserved a stepmother like Sophia. Someone who could help his niece navigate through the *ton*'s fickle proclivities. Briefly he closed his eyes and thanked Providence. Prayer had been foreign to him for many years but after Hannah arrived and portions of his heart began to heal, he saw the goodness of God in so many things. He had invited his old nanny to come live at his estate and she had slowly but surely revealed to him the beauties of personal faith.

She refused to travel to London, though. Said the place sucked belief out of her. He smiled, thinking of Miss Nelly Smith. Would Sophia like Nanny? Would Sophia ever visit his favorite estate? Rennington was south of London, by the Celtic Sea near Devonshire.

"Your Grace." The subject of his thoughts sidled up to him, bringing lavender and roses to his nose, warmth and tingles to his skin. "I'm happy to see you made it."

"Are you?" He raised a brow, trying hard to ignore the ridiculous fluttering in his stomach. She looked as lovely as when they'd left earlier that night for the play. Not a hair out of place. She refused to meet his eyes, though.

Biting back a grin, he swiveled to the front of her, blocking her view of the dance floor and forcing her to look up at his face.

"I asked you if you're truly happy that I am here." He searched her eyes. They were wide but untroubled. As per usual, she did not show her true feelings. What would happen if he reached over and touched her cheek? If he allowed his thumb to caress her skin, to see if it felt as velvety as it looked? If he touched her lips, to see if she wore lip stain or if they were naturally the color of a sun-kissed berry ripe for picking?

Sophia surely felt his perusal, for the color in her cheeks deepened, but she did not look away from him. "I am happily surprised," she said at last. "There are more layers to you than I expected."

The strains to a waltz began, and Edmund held out his hand. "There is a layer right now that wishes to dance. Will you join me?"

It seemed as though time stretched on an invisible thread suspended between them, blending with the music, weaving into a palpable moment in which he didn't dare breathe as he awaited her answer.

She blinked then, and her mouth curved upward. "I should be happy to dance with you."

She placed her hand in his, and he gently led her to the dance floor, mindful of how small her palm felt, how delicate. Then they were joined, his hand about her waist, their fingers interlaced, and they were moving across the floor. Swirling around other couples, but he could not take his gaze from her.

Her skin was as warm and as soft as he imagined it would be. There was a lightness to her gaze, but the barest tension about the corners of her mouth, as though she worried about something.

"I shall not step on your toes," he assured her. At one point in his life, he had been considered an excellent dancer, despite his large size.

"You would not be the first," she rejoined. "And after all these years without music, I doubt you have the waltz down."

"Without music?" They twirled past a potted plant.

"My dear Mrs. Seymour, I do not live a life without music."

"Without dancing, then," she amended.

He laughed and pulled her closer to him. He heard her soft little puff of breath at the contact, and felt a deep, masculine satisfaction. "I have not gone without dancing either."

He maneuvered her to a side door and they waltzed out of the main ballroom, onto a balustrade that overlooked a dark garden that had not been made open to guests. They whirled to a stop inches from the rail, her dress sweeping against his legs. He kept his palm against her waist, and slid his other hand from hers, up her arm, to her shoulder. She watched him, waiting, uncertain.

"Did you know that you are the most beautiful woman in London?"

"There is no need to flatter me, Your Grace. The banns have been read. You shall not lose your perfect duchess."

He frowned, hearing something in her voice he couldn't identify. Sarcasm? He allowed his fingers to meander the contours of her collarbone, tracing its delicate curve. Her skin was warm from dancing. A tiny catch of breath snagged his attention to her lips, which were parted ever so slightly.

"I speak the truth." He lifted his gaze to her eyes, amazed at how clear they shone beneath the moonlight. "And your eyes are like the Celtic Sea, changing colors with your mood."

"You are poetic tonight," she said lightly, but she remained beneath his fingertips, unmoving and still. "I assure you romance is not necessary."

"Perhaps I am not the type to do necessary things."

"You are the type who lures young widows out onto moonlit balustrades with potentially rakish intentions?"

He chuckled. "That is a monstrously long sentence and an unfair accusation."

"But is it the truth?"

"That I am rakish? Far from it." Was it his imagination or did she move closer to him?

"What were you like when you were younger?"

Suddenly, he did not like the bent of this conversation. What had prompted him to bring her out here? Some insane impulse, little thought out. But the way she looked at him, questioning and serious, made him want to answer. "I was trusting. I had a faith in God and in people."

Her arm rose and before he understood what she intended, she traced his cheekbone with a finger. Slow and gentle, tender, even. Moonlight washed across her face in pale abandon, and she trapped his gaze with her own.

"I am sorry for what happened to you."

He reached up and encircled her wrist, mindful of her smaller size. "I am not. It made me who I am."

"Cantankerous?" she whispered.

"No." He threaded his fingers through hers, while his left hand pulled her closer to him. "Resolved." His heartbeat echoed in his ears as he leaned forward and brushed his mouth against hers, ever so slightly, the barest hint of his breath mingling with hers, the barest warmth of their lips touching before he ended the kiss.

His forehead rested against hers as he tried to calm the beat of his pulse, but she smelled so good, like peace and goodness and roses, and with a groan, his lips found hers again.

She was pliant and something that had been tightly locked up within him unbound. In that second, he was flooded with the feeling that everything was right in his world. Sophia fit perfectly against him, their mouths melded in sync, and Edmund surrendered to his feelings.

The kiss lasted but a moment, for Sophia yanked away from him, a curious sheen to her eyes. He stepped back, struggling to contain his emotions. Sophia seemed to have no such problem. She touched her hair, tucking a few stray strands behind her ears.

"Your Grace—"

"Sophia, I—"

They spoke in unison, and stopped. He cleared his throat, urging her to go first.

"I would like to remind you—" and her fingers found the chain about her neck "—that our arrangement is in name only. You are not to kiss me."

Her words sparked a fire in his blood. His hands clenched at his side. "Forgive me." The words scraped from his throat, rough and unrefined.

Even in the muted light, he could see her complexion deepening. "The forgiveness is mine to ask. When we made this arrangement, I'll confess that I did not imagine you had any desire to kiss anyone. You seemed firmly ensconced in your hermitude, active in London only for Hannah's Season."

"I was," he said in a sharp tone, angry with her, angry with himself.

And as his temper rose, he understood that he could not kiss this woman, or any woman, ever again. There was too much that could go wrong. He knew that he was like his father and his brother. They had all been fiercely angry. Because of this commonality, he could not allow himself to be, as Sophia put it, a true husband.

He would only hurt her.

"Our arrangement will stand," he said hotly, hating that she was right and that his temper was mounting.

"Thank you," she said softly.

Thank you? His jaw ached. She had disliked his kiss. Even if he didn't want their marriage to be anything more than a contract, he still had his pride. How humiliating to feel unwanted, and even more, like a terrible person for wanting to kiss her again.

He hadn't felt self-loathing in so long that it took him a moment to recognize the visceral emotion flooding his system. He inclined his head, spun on his heel and walked out.

Chapter Thirteen

A kiss should not leave one's lips tingling overnight. Nor should it cause an inability to sleep.

And yet that was exactly what had happened to Sophia. She returned from the rout, citing a megrim, and spent the remainder of the night unable to sleep, eventually settling for a book in the library. At some point, sleep claimed her, but it had been discordant and unfulfilling.

She woke on the library couch, a crick in her neck. After a steaming cup of tea and a small breakfast, she went out to her garden. She sat on her bench and watched the bees play in the roses, chastising herself that she was imagining the burn of Edmund's kiss upon her mouth. Her lips were merely wind chapped.

Soon after breakfast, Betsy brought her a note from Edmund. The morning had been kind thus far, filled with sunshine and a floral breeze. She opened it, and as she read, her mood lifted. Edmund had asked her to meet him at her mother's for important news. Good news, he wrote.

Which surely meant Father wasn't dead. And while

her heart leaped upon reading the words, there nevertheless still existed a deep guilt for kissing Edmund. For wanting to kiss him. For still feeling the imprint of his lips upon hers.

And for upsetting him so much that he had immediately left the rout.

She fingered the locket about her neck. Would Charles have wanted her to marry again? To enjoy kissing someone else? They had never discussed the subject, though they had exhausted many other fields of study. Philosophy, some sciences, though that was more Frederika's area of expertise. Literature galore. Current laws, past laws. There had been no subject prohibited from their discourse.

Except the future.

They could not have foreseen that he would die three months after their wedding.

Sighing, she stood and went inside to continue supervising the packing of her personal items in preparation for her move to Edmund's townhome. Stuffing down her sadness, she called for Betsy and Tom, and got to work.

When afternoon rolled around, Tom summoned a hackney and she rode over to her mother's new town house. She found her family in the parlor. Edmund had not yet arrived.

"My darling, sweet girl." Mother fanned herself, cheeks pink, but did not rise from the chair in which she sat. Piles of yarn covered her lap and spilled onto the floor. "We have so much to speak of."

Sophia felt her brows go up. Quickly, she schooled her features. "Do we?"

"I suppose you did not read the papers this morning?" Eliza's hands were clasped in her lap and she wore the unmistakable air of one containing so much excitement that it was bound to spill over at any moment.

"Why would she?" muttered Frederika, her dark head bent over a drawing.

Sophia moved into the room, stopping by the desk to look more closely at her sister's handiwork. As her brain registered what she was seeing, her mouth dropped.

"I am greatly disturbed," she said.

"Don't be." Frederika glanced up, saw her expression and broke into a smile. "It is a homunculus. I can explain it more, if you'd like."

"Do not fall prey to her seemingly innocent words," said Eliza, who had followed Sophia to the desk. "Our darling sister tricked me earlier and I wasted a good portion of my day listening to a lesson on human anatomy."

"The brain is a fascinating organ. As are the other viscera." Frederika's gaze took on a faraway gaze Sophia recognized as absorption. Biting back a smile at her eccentric sister, she patted Frederika's shoulder and turned to Eliza.

"At what time does the duke plan to arrive?"

"Any moment now." Eliza linked her arm in Sophia's and they walked to the couch. "Rennington sent word this morning and Mother has already fainted twice."

"Almost a third time, too, if Eliza had not loosened my stays," put in Mother with an entirely too eager tone. Her eyes were bright, and though she worked a darning needle, Sophia saw little progress in her lap.

They sat, and Sophia became aware of a certain constriction in her throat. Nerves, perhaps. She wet her lips.

Eliza must have noticed her angst, for she leaned forward and poured a cup of tea from the table in front of them. "Here, this will settle your nerves."

Sophia patted her sister's knee, warmed by her concern. If Sophia was the paragon of perfection in the family, Eliza was the mother hen. She tried to take care of everyone, and Father's absence had hit her the hardest.

"Thank you. How is Mother?" As one, they looked across the room to where Lady Worland sat in a high-backed chair. She hummed whilst chewing her lower lip.

"She's not been herself since Father disappeared. She tries to hide it, keep up appearances, but…" Eliza's voice dropped to a whisper, fraught with sorrow. "I have heard her weeping in the night."

A pang cramped through Sophia. How well she knew the loneliness night could bring. "I wish I could do more."

"Oh, but you have." Eliza took her hand and squeezed. "You have saved us from ruin by agreeing to marry Rennington. And have you noticed the furnishings here? There are so many expensive items that I am afraid to move."

"I'm not," piped in Frederika.

Eliza rolled her eyes. "You do not fear anything."

"A truth wisely spoken." Pride swelled Frederika's tone, and Sophia couldn't help smiling at the intrepid girl. She would be a bluestocking, no doubt. Perhaps she would not ever marry, but she would be happy.

Sophia worried more for Eliza, who had stars in her eyes and romance on her mind. Such impracticality would surely not be rewarded.

"As I was saying," continued Mother, her eyes on her work, "we have much to discuss. Namely, that you have fallen in love with the duke."

A tickle exploded within Sophia's throat, and she began coughing in earnest. "In love," she managed to rasp, gratefully accepting the teacup her sister handed her.

"Yes, the *ton* is all atwitter about you two." Mother's cheeks bunched in a satisfied smile. "You attended a ball last night, did you not?"

Sophia nodded, still recuperating from the cough.

"Well, someone spotted you two waltzing out onto the balustrade." Mother looked up then, pinning Sophia with such a knowing look that she immediately felt a hot flush suffuse her face. "And you kissed."

Surely her face must be flaming. She sipped her tea, aware that Eliza watched her with a sympathetic gaze.

"Well—" and Mother's lips pursed in an annoying way that showed her pleasure at the entire situation "—society is convinced you are a love match."

"It's very romantic," said Eliza. "Even if untrue."

"Romance is superbly untrue," added Frederika from her place at the desk. "It's all a matter of physiology, of certain humors affecting the brain. That's why love fades over time, and people must rush out and find someone new to experience romance all over again."

The room was silent as they digested Frederika's cynical words. Mother was the first to recover. "Why, young lady, I am just as in love with your father as I ever was. More so, if you must know. Time hones love."

Frederika turned from her place at the desk, eyes flashing. "If love is so strong, so lasting, then where is Father? I do not see anything resembling love with a father who leaves his family bankrupt and dependent upon the goodwill of others. And then our dear sister, still mourning the death of her best friend, is forced to marry to save us all. That is not love."

Sophia gaped at her sister, shocked into silence. How angry Frederika was, how defiant on her behalf. Everything within her longed to hug her sister, but then she looked at her mother, and felt grief anew, for her mother's face had hued to a pasty gray color.

"Am I interrupting?"

As one, their heads swiveled to the door where Edmund lounged, a cutting look in his eyes.

Edmund did his best not to stare directly at Sophia. He did not wish to make her uncomfortable again, and after a sleepless night of self-recrimination, he had determined to leave the matter behind him.

At least he had good news to give them. And as he scanned the room, he knew they needed good news. The youngest sister, whose name he had forgotten, terrible fiancé that he was, glowered at him.

The other sister, Eliza, sat quietly beside Sophia, eyes red rimmed. Lady Worland did not look well, though she seemed to be recovering rapidly. And Sophia. He let his gaze rest briefly on her, a butterfly on a flower, hardly there long enough to take stock of her expression but quickly enough to see her perusal.

"Come in, come in," said Lady Worland. She lifted the darning off her lap, set it on the side table and stood. "You must sit and let me pour you some tea. Would you like biscuits? Tarts? The cook you've hired is an exquisite baker." She smoothed her hands across her skirts, obviously rambling, and Edmund felt a start of sympathy for her.

"Madam, I am perfectly fine." He found a seat on a

couch adjacent to the two other girls. It was small and uncomfortable, as most furniture in parlors were. "I wanted to give you this news in person. Perhaps you should sit down," he said to Lady Worland. An unnatural pallor tinged her face.

"Mother, do please sit," said Sophia.

The sound of her husky, well-modulated voice scattered awareness through Edmund. He shoved the reaction away, focusing on the mother.

"Your husband has been found. It took some work, but it appears that he was kidnapped."

"Kidnapped?" Lady Worland's hands flew to her cheeks.

"That is the stuff of fiction. How is it possible?" asked the youngest girl.

Ah, the part they would not like to hear. He would skip it for now and let their father tell the tale. "However it came about, your husband—your father—is in Scotland, supposedly as an indentured servant. He is there against his will. I have made arrangements to pay for his release."

"Oh, this is terrible." Lady Worland began making a strange wheezing noise that might be amusing if he were not concerned for her health. Both Sophia and Eliza rushed over to their mother, but the youngest sister started laughing.

She had a melodic laugh at odds with her intense expression that Edmund immediately liked. Surely the situation was not dire if the girl laughed.

"Frederika, do stop," chastised Eliza.

"She's fine." Frederika shook her head. "Mother, please breathe through your nose and quit gasping for air like a fish out of water. There is more than enough oxygen in this room and you are not an asthmatic."

Sophia shot Edmund a look he could not decipher, but it might be close to an apology.

"Shall I call for water?" he asked.

"That would be most kind," said Sophia, and he thought he heard thankfulness in her voice. The water arrived and after Lady Worland calmed and everyone sat, she cleared her throat.

"I shall leave immediately to retrieve your father," she said.

"I'm going, too," said Eliza.

"It is a long trip," warned Edmund. He glanced at Sophia, wishing he could know her thoughts. "Even if you leave as early as tomorrow, you will miss our wedding in a fortnight."

Quiet ensued. Sophia smiled, though it seemed less wide than usual. "You all must go, of course. I shall be fine."

Eliza grasped Sophia's hand, and Edmund noted the compassionate expression upon Frederika's face.

"I will stay, if you want," said Eliza.

"Nonsense." An indecipherable emotion flashed across Sophia's features. Did her sisters see it? "No matter what London gossips may think, the duke and I are simply making a legal agreement. There's no need for your attendance."

Frederika was strangely quiet at her desk, and Eliza's fingers clenched in her lap. Only the mother seemed unaware of the tension in the room.

Her knitting continued, clacking into the silence with an erratic echo. "How dire is his situation? I have several things to put in order and I'd rather hire a hackney than ride a mail coach. This will take time, but I know it must be my loving face that he sees first. He must know we've come to rescue him."

Edmund waved a hand. "Travel arrangements have already been taken care of. My coach is at your disposal and I shall send footmen and maids to assist you in your journey."

Lady Worland dropped the needles, gasping. "That is most generous."

"Sophia's happiness is important to me." The moment the words left his mouth, he regretted them. His neck burned and he had the awkward sensation of reliving his first dance at a ball. "Our agreement is that I help her family. And so I shall help you, as she has helped Hannah."

That was better, right? Mouth dry, he offered a stiff, courtesy smile. "I shall go now so that you may pack. Send word when you wish to be picked up. The coachman will have the information needed for your safe travels."

He stood and was in the hall before anyone could stop him. Striding to the door, he let himself out and found his curricle awaiting him. The benefits of dukedom, he thought wryly.

"Wait." Sophia followed him out of the house and though her steps were hurried, she retained the grace he found so attractive.

He climbed into the curricle.

She stopped at the curb. "Will you drive me home?"

A jolt of surprise shocked him into saying, "With pleasure."

He gave instruction to the driver, and a footman assisted her into the curricle. She settled beside him in a flounce of skirt and perfume. The curricle started off, clattering through the streets. What to say? He was at a loss. He pushed the memory of last night's kiss from his mind.

"It's a beautiful day." There. An innocuous conversation proved best.

"Indeed," she answered.

He stared straight ahead, noting the bright blue of the sky and warm afternoon temperature. "Good for roses."

A soft little laugh escaped her. "Yes, it is. I shall miss my roses."

He let himself graze her with a glance. "You are giving up much for your family."

"You are giving up more." Her fingers plucked at her skirts. "I feel badly regarding last night."

The admission caught him off guard. He cleared his throat, staring ahead as their driver navigated the busy streets. "There is nothing to feel about it."

"Edmund."

He felt a tug on his sleeve. He looked down. She was peering at him in earnest, a serious tilt to her mouth. "In truth, I enjoyed the kiss immensely, but it was unexpected and it doesn't fit within the trajectory of my life."

"I understand." And he did, for he had not planned on her presence in his own life. He gave her a small smile to put her at ease. "Let us move on to other matters. We have given up looking for a similar contract in my father's old office. We will assume that your copy is the only one. Would you like it destroyed?"

"There's no sense in keeping paperwork. We have made our plans. My reputation is intact, my family is cared for and Hannah shall have a proper chaperone until she marries."

"And I will not need to worry about eager mamas pawning their husband-hungry daughters off on me."

They both laughed and for several minutes they rode in companionable silence. In the afternoon London streets were busy with carriages, barouches and hackneys. Ladies in their finery walked about to various stores. Gentlemen strolled the streets as well, greeting each other, while their servants carried their goods behind them.

It was a bright spring day. Perfect for pleasurable outings. "Do you need to shop for anything?" A thought occurred to him. "Perhaps assistance in packing your things?"

"No, all is under control. But what of our wedding? Have you obtained the license?"

Edmund grinned at her. "Whatever you may think of me, Mrs. Seymour, I am not an irresponsible man. All is ready for our nuptials in a fortnight. It shall be a small affair, as I think you'd prefer."

"Indeed."

He looked at her more fully. Her lips were compressed and the more he began to know her, the more he felt he could somewhat read her feelings. She tried so hard to hide them and he couldn't understand why. There was a certain liberty that came with freedom of expression, and he wasn't sure how to unbind the shackles she locked herself in.

Or even if he should.

His carriage turned onto a new street. It was less busy. They were nearing her townhome. Even though he had been dreading seeing her again, her confession had eased the knot in his chest that had plagued him all night.

"I am sorry your mother will not be at the wedding," he said tentatively.

She shrugged. "It is nothing. Our wedding is a formality."

"That's true, but I'm sure there's a part of you that wishes your family to be with you."

She sighed, looking down at her clasped hands. She did not speak.

"What was your first wedding like?" Did he really want to know? But she needed to speak. He could see her holding herself in, caged, and what he wanted was for her to be like her roses. The wildness she truly found beautiful. She had been pruned her entire life, rearranged and ordered for maximum effect. He wanted to put his hand over hers, the way she had comforted him only nights ago, but he resisted. Now was not the time.

Her silence was palpable. She might not answer.

But then another exhalation filled the air, and she spoke. "The wedding was larger than usual. Despite his quiet ways, Charles had many friends across many spheres. He was older, you know."

"No, I didn't realize that." He had assumed them to be a young couple in love.

"Yes, he was past thirty when we met. I was eighteen. We were a perfect fit, though, and I knew I wanted to marry him by the second time he called on me."

Edmund frowned. "That quickly."

"Sometimes love happens that way." A tiny smile edged her lips. "My parents expected more from me. Evidently to at least marry a titled man. We have all repeatedly wondered why Father did not pull out the betrothal at the start of my Season. Not that I would have allowed him to force my hand in marital matters."

"Were they disappointed in your choice of a third son?"

Only the slightest catch of breath gave hint to her feelings. "Yes."

"And now you are marrying me."

"It is certainly everything my mother dreamed of. Now that we know my father is alive and well, her happiness shall be complete. Until Eliza's coming out. Then she shall be on tenterhooks trying to secure better than a third son for her next daughter." Sophia's shoulders lifted in a shrug, but Edmund couldn't but feel that she was still on the precipice of some indefinable emotion.

They were almost to her house. "I can send someone else to retrieve your father. Your mother and sisters need not go."

"Oh, no, they have missed him so. As have I."

"Would you like to go with them? We can push the wedding back."

"No." Her headshake was firm. "I have already informed Lord Windley to find a new tenant and have given him the date of my departure. Our plans have been set."

The carriage slowed in front of her townhome. Edmund wished to make her smile but had no idea how. "I am very serious that our plans can change. You are important, Sophia. Your feelings matter."

It was one of the many truths his nanny had taught him. To his surprise, Sophia turned to him with shining eyes. Almost as though she might cry. A band of commiseration tightened across his chest.

"Thank you, Edmund. That is a most kind and thoughtful comment." Even though the carriage had stopped, she did not get out. "It is true that I am sad they won't be there. I am a little afraid. After all, I am linking myself to you for life. There is no going back after this. My family and I will be at your mercy and my independence is changing forms."

"I can understand your worry." He felt his brow furrowing. "Have you seen the betrothal contract I drew up?"

"Of course. I am also not an irresponsible woman." Finally, her face was relaxing and there was perhaps a small twinkle in her eye. "You have been most generous with me. I shall not want for funds."

He tipped his head. "I wanted to make sure you had plenty of pin money for your charities."

Now she smiled, a true and bright smile that lit dark places within him. He could not have chosen a more suitable woman to wed.

"But what of my wardrobe?" She grinned wider. "You know how I do love to be fashionable."

"I only ask that you not push your stylish bent upon me." He pulled upon his neckline, purposefully making it crooked. "I prefer to set my own fashion trends."

She laughed. "Very well. I shall be the polished gem and you shall be the uncut diamond." With that, she held out her hand to the footman, who had been waiting quietly for her, and dismounted. She gave Edmund a little wave, and then walked up to her house and let herself in.

All the way home, Edmund fought a growing disquiet that his life was moving in a direction he had not anticipated. The feeling inside was a curious mix of elation and terror, suspense and calm. In a fortnight he would be a married man, something he had thought never to be.

Would that he not destroy his marriage the way his father and brother had destroyed theirs.

Chapter Fourteen

It rained the day of Sophia's second marriage.

She watched rainwater sluice down the pillars of the church from her perch in the open doors. The grayish cast to the sky mirrored her emotions. She could not drum up excitement nor happiness, but instead, her heart felt the weight of this decision. She watched the downpour express her emotions, for she did not dare cry in front of anyone.

Imagine the scandal.

Caroline, Lord Boxing and Lord Windley were to be witnesses, as only they had been invited. It had been quietly explained to them that there'd been an important matter taking Sophia's family to Scotland. Thankfully, their guests did not ask probing questions.

Hannah glowed with excitement. Sophia could hear her excited chattering as St. George's had an interior that allowed for excellent sound effect. Indeed, the church was known for its simplistic beauty.

Simplicity for a simple marriage.

If only the marriage still felt uncomplicated. The more she began to know Edmund, the more she liked

him. Even when he was being heavy-handed or brooding or flirtatious. His kindness undercut that aura of
anger that used to surround him. But the closer she became to him, the higher her chance for pain.

She fingered her locket. She had considered taking
it off for the wedding. Charles was gone. It had been
many years and she was silly to still cling to a memory.
And memory was all she felt now. It was not as though
she still felt in love. Rather, the locket represented what
she had lost.

It reminded her to never lose again.

If she let herself like Edmund, would she fall in love
with him? Her heart hammered within, and she felt a
rushing of blood to her ears. The loss of a husband was
a pain she did not wish to ever feel again.

And yet, Edmund's kindnesses, the gentle tone he
used with her, wooed her. Even when he was surly and
irascible, there was a vulnerability about him that she
could not help but relate to. His kiss…she had felt the
deep emotion coming from him. She had felt his caring
to the very marrow of her bones and even now, sometimes her mouth wondered what it would feel like to
kiss him again.

Might he kiss her today? She swallowed the panic
rising to her throat, forcing herself to let go of the chain
about her neck and stand. Her legs wobbled a bit and
she wished heartily her sisters and mother were here.
They always made her feel stronger, more in control.
But they had left almost two weeks ago, and she was
alone. Even though only days ago Edmund had told her
they were on their way home, their father safely with
them. Still…alone. She sucked in a deep breath, holding it for a count of five, before releasing.

Not completely alone. She had her faith in God, and she had her dear Caroline. Perhaps her friend did not know the truth about the marriage, but she was here to support Sophia, and for that, Sophia was grateful.

She prayed for strength and then walked up the aisle to wait for Edmund's arrival.

The ceremony was passing so quickly. As the minister said the vows, and they repeated them, she couldn't help but compare this wedding to her first one.

That had been a true love match. The wedding had been held at the Windley estate and there had been gaiety, balloons and even fireworks. Many of their guests had stayed for the weekend to enjoy festivities and Sophia still recalled the open joy she had felt at being forever united with her dearest friend.

She studied Edmund now. His eyes, so very serious. His mouth somewhat grim. She hoped he would not regret this marriage. What if he found a true love in time? By marrying Sophia, he lost all hope of a real life with a woman he loved.

She squelched her guilt.

They had made their choice. That was the gist of the matter, and there was nothing else to be said or done about it. She squared her shoulders, clutching her tiny bridal bouquet tighter. She hadn't planned on even having flowers, but Caroline brought them and insisted. For her friend's sake, she acquiesced. They did smell lovely. She inhaled, and she saw Edmund's eyes flicker.

Was he as nervous as she was? As the ceremony ended, they recited their final lines of dedication and commitment, and then Edmund leaned forward. For a fraction of a second, Sophia was sure her heart stalled. Or perhaps skipped a beat.

His breath fanned her face and then he deposited a lone kiss upon her cheek. It was chaste and it was quick. Then he was straightening, and the service was over.

They were legally married.

They turned and Caroline's face showed no happiness. A look of concern wrinkled her forehead. Sophia gave her a small smile, an attempt to ward off that expression, but Caroline only nodded, as though acknowledging Sophia's effort. While Edmund endured his friends' jovial slaps on the back, she left his side to hug Hannah and Caroline.

"What haven't you told me?" her friend whispered against her ear. Sophia pulled away from the hug, looking down at her flowers, which were bright and lovely.

Moistening her lips, she met Caroline's concern with calm. "You needn't fret. Our marriage is not a love match, but rather an arrangement to stabilize both of our futures. We are well matched, and we understand each other."

"Do you?" Caroline's expression took on a thoughtful glaze.

"Yes. We do." Sophia glanced at Edmund, noting his proud posture and how even dressed for a wedding, he somehow looked like a disreputable pirate.

Caroline laughed, startling Sophia. "Well, that smile says it all."

"What smile?" Sophia touched her mouth.

"The one you are trying to hide." Caroline patted her shoulder, still tittering in a supremely obnoxious way. "Never mind, dearest. I must be off. Salutations on a most advantageous marriage."

Her friend pranced off to rap Edmund on the shoulder with her fan. "Such a boring kiss, Your Grace. You really must do better." She gave Sophia an overexaggerated wink before exiting the church, Hannah in tow. She was to spend the day with Caroline to give Sophia and Edmund privacy.

Despite herself, Sophia grinned.

"What's gotten into Lady Montfort?" asked Lord Boxing, scratching his beard in confusion.

"She's opinionated." Sophia shrugged, and then held out her hand so that Lord Boxing could give it a celebratory kiss.

"My congratulations on your nuptials," he said. "I have always hoped the best for you."

"As have I," put in Lord Windley. He took her hand next, his touch gentle. "This is a pleasant union and I am happy for the both of you. Charles would approve."

Sophia felt a hot flush upon her neck, and her heart flip-flopped in strange ways. To hear her former father-in-law's approbation made her feel better about the entire affair.

"Thank you," she managed to say, and then before she knew it, both the men had left and she was alone with Edmund.

Her husband.

"I have a carriage awaiting us," he said quietly, his gaze probing, his eyes dark. "I thought we might go to Gunter's for sweets. And then, I am game for whatever you wish to do."

"A rainy promenade in the park?" She sent him a teasing smile because her heart was beating erratically and if she didn't tease, she might cry, or she might ask him to kiss her again, which would be terribly unladylike and crude.

Yes. Completely unlike herself.

"A promenade, if you wish for it." But his voice was stiff and he was clearly less than pleased with her suggestion.

Hiding her smile, she linked her arm through his. "Well, we've done it. We are married, and I shall not force you to prove your matrimonial commitment through the sacrifice of your comfort. We shall not parade ourselves about the park, but Gunter's sounds lovely on a rainy afternoon. And then perhaps we could take in a play?"

"Or a musicale?" he asked.

"Yes, because you have both listened to music and danced despite your absence from societal events these long years?" She'd been meaning to get to the bottom of his comment that he would not trod her toes when they had waltzed.

He led her to the church exit, their arms still intertwined. His warmth was quite pleasant. It permeated through the sleeves of her gown and chased the chills of the day far from her heart.

"Do you know that my estate, Rennington, is by the sea?"

"I believe you've mentioned it," she murmured, remembering how he'd compared her eyes to the Celtic Sea. She'd never seen that coast, but now a curious hunger took hold and her imagination searched for images of its beauty.

"It is my home," he said simply. They stepped out of the church, and his carriage truly was awaiting them. The vehicle was a resplendent nod to Edmund's station, the crest commanding and ornate, overlaid in gold trim. "When I am there, I am happy. At least once a week an orchestra comes in and plays throughout the day. Hannah and I like to dance. She has country friends, people who know little of our pasts, and they call often. My life outside of London has been fulfilling."

Sophia allowed him to help her into the carriage. She sat on a comfortable seat, noting the pleasantries within, like the soft blanket and pillow next to the window. The seat was a plush, welcoming fabric. "This is a different carriage?" she asked.

"Yes, I sent your family in my other one. They should return any day. I had a missive this morning that all is well."

"Wonderful."

"And your things have all been moved to my London house. You shall have the master bedroom."

"You are efficient."

"I am."

Quietness suffused the coach. Edmund had sat across from her, and their eyes met at the same time, cultivating a laugh from each.

"I confess," he said, scrubbing his chin in a nervous way, "that I have no earthly idea on how to be a husband."

"Go about your business and keep my pin money in ready supply."

"Is that it? And here I thought I must make conversation."

"Only if you like your wife."

One of those short, hearty laughs burst from Edmund. He stretched his legs, eyeing her with heavy-lidded eyes. "I do like my wife. Very much indeed. Perhaps more than I've liked any other woman."

A hot, visceral flush spread through Sophia. Her cheeks burned and she suddenly realized how very striking Edmund was, with his curling, overlong black hair and his strong nose and jaw. The lips, how gentle they had been against hers, at odds with the rugged planes of his face. She looked down at her lap. Marriage to him was infinitely more complicated than she had expected. For so long she had settled with the comfortable expectation of a quiet life.

But now, her future was unknown. Unpredictable. And far more invigorating than she could have ever imagined.

Sophia's family were to arrive anytime now. Edmund paced his library, every so often glancing out the window for the carriage. He had hardly seen Sophia since their wedding. They'd passed a pleasant wedding day, and then he'd continued his many duties as a duke while Sophia took her role in Hannah's life seriously.

They had gone out every night and had not invited him once. He could simply insert himself into their adventures, and a puckish part of him longed to do so, but there was also the other part that needed distance from Sophia.

Every time he saw her, he felt the punch of attraction and a longing he couldn't define. Scowling, he went to his desk and continued working. The vouchers from Almack's mocked him from the corner of his desk.

A commotion propelled him to the door. He went to the stairwell, looking down into his hallway as Reed opened the great doors of his townhome. Pattering sounded behind him and Hannah came bounding toward him, her eyes alight.

"They're here," she shrieked, rushing past him and flying down the stairwell. "Eliza!"

The family poured into his house. He made his way slowly down, observing their interactions. Eliza and Hannah embraced, squealing and laughing. Lady Worland bustled in next, already talking although he couldn't tell to whom. Perhaps to Frederika, who walked in behind her with a pensive expression. And then Lord Worland came through the door.

The man did not look as bad as Edmund had feared. A certain gauntness shadowed his cheeks but there was a jovial air to his nature that showed itself in deep crinkles about his eyes. As Edmund stepped off the final stair, all talking ceased. The family filed all the way in and Reed shut the door.

The girls dropped to a curtsy, and Lord Worland made a deep bow.

"Your Grace," he said, his voice gravelly. "I am indebted to you."

As though realizing the relevance of what he'd just said, Sophia's father grimaced. In truth, the man was indebted to many and because of that, he had endangered his family. Nevertheless, Edmund inclined his head in response.

"We are related now," he said, and what a startling epiphany that was.

"Eliza, you must come see the new prints I obtained." Hannah, as usual, was oblivious to the atmosphere of the room.

Eliza looked at her mother. "May I?"

Lady Worland gave her approval, and the young women raced off.

"Have you eaten supper?" asked Edmund.

"No." Frederika hugged herself, looking out of place. Sympathy for her nerves filled him. She did not seem the type to enjoy loitering in a ducal townhome.

"Come. I shall order us a repast. Your trunks will be taken to your town house." They walked up the stairs to the second floor, where his parlor was located. It was a large, bright room he rarely used but perhaps they'd find it comfortable. His housekeeper met him at the top of the stairs. After giving her instructions, they all settled into the parlor.

"Where is Sophia? I would dearly love to see her." Lord Worland twisted a hankie in his lap. His wife reached over and stilled his busy fingers with a gentle tap of her hand.

Edmund settled into a wing chair. "Sophia has been sent for."

"All will be well, darling," murmured Lady Worland. From the corner she'd chosen near a large window, Frederika made a sound that seemed suspiciously like a snort.

Edmund frowned. There was tension in the room, and Lord Worland was clearly not at ease. Several maids came in with platters of sandwiches and biscuits. They poured tea and Edmund let them eat in silence while he contemplated the situation. Obviously the baron had apprised his family of his situation. It was a sad day when one succumbed to the addictive greed of gambling.

Beyond that, the baron's gambling had been kept secret. Edmund shifted uncomfortably, for he had his own secret, which had remained hidden for years, and he intended to keep it that way. Nevertheless, he felt a sympathy for Sophia's father.

Rustling sounded to his left and Sophia appeared in the doorway. She wore a rose day dress that brought color to her pale skin. Her gaze lit upon Lord Worland.

"Father," she said, emotion clogging her words. The baron stood and they embraced. Their mutual affection was evident. Edmund felt a tug of envy, for how often as a boy had he wished his father might hug him? Or even touch him with hands of love rather than hands of anger? His brother had tried to give him the love that lacked, but in the end, his brother had become exactly what he hated.

Edmund shut the memories away. The secrets. They brought nothing but a throbbing to his temples and a sickness to his gut. He focused on Sophia's face as she pulled away from her father, still grasping his arms as though he were mist that might fade if she looked away.

"Are you well? What happened?"

"My dear girl…" Lord Worland's voice faltered. Edmund braced himself, for he knew the man's confession must cause him a great deal of pain.

"What is it? You are too pale." Sophia touched her father's cheek, concern marking deep grooves around her mouth. Edmund had never seen her frown before, and his chest constricted. His arms ached to hold her. To comfort her.

He cared about her.

It was not a bad thing, he told himself as he watched her lead the baron back to the couch. Once sitting, she poured him more hot tea before taking a seat beside Edmund. His fingers itched to cradle her hand within his. He ignored the feeling. Caring did not mean he had to touch her.

"Now," she said calmly, though he saw her white-knuckled clasp, "How did you end up being kidnapped? Do tell me all."

Frederika made that sound again, and Sophia's gaze shot to her sister. But Frederika was staring out the window at his rose garden.

Lady Worland turned to Sophia. "Your father is... well, he struggles, dear heart."

"Struggles?"

"With horses." Lady Worland shot a gaze at the baron. "With gambling."

An uncomfortable silence filled the room.

Sophia made a delicate throat clear.

Lord Worland's hands were twisting again, and the sorrow upon his face was so palpable that Edmund almost felt sorry for the man.

"I thought I had it, the winning horse, that is," he said weakly. "Then I lost our fortune and needed to regain it, but I had a bad run. I knew if I tried one more time, I'd win. I knew it, to the bottom of my soul. Those creditors didn't give me a chance to prove it. Instead of throwing me in Fleet, they indentured me to a blacksmith in Scotland."

"Did you go willingly?" asked Sophia.

"No. They captured me, covered my eyes, and I was restrained at all times."

"I see." Her eyelids flickered. "If you all will excuse me, I need a moment." She rose gracefully from her seat and glided out of the room, her back straight and stiff.

Lady Worland began to weep, and her husband pulled her into an embrace, tears glistening in his own eyes. "She will never forgive me," he said.

Edmund stood. "Please, help yourself to more food. I will attend to Sophia."

Perhaps he could never be a husband in truth, but he well knew how to be a true friend. And at the moment, Sophia needed someone to count on. Someone like him.

Chapter Fifteen

The perfection of Edmund's garden grated on Sophia's nerves. The rows were carefully tended, the stems meticulously pruned. His garden stretched out in a tiny, perfect square, encompassed by tall walls of stone and hedgerows.

She touched a deeply scarlet bloom, marveling at its rich-hued scent. How orderly this place. How neat and perfect and unsurprising. Was that why Edmund made it such? Because his world had splintered into pieces, falling about him in jagged chaos, and he had needed a space where everything had its specified purpose?

She rubbed the rose petal betwixt her fingers, her chest aching with suppressed tears.

"Sophia." Edmund's resonant voice pierced the quiet of the garden. His footsteps grew closer until his cologne reached her first. She felt his warmth at her back. She could not look at him. Throat tight, she continued to knead the rose petal.

"I am sorry," he said, his apology a whisper at her ear.

"We might have ended up in the poorhouse. Or

worse, on the streets." The words strangled out from her, taut and unyielding.

"Yes."

"All because he was betting on racehorses. Gambling."

"There are those who develop a taste for gambling and cannot stop."

"Even at the endangerment of their family?"

"Some say it is a sickness."

She whirled then, her heart pumping in dangerous, angry beats. "That does not change what he has put us through. If not for you—" Her voice broke. Alarmed, she stopped speaking.

"Everything will work out for good." Edmund put his hand on her shoulder, his irises dark and deep. "Is that not what the Bible teaches? Our faith? That God will help us in times of need."

"Faith." She pressed her lips together, sifting through her thoughts in order to express what she needed. "My father taught me to trust in God. To do good and to be honest. But he has lied. He has betrayed his entire family and for what? Greed? To gain money? How can I ever trust him again?"

And that was the crux of it all, wasn't it? The man who had taught her so many honorable things was in fact himself dishonorable. Her heart twinged, knowing that wasn't completely true, but she held her anger in her palms and refused to let it go.

Edmund's expression was unusually thoughtful as he took one of her hands. "Come with me."

Silently she followed him, the warmth of his hand curling around hers, anchoring her soul. They walked the stone path as it wound around an ivy-covered wall to expose a small alcove wherein sat a table and chairs. He sat and patted the seat beside him. Reluctantly, she followed suit.

"I do not need an optimistic lecture," she said. "I simply needed air."

"Do you want me to leave, then?"

Did she? She took in the scene around them, the fragrant area creating a tiny alcove that gave the impression of solitude. Besides rosebushes trimmed like perfect little sentries around them, there were bright blue and yellow flowers growing within the vines. "No," she said at last, surprised by her own answer. "Please stay. Did you design this place?"

He nodded, his gaze following hers as she admired it all. "There isn't much room in London for private gardens. Many of the peers have communal gardens, but I wished for privacy. I did not need anything huge or ostentatious."

"Did your wish for privacy stem from what happened after your brother died?"

"It did." He inhaled deeply, and when she looked at his face, she saw the love he felt for this place engraved in his smile. "I do not wish to speak of the past, though, but the future."

"Is the past a dead horse, then?"

"More like a buried horse."

"Never to be resurrected? I think sometimes we must examine the bones of a thing to make sure it never dies again."

"I had no control over the horse, therefore examination changes nothing."

She was sad to see the smile leave his face. "I believe I know exactly what you mean, Your Grace. It seems that for all my careful choices, I have had no say in what has recently occurred."

"You are angry with your father."

"Do you think I should be happy with him?"

He chuckled. "Calm yourself. I did not say such a thing."

She tried in vain to subdue the flush of anger skidding along her skin. "Then why are you stating the obvious?"

"Because you showed little to no emotion when he explained the circumstances. I realize this is rather forward of me, but I must point out that not telling him how you feel could be truly detrimental to your relationship."

Sophia's jaw dropped before she quickly snapped it closed. Advice? The *Beast of London* was giving her advice?

He held up a hand, noting her look and reading it all too well. "Trust me when I say that anger brings little good, whether let loose or tightly constrained."

"Sometimes anger sparks necessary changes."

His mouth quirked. "Exactly. But if you do not tell your father how you feel, do you think anything will change?"

"Did you hear him? He still believes he would have won the money back. He expressed no sorrow for what he has put us through."

"Perhaps he does not understand the full anguish you feel? As I said before, it is a sickness, I think, what your father carries."

"A sickness." She crossed her arms, feeling guilty as she did so for being unreasonable. But not completely. "Had we not found that contract, which put us in contact, had you not desperately needed a chaperone, which led to our marriage, my family would have been ruined."

"I can share good news, if you'd like."

She kept her back to him, but she was in dire need of good news.

"I have received our vouchers for Almack's."

She spun around, joy ricocheting through her so quickly she felt dizzy. Her family *hadn't* been ruined. Hannah's season wasn't either. She should be grateful for both. "Positively splendid. There is a ball this Wednesday. We shall attend. I must go to Hannah and ensure she has the correct clothing to wear. This is her statement to those she wishes to impress."

"Hannah wishes to impress?"

"But of course." Poor Edmund. He did not see how the next few years could affect Hannah's life. She patted his hand. "These are those of polite society who pass muster. They are people of good reputation and good money."

"Are vouchers all it takes to make your anger pass?"

Sophia shrugged, heaviness still on her soul. "I'm trying to be grateful for what I do have. I'm quite happy to be distracted by a dance to plan for."

"Do you think I should come?"

Above, a cloud passed over the sun and dropped shadows upon Edmund's features. For the first time since he had come into the garden, he sounded vulnerable. She was overcome with an insatiable impulse to touch him, to assure him, but of what?

"There is no need," she answered.

To her surprise, he frowned. "But what if there is a want?"

Taken aback, she tilted her head.

"I suppose," she said slowly, "that if there is a want, and it can be fulfilled, then perhaps it should be."

"In that case, I have a great many wants." The way shadows slanted across his face struck a shudder through Sophia. He was flirting, but not in a lighthearted manner. His eyes glinted, and in them she thought she saw the same struggle that currently raged within her.

She'd gone seven years without physical closeness, without emotional intimacy, and now she found herself within the maelstrom of the duke's intricate emotional nature. She moistened her lips, meeting his heady gaze with a practiced aloofness.

"Let your moderation be known unto all men."

His brow lifted.

"It is in the Bible, Your Grace. Fulfilling one want at a time seems best."

He only nodded.

And so it was that on Wednesday, the Beast of London went to Almack's to fulfill his apparent want of dancing.

Sophia found a great deal of amusement in watching him navigate the stuffy atmosphere of pretention and faux smiles. Although he insisted he wished to go, she could see now as he drifted past during a reel that he was overtly miserable. Not only that, but he kept glaring at every young man who tried to speak with Hannah.

Sophia took her gaze from Edmund and found Hannah in the crowd nearby. Potential suitors surrounded her. She tossed her head often, laughing gaily, eyes sparkling, and satisfaction permeated Sophia. She had taught her charge well. One couldn't be simpering but neither could one be brash. Hannah was striking the perfect notes and her admirers knew it.

She was smart enough to include some other young ladies in the group so that she did not alienate anyone. Clever girl.

"You are smirking." Edmund's low voice at her ear sparked a delicious shiver down her spine.

"I am admiring my masterpiece."

He grunted. "She does seem rather toned down since you've taken your pruning shears to her."

Sophia wrinkled her nose. "Pruning shears?"

"Yes, shears. She was already a masterpiece, you just had to cut the extra, unneeded pieces away."

She sighed, refraining from the eye roll she felt he deserved. "Very well. You win. Shears it is. But look at her."

"She's magnificent."

"Yes. You have done a wonderful job raising her."

A hint of color crept over his sharp cheekbones. "My nanny did the brunt of the work."

"Nonsense," she said briskly. "Hannah is very much your copy."

"In only the good ways, I hope," he muttered darkly.

Sophia grinned. "Unfortunately, no."

"Who is that?" Edmund's voice underwent a change, lowering to a growl. Sophia followed the line of his eyes to a young man who had managed to corral Hannah's spirited conversation to himself. Edmund made a rather uncouth sound and she quickly jabbed him in the side with her elbow.

"Stop that at once," she whispered in a sharp hiss. "Try to smile."

"I am," he gritted out.

She chanced a look at him and folded her arms. "I did not say bare your teeth. You are truly incorrigible, Edmund." Taking his arm, she pulled him in the direction of the supper room.

"Where are we going?" His head whipped back to spy on Hannah again.

"*You* are going to get some food. I will join Hannah and find out who that young man is."

Edmund stuffed a stale biscuit in his mouth, then washed it down with tepid lemonade. Why on earth was Almack's so popular? He could think of several places that offered better refreshments than this. Like his own home. Feeling the rigidity in his face, he tried for another drink of the lemon swill.

Swallowing it down with a grimace, he eyed the doorway to the ballroom. How long did it take to ferret out the name of the swine who was trying to gain Hannah's affections? He crossed his arms and planted his feet. Let that young man prove himself.

His mind went back to Hannah's mother, Naomi. If only she'd had someone to vet his brother for her. Had she looked into his history, and even their father's, she would have found a pattern of moodiness and passive aggression. But alas, Naomi had been an orphan raised by relatives, just as Hannah was, and had no one to care for her future. Her relatives had only been too eager to be rid of her.

And though Hannah was similar to her mother, she lacked the innocent and delicate temperament that had blinded Naomi to his brother's faults. Hannah was strong-willed, feisty, and he'd be surprised if anyone charmed her so much she didn't see the truth of their nature.

Nevertheless, he planted his feet squarely facing the doorway as he waited for Sophia to return. A servant came and took his glass. He crossed his arms. Who dared spirit Hannah away from the group, knowing she was his niece? The bold chap better come up to snuff.

A gentleman and lady who looked familiar started toward him, but then abruptly changed directions. His brows lowered. Good. He had no intention of speaking to anyone until he ascertained Hannah's safety.

It felt like hours before Sophia returned. She swished into the room with a beatific smile, her face glowing with what he could only presume was satisfaction.

Drawing out her fan, she rapped him on the arm before opening it and fanning herself. "I never realized how dark your face gets when you're glowering. It's as though the blood has left your brains and pooled in your cheeks."

Edmund's temple throbbed. "What news?"

"Do you think first you should swallow some oxygen? I daresay, Your Grace, if you have an apoplectic fit, I shall be most disappointed."

He scrubbed a hand through his hair, raking hard enough to wince. "This is far too stressful."

Sophia laughed in a tinkling, harmonious way he found soothing. "Buck up. Your constitution will be just fine. I shall get you a drink, hmm?"

"This place has nothing good to offer."

"On the contrary. Almack's is the ideal place to find a husband. Which is Hannah's goal."

He made a sound.

"Quit growling. She shall be happy, if I have any say

in the matter." She flashed him such a bright and open and utterly charming smile that the hard knot gripping his insides began to ease. "The gentleman speaking to her is Mr. Paul Aimsley. You may remember him from the park?"

"Heir to an earldom."

"No, that is his older brother. He has plans to purchase a commission as an officer. Though..." She paused, tapping her fan against her dress.

"What?" he asked sharply.

"Well, his is an old lineage. I don't know the finances of the family."

"He's out."

"Now, Edmund, be reasonable. Hannah, if not an heiress, will be properly settled, correct?"

"I don't want anyone marrying her for money."

"He has plans to be an officer. That is hardly a man looking for a rich bride." She tugged at his hand. "Come, we must go back to the ballroom. I'm being remiss in my chaperone duties."

Edmund found himself dutifully following his iron-willed wife into the ballroom. Immediately music engulfed him and he trailed Sophia's determined march. They found Hannah dancing a quadrille.

With that man-child. Mr. Paul Aimsley. He sported a foolish grin on his placid face. Edmund shook his head. Sophia nudged him.

"Stop frowning."

"I can't. I shall dispatch a Runner immediately but I can already surmise that this Aimsley fellow is unsuitable."

"Nonsense. I'm sure he shall call tomorrow. Hannah will decide."

"Hannah? She's a child. She cannot be trusted to choose her future."

"I beg your pardon?"

"You heard me." He skewered Aimsley with a glare. "Hannah will respect my choice for her."

"You cannot be serious." Sophia's voice quivered.

"Indeed I am. My responsibility is to see to her long-term happiness." Even if it meant circumventing temporary happiness. He felt the disapproval radiating from Sophia but set his jaw. He had married Sophia for her reputation, not her opinions. Under no circumstances could he allow what happened to Naomi to happen to Hannah. He'd protect her at any cost, and the secrets of the past would remain buried. For Hannah's sake.

Even still, a feeling akin to regret coiled in his gut when Sophia left his side without so much as a goodbye.

Chapter Sixteen

Gossip was a terrible thing.

Sophia had just taken her first sip of tea when Mother said, "So you've had a row with the duke, have you?"

Coughing, she swallowed and set the cup down. "Whatever do you mean?"

Eliza grimaced from her place at the parlor window. "The gossip column told a tale."

"It's not hard to imagine," Mother said in a snitty tone. "He's a complex man."

"Mother," Sophia said in reproof.

"I knew he'd be difficult from the very beginning." She smiled in satisfaction at her judgment.

Sophia shook her head. Her parents had invited Edmund and her over for dinner this evening. He'd had matters to attend to for the day but he was set to arrive soon. In the meantime, Sophia had met her sisters on Bond Street to do some afternoon shopping. Their expedition had been quite fun, especially with the money Edmund insisted she have for her own use.

"He is not difficult and no matter what the columns said, Edmund and I are on perfectly good terms." Even if he was being utterly ridiculous when it came to poor Mr. Aimsley. The sweet man had come calling two mornings in a row and one could see why Hannah was so smitten. The man had kind eyes and a dry wit. He did not stand out as outrageously handsome, yet Hannah was drawn to him and seemed to enjoy their brief interludes. A sparkle lit her eyes whenever his name was mentioned. Sophia and Eliza had chatted about the burgeoning romance while shopping.

"Good terms or no, thank goodness for that contract." Mother lifted her chin in a suspicious way, as though far more pleased with herself than she should be. Sophia's eyes narrowed.

"It's a mystery how you found that old thing, and even more startling that His Grace went through with the marriage." Father came into the room, and Sophia suppressed the dart of anger that pricked her heart. "I thought we destroyed it."

Sophia's jaw dropped.

Father paid her no mind, settling beside his wife with a hearty expulsion of breath, as though he had not been missing for months, leaving his family defenseless and penniless.

She managed to find her voice. "We?"

Eliza stood and left the room. Frederika, who had been reading at a far corner window, followed. Sophia felt her own mouth flattening.

"Why, the duke's father." Father laughed, slapping his knee. "Your mother didn't tell you?"

Mother was knitting furiously, her gaze refusing to lift.

"Martha." Father's voice lowered. "Do they not know?"

"You left me no recourse," she said stubbornly. "I have held on to the contract for such a time as this."

"But you knew it was made in jest." Father's eyebrows furrowed. "A silly wager between men too deep in their cups to be reasonable."

Mother sniffed, raising her nose and giving Father a starched expression. "Nevertheless, I kept the contract with our papers at our barrister's office, and as it turns out, my preventative measure came in handy. Do you know to what great lengths I had to go in order to save our family? Your daughter—" and she gave Sophia a pointed look "—told His Grace no when he proposed."

"I'd hardly call it a proposal," said Sophia dryly, though the more her parents conversed, the more her temper heated.

"Sophia sent him a list of *other* women to help him with his niece. She refused to marry a perfectly good candidate and for why? Sentimentality over a man she barely knew."

Sophia sucked in a quick breath, surprised by the lancing dagger of pain her mother's words engendered.

"And I am not trying to hurt you, dear heart." Her mother rushed on, oblivious. "But I would go to any lengths to keep us from ruin."

"Ruin?" Father wore befuddlement like a coat. "Why didn't you go to my aunt Sally in Bath? You two have always been close, and she's lonely."

"Because, Lord Worland." Mother slapped her knitting on the couch, between her and Father. "My daughters deserve Seasons and that is what I have made certain they'll get. What did you expect me to do when you disappeared?"

Sophia's entire body felt on fire. Her cheeks burned.

"Did you manipulate the terms of my marriage? You knew the contract to be a jest. But how did you…" She trailed off, knowing there were dots to connect but failing to draw the lines.

Mother waved a hand. "I spread the word about His Grace's more beastly aspects. Add in an unruly chit of a girl with no refinement, and I knew he'd need Sophia. You may recall he had engaged a chaperone for the girl? That was my cousin and she was only too happy to give up the post. Apparently Hannah is a difficult young woman to corral."

"Were you ever even in danger of poverty? Ruination?" Sophia felt sick, a deep nausea pervading her stomach and clinching her throat.

Mother's eyes flickered, the first indication that she felt any guilt at all. "In a sense, my darling. Ruination, certainly. Our lives would have assuredly changed for the worse. No one in polite society would accept us if they knew the details of our circumstance. I simply made certain His Grace knew you could solve his problems, and in turn, he would solve ours."

Sophia closed her eyes in an effort to retain her temper. Edmund could never find out that her mother had contributed to Hannah's social distresses, nor that the contract had been a farce. He might think Sophia involved. He might think her a schemer, the worst sort of woman, the kind of person he felt populated the *ton*. Fake and grasping.

She opened her eyes as she inhaled deeply, attempting to calm her nerves.

"My lord." A servant entered and bent to whisper in her father's ear.

"Wonderful. The duke has arrived." Her father held

out a hand to her mother, who took it with a smile as though nothing had happened. As though the world Sophia thought she inhabited still existed. When Sophia's father held out his hand to her, she refused to take it. He tipped his head, studying her for a moment, and then he and her mother went to meet Edmund and Hannah.

Discovering her mother's involvement in her present circumstances hurt almost as much as knowing her father had been living a secret life, that he had courted dishonesty and greed and in the process, almost destroyed his wife and daughters.

She took deep breaths to calm herself, struggling with the rapid beating of her heart and the anger flushing through her system. Was this how Edmund felt all the time? Had what happened to his family so shocked his nerves that he had found himself in a perpetual stage of fury? It felt as though her parents were her enemies now. They had betrayed her.

She could suddenly see Edmund's perspective toward the *ton*. Though he had not given her specifics and she had been too young at the time to hear the slanderous details, she gathered he had been active in society before the death of his brother and sister-in-law. Then they had been murdered and Edmund found himself unexpectedly and unfairly shunned.

No wonder he was loathe to venture out. Perhaps everyone he met seemed a nemesis.

She gathered her skirts and her courage and ventured toward the dining room. Edmund was seated next to her father. She took a seat next to him, appreciating his familiar scent and the comfort it brought. At least he was real. He had never pretended to be anything other than himself.

He turned to her, bending his head in greeting, and she noted the uneven folding of his coat lapels. Her mouth tugged in amusement. Yes…he was most assuredly his untidy, uncaring self.

"I thought perhaps you might miss dinner," he said.

"I am upset." Their eyes met, and the blackness of his irises arrested her so that her breath caught.

"As am I." He broke their stare, his voice quiet. "My Runner visited this afternoon. It seems Aimsley has no money for a commission. His parents are scraping by, relying on the elder to marry an heiress, and then they will buy him his papers. He is not suitable for Hannah. As I suspected."

Her heart sank to even further depths. "I am disappointed to hear such a thing. Hannah finds great joy in his presence."

Edmund made a sound in his throat, disapproval, no doubt, and then turned to Father. They began to speak of politics. Mother sat directly across from Sophia. Hannah sat next to Mother, and her sisters were separated, one on each side of the table. Frederika was, as usual, quiet and contemplative, her gaze heavy with thoughts Sophia was sure she'd never comprehend.

Eliza and Hannah politely listened to Mother prattle on about the latest scandal while exchanging wry glances. Apparently a known rake had absconded with a girl of good fortune to Gretna Green for a quick marriage. Or so it was surmised. As they had not yet returned, the nuptials could not be verified and so merited much discussion.

Sophia pursed her lips, looking down at her place setting. How could they all sit there, so relaxed, in the town house Edmund had provided, with the food Edmund had provided, and not apologize? Her father was his usual hearty self, speaking with Edmund without the slightest care in the world. And Edmund himself maintained a relaxed air. Certainly more lenient with her father's failures than she could force herself to be.

Even if his gambling was a sickness, even if there were some element outside of her father's control, could he not at least acknowledge the pain and worry he had caused his family? She stared incredulously as he belly laughed.

Perhaps Edmund was right. A solid certainty took hold. Perhaps Father needed to be told what exactly he had done to the family. He needed to see that she was hurt, betrayed. Sophia glanced at her female family members. Wasn't there strain upon their faces? Pain hidden in their eyes?

She cleared her throat. The conversations continued. And so she took a spoon to tap her glass, but her tap hit harder than she expected, and the glass shattered in a sharp and tinny sound.

Edmund's head jerked to the right. Glass splattered across the dishes, bouncing onto plates and clattering against other glasses. Beside him, Sophia stood, a strangely resolute expression upon her beautiful face.

"I have something to say." Her voice trembled.

Was she taking his advice? Now? He winced, foregoing any anticipation of a calm, family affair. It had been odd how he'd looked forward to this dinner, how he'd felt eased by the warm greeting Lord and Lady Worland gave him when he arrived. How long it seemed since he'd felt part of a family that loved one another.

Yes, he had Hannah, but there was something to be

said for a large family dinner, for laughter and companionable conversation. Not only that, but he'd been looking forward to the food. The day had been long and tedious as he reviewed estate accounts and sundry other items that came with being a duke. Everything was running smoothly, his life had moved into order and he'd married a woman who brought stability and interest to his days.

Things had never been better.

But now…he found himself holding his breath. Sophia looked as fragile as the glass she had unwittingly shattered.

"Sophia." Lady Worland shook her head at her daughter, her gaze darting to Edmund as if trying to ward off his attention. "Later. After dinner."

Two maids came and began picking the glass off the table. Lord Worland waved them away. "Let her speak," he said.

"Father." Sophia's throat moved, as if swallowing her fear, or perhaps tears. He could not imagine this formidable woman crying, but at the moment, anything seemed possible. "You and Mother have taught me a great many things. How to smile when I don't wish to smile, how to ignore my feelings in favor of the perfect facade."

"That's not true," interjected Lady Worland, her chin trembling.

Lord Worland held up a hand. Edmund admired his reserve. "Continue, Sophia."

She clasped her hands and Edmund was sure he was the only one who could see her whitened knuckles. "You also taught me a true love for others, to care for their well-being in accordance with God's calling in our lives.

You, particularly, Father. And yet you have lived a secret life. How could you betray us that way?"

Lord Worland's eyes widened. His jovial air dissipated as the full import of his daughter's words took root. "Are you angry at me, my girl?"

Sophia sat abruptly, her cheeks pale. Edmund longed to embrace her, but hadn't he told her she should express her true feelings? He hadn't expected it at dinner, though. His stomach rumbled.

"Do you expect me not to be angry?" She gestured wildly to her sisters and mother. "What about them? Have you considered for one moment how they felt when you did not return home? Have you thought of Mother's tears? My sisters' worries?"

Lord Worland's eyes fluttered closed. "I have tried not to."

"Well, perhaps you should stop trying," she said hotly. There was a pitch to her voice he'd not heard before, a quavering desperation that proved to be a precursor to tears. He watched as one rolled silently down her cheek. His hands fisted, his jaw hardened.

He hated that his happy, peaceful Sophia felt the scorching burn of betrayal. If only he could take it for her, take the pain of everything.

"Perhaps you could bother to offer an apology," she continued. "Not only for the worry you've caused us all, but for losing our fortune. Gambling, of all things."

"Watch yourself," Lady Worland put in sharply, her hand reaching for her husband's. "He's tried so hard to overcome this dreadful habit."

"No wonder you were not surprised at our change in finances." Sophia folded her arms against herself. "Father, you taught me to be Godly, to seek God's will above everything, and yet all this time you have been hiding a terrible secret. We are betrayed by your dishonesty. *I* am betrayed. You are not the man I thought you were, and I should not have thought so highly of you."

Edmund's heart twisted at the cutting words. Lord Worland's throat bobbed, and his eyes grew shiny.

"It was never my intention to hurt any of you." His voice wavered with emotion.

"But you did. And then you return, acting as though we have not gone through the worst eight months of our lives. But for when Charles died, I have not felt so much pain and consternation as I have these past months. Not only did I fear your death, but my entire life has been disrupted." Sophia's tone dropped. "I had to marry, when I wished to never, ever marry again. You know how much I loved my husband." Tears streaked down her cheeks.

Edmund could look no more. There was a yawning pit hollowing out his insides, severing away any unacknowledged hopes he had for the future in slicing, jagged strokes.

"Now I am a wife. I have moved from my home, changed my entire lifestyle, because of your selfishness. If you had controlled yourself and been wise, if you had been the person you pretended to be, none of this would have happened. My sisters would have Seasons with good prospects and my life would be as I chose it to be. You took our choices away. And you don't even care." Her hands gesticulated wildly. "How can you sit there laughing as if nothing happened. My entire life has been altered. We are forever indebted to Edmund. Because of you."

She dropped off suddenly, pushing out of her chair

and heading toward the doorway. She stopped then, and her face was no longer pale, but flushed. Her eyes flashed. "I am going to my new home and I will pray that I can forgive you for the havoc you have wrecked upon this family."

She left then, and the family sat in stunned silence. Eliza and her mother were both crying, one silently and the other with huge wheezes and rolling tears. Frederika had no tears but her mouth was tight. Hannah stared at her plate. Lord Worland had closed his eyes and hardly moved.

For his part, Edmund felt rent in two. He had hoped that Sophia might come to like him the way he liked her. He had thought her happy enough, but now he realized she would never be happy. She would never want their marriage. She would never want him.

Which was a ridiculous thought, as he certainly did not care if she wanted him. That was not part of the agreement. And yet there remained a vulnerable, pulsating hurt within because he had no idea if he could ever give Sophia the happiness she deserved.

Not as a husband to a wife, but as a friend to a friend.

Without a doubt, if anyone deserved to know their worth, Sophia did. Despite the bitter flavor permeating his sense of self, he determined he would rectify her perspective. Sophia would have no cause to regret their marriage.

He'd make sure of it.

Chapter Seventeen

$\mathbf{W}$ho would ever guess how exhilarating anger could be?

Sophia flounced into Edmund's home, *her* home, flush with a zinging satisfaction. Every part of her felt alive. Triumphant, even. Mr. Reed took her coat and she practically flew up the stairs to the parlor. Her stomach grumbled, perhaps the one part of her that did not feel happy as she had missed the evening meal.

Perhaps *happy* was not the correct word, per se, but she did feel something close to an elated contentment. All these weeks she'd pitied Edmund for living in his anger-induced grumpiness, but now she realized that such strong emotion gave a level of power she hadn't anticipated. She could still see their shocked faces.

She went into the parlor, paced, then left. Her father's expression flashed in her mind. He had not only been shocked, he had been hurt. Her stomach fell a little at the realization. She walked to her room, where she found Betsy readying her bed for the night. After a brief conversation regarding the adorable yet fiercely protective mastiffs now living at the boarding homes for the fallen women, Sophia went back to the parlor.

Restlessness pattered through her blood. She had no intention of hurting anyone. But Edmund had been right. It was important that her father see the effect of his decisions. That he feel the brunt of his foolish misdeeds.

She sat on the couch in the parlor, the brocaded one by the window. She felt no pleasure in her father's hurt. Without asking, a maid brought in tea. Mr. Reed asked her about food, and she decided she should eat a little something. He kindly informed Cook and it wasn't long before she was brought a delicious artichoke soup.

When Betsy came in to check on her, Sophia sent her to bed, assuring her she could handle her nighttime routine herself.

Edmund found her in the parlor much later, when dusk had withered to deep shadows and a sliver of moonlight peeked through the curtains. She hadn't left her spot, instead finding a book to read as she slowly came down from the titillating height of losing her temper for perhaps the first time since childhood.

She set down her book and pulled out her locket, flipping it open to study Charles's visage. How long ago her marriage felt, and truth be told, she was no longer in love with him. She should not have brought him up earlier. Her heart might always ache for him, but the ache had changed to a dull thud, and it had not made her heart stop beating.

She took in his light blue eyes and ash-blond hair, cut in the style of when the portrait was rendered. How very dear he would always be to her. A dear friend she would always remember. But tonight had taught her something: though his earthly life had ended, hers had not.

"You look content."

The deep voice brought her attention from studying the picture to the man lounging in the doorframe. He looked even more tousled than at dinner, and his hair hung about his face in disarray, as though he'd gotten into a scuffle. A glowering quality imbued his countenance.

"Edmund." Seeing him brought unexpected joy to her heart. She dropped the locket and stood up to greet him, but he waved his hand, beckoning her to sit back down.

"I shall join you." He strode into the room, tall and strong. When he sat next to her, the tempo of her heartbeat changed. But of course, she was glad to see him. It was normal, she assured herself.

Before she could conversate, he reached over and lifted the locket from where it lay nestled against her dress. How very odd to see his aristocratic, long fingers holding her jewelry. Using his thumb and forefinger, he flipped the locket open to expose Charles's guileless smile.

"Your husband?" His voice sounded raspy, as though he'd overused it.

Concern reared. "Yes. Are you well, Edmund?" She tried to ignore the warmth emanating from him, as he was sitting much closer to her than usual.

He did not answer, appearing to be engrossed in studying the picture. A pang of discomfort struck her, though it was ridiculous. Suddenly she did not want him looking at Charles, but she could not say why.

She slipped the locket from him, a gentle tug to slide the golden oval from his fingers. "I keep his picture around my neck. It is silly, really."

"You must have loved him very much." Edmund's eyes searched her, excavating, and his attention touched her heart.

"I did." She tucked the locket beneath her bodice. "We were well suited. Despite any reputation I may have garnered, at heart I was as happy in a quiet home as he."

"But did he not choose to go into law?"

"He did." She smiled, but sadness kept the smile from fullness. "To help others. He chose low pay to take on those who could not afford services."

"He sounds like a saint," Edmund said.

Surprised, Sophia lifted her gaze. "He was far from perfect. He did not like to socialize and you do know how I enjoy parties and friendships. I often went alone, leaving him at home to read."

"I maintain my original opinion." The creases at the corners of Edmund's eyes smoothed. "Have you eaten supper?"

She nodded, the events of the night barreling back into her mind. "Mr. Reed did an excellent job at seeing to my needs. Tonight is the first time I have not seen him look paralyzed with terror."

"He's lasted longer than I expected." Edmund's brows furrowed. "I used to terrify my servants more effectively."

Sophia laughed. "I would believe you if I had not heard otherwise."

"Otherwise?" Edmund's face took on a pensive expression, reminding Sophia anew that he was not a man to be trifled with. And oh, how her family had trifled.

She shoved down the nervousness threatening to take over. There was no reason for Edmund to think she had been involved. None at all. He would not blame her. Would he?

"I don't like keeping servants too long in the city. They gossip and get overly comfortable. It sounds as though Mr. Reed is no longer on his toes."

She did not like the look in his eyes. "You cannot distrust everyone."

"Although you may have heard good things about me, the pertinent point is that you did indeed hear things. Servants talk."

"They are also loyal," she pointed out.

"Are they?" he mused, and a thick tension spiked the space between them.

"I suppose I understand, to a small extent, how you must feel." She moistened her lips, wanting him to look at her, but he simply stared down at his hands. "To trust someone and then have them betray that confidence. It is shattering."

She stopped. She wanted him to say something about the night's events. Did he think her uncouth? Improper? Her actions had certainly been out of character and not the behavior he expected from a duchess. She chewed her lower lip, wondering at his current opinion.

He tilted his head to look at her from beneath heavy-lidded eyes. The strength of that stare melted her thoughts into a puddle of mixed emotions.

She swallowed and said the first thing that came to mind. "Have you also eaten?"

"I left your parents' house early and met up with Boxing at White's. We dined there."

"And Hannah?"

"She will be Eliza's guest for the night. I confess that I am happy she has found such a true friend."

"Eliza is sweet and not temperamental. A bit fanciful but kindhearted. She and Hannah complement each other."

"Eliza takes after her older sister."

Sophia grimaced. "Not after tonight's debacle."

She willed him to say something, but his features tightened and he stood. "I find myself exhausted. If you will excuse me, I shall see you in the morning."

"Of course." She nodded, ignoring the disappointment spreading through her. "Do not forget that tomorrow night is the Kerrington ball."

"I do not know them." A shadowed expression crept across his features.

"They are very kind people who have given extensively of their time and money to Lord Windley's projects. You might like them."

"Perhaps." He paused at the door. "Should Mr. Aimsley come calling tomorrow, he is to be turned away."

"Of course. Hannah is not here."

"Even if Hannah is here, she is not to see that man anymore. Without a commission, there is no way he can support her or give her a future."

Sophia schooled her face into an impassive mask. "Have you spoken to her about this?"

But he did not answer, and Sophia was left sitting on the couch to contemplate how she'd navigate between two unyielding natures in the following days.

Edmund had vastly overestimated his influence on Hannah. He considered the issue of Aimsley settled until a week later when the man showed up to call on his niece. The young cur had the audacity to bring flowers. Although he'd been sent away thrice before, Hannah just happened to be in the hallway as Mr. Reed instructed Aimsley that Hannah was not receiving callers.

Edmund had the misfortune of being in his study overlooking the books when he heard her screech. At first he thought a cat lay dying in his hall, but then he realized it was Hannah yowling with rage.

He shoved to his feet, annoyance propelling him across the floor in seconds. The scene in the hallway was not reassuring. Hannah faced off with Mr. Reed. The butler sported a stubborn look rivaling any Hannah could muster. Grudging admiration for his servant scurried through Edmund as he neared the group.

"What seems to be the problem?" The front door was closed. Good. Mr. Aimsley had not been let in.

"This—" Hannah ground her teeth "—*servant* will not let my caller into the house."

From the corner of his eye, he saw Sophia emerge from the parlor. Concern drew her brows together. Throat tightening, he fastened his attention to Mr. Reed. One almost felt bad for the man. A flush suffused his face and his Adam's apple bobbed with panic.

"Well done, Mr. Reed." He gave the man a swift nod. Perhaps Sophia had a point regarding loyal servants. "You are dismissed."

"I beg your pardon?" Hannah planted her hands on her hips, her eyes darting from the butler's retreating form to his face. She whirled to Sophia. "Did you know about this?"

"I make the rules in this house," he said, causing his dervish of a niece to pivot his way. "Mr. Aimsley is not welcome to court you."

"I demand you let him in."

"He is not suitable."

Hannah's eyes blazed. Without a word, she rushed past him and up the stairs.

Sophia emerged, her eyes a little wider than usual, her mouth a soft, pink bow. "Do you think this is for the best?"

"Yes." He smiled at her. This past week he'd made an effort to woo Sophia. Not romantically. He could never allow himself to love a woman that way. But he could love her as a friend. When he'd seen how she looked at the miniature of her late husband, he'd realized that Sophia had become very special to him and that he wanted her to look at him the way she had Charles. With admiration and caring.

Who would have thought a woman firmly ensconced in the ways of the *haut ton* could affect him so, but she had, and deeply. After all, she had flouted her parents' wishes to marry a third son who offered little in the way of riches or status.

He had embarked this past week on making her feel valued because he did not want her to regret their marriage. He had caught her curious glances, but ignored them. Thus far, he had attended social events with her, attempted conversations with people he did not like, and brought her flowers.

She had particularly enjoyed the lilies, he thought with satisfaction. As she would enjoy the other surprise he had for her.

"I am worried," she said, her gaze playing over the stairwell recently tromped upon by his niece. "Hannah is strong-willed and Mr. Aimsley is the only one she's shown any interest in at all. She has a tendre for him."

"You think she will defy me?"

"It is possible." She smoothed her dress. "Well, I

shall do my best to introduce her to others. But you must know, one cannot always control who one loves."

"Love?" Edmund scoffed. "That is not love. It is too soon. Hannah's propensity for impulse and intense emotions lead her to believe Mr. Aimsley is the only one for her. That's simply not the case."

"And do you think I have propensity for impulsive decisions?"

Surprised, Edmund noted that her stance was stiff, her fingers curling into the folds of her dress. He rubbed the back of his neck.

"No, I have not observed that you have a temperament similar to Hannah's."

"And yet I knew I loved Charles and wanted to marry him within a month of our acquaintance."

"Infatuation. It would have faded over time."

"Infatuation? Really, Your Grace." Her brow arced in a steep curve.

"It seems to me you only use the term *Your Grace* when you are miffed with me," he remarked dryly. "Have I said something to offend you?"

"You are intimating that I am not self-aware enough to know my own heart. You presume your opinion is more valid than my thoughts, and you are doing the same to Hannah." Her hands went to her hips, a surprise motion showing her pique. "Do not underestimate the power of love."

"But this is not love."

She threw her hands in the air and turned back to the parlor.

"You will leave in the middle of conversation?" he asked to her back. Sophia's new penchant for showing annoyance amused him. How many layers she had.

He could spend a lifetime and still discover more. The thought was unsettling.

She spun around. "Is this a conversation? You are set in your conclusion, and it is obvious you have little to no regard for Hannah's or my feelings."

He crossed his arms, his amusement quickly fading beneath her accusation. "I never said such a thing."

"You intimated. I used that word already, Edmund. Perhaps if you listened to what I said, you would know that."

"Your snippiness is not attractive."

"Neither is your stubbornness."

They glared at each other, a silent standoff in which he did not want to give ground and yet…he felt he must. He didn't want to fight and he wouldn't change his mind about Aimsley's suitability, but that didn't mean he disregarded Hannah's and Sophia's feelings on the matter. Apparently he was not the only stubborn one in this house. Someone could have warned him of Sophia's obstinate streak.

Nevertheless, she looked beautiful, almost like an avenging angel with her hands back on her hips and the light from the windows a halo about her hair.

"I have a surprise for you," he said.

"You are changing the subject."

"Because we will not agree on this matter of Aimsley."

"I'm more upset that you are discounting my opinion."

He raked his hand through his hair, unsure how to respond yet amazed that Sophia, paragon of hiding her feelings, was actually admitting to being upset. He felt strangely honored, as though she were comfortable enough with him to express her true emotions.

Sighing deeply, he reached for her hands. And surprisingly enough, she let him take them in his. "I do not mean to discount how you feel. I cannot agree with you that Hannah is truly in love, and I cannot support a courtship with a less than adequate future."

"But there is a future, just not the one you want for her."

He dipped his head in acknowledgment. How small and fragile her hands felt within his. His thumb caressed her soft skin as he considered an answer.

"I want what is best for her," he said finally. "I am not convinced Hannah can choose for herself what is best when her judgment is clouded by emotion."

Sophia frowned and he saw sadness in her eyes. What a clutch of pain that look triggered within him. Using one hand, he reached up to cup her chin. "Do not look so sad. I have a surprise for you, remember?"

Her lips lifted slightly, and he was close enough to see her pupils dilate. He could kiss her again. The thought nudged him, but he willed it away.

"Very well. Where is this surprise? Though I must confess that I feel you have been spoiling me."

"You deserve spoilage."

"Then I shall turn very rotten indeed, and perhaps you will no longer want a mollycoddled duchess."

He laughed, relieved to see the glimmer of humor lighting her eyes. Releasing her, he held out his arm and she linked hers through it. "Nonsense. We are legally bound together for the rest of our lives. I shall not be able to get rid of you."

He drew her to the garden, enjoying the pliant way she trusted him to lead, and the scent of her perfume that lingered on his skin.

"More roses?" she inquired as they walked the path to the secluded niche he had created years ago.

"You could say something like that." They reached the opening, and she gasped in surprised wonder. His heart swelled, overcome by emotion. He had done something right. "I thought you might miss your own garden, and I remember that you crave chaos in nature."

She looked up at him, her eyes shining and her face bright. "Not chaos. Authenticity. The natural order, not something trimmed and hacked to look a certain way." Her hands went to her cheeks. "This is so lovely."

His gaze traveled the little area, trying to see what she saw. He'd spent a few hours with a gardener organizing the flowers in haphazard ways that mimicked a natural setting. There were roses, of course, but also lavender, foxglove and delphiniums. They nestled within each other, lush and redolent.

"Edmund." Her hand slipped into his, a warm caress in the cocoon of his hand. "I have a confession."

Chapter Eighteen

Sophia's heart hammered beneath her sternum. The profusion of flowers scenting the air in sweet tones touched her emotions and on impulse, she had blurted out something she'd been desperately trying to hold inside.

"By all means." Edmund gestured to the small table and chairs in the center of the flowered nook. "I have time to spare."

Throat dry, she sat. Her fingers played in her dress, sliding along the silky folds as she contemplated how best to frame her words. It had been a week since her outburst with her parents. She hadn't seen them nor visited since. She couldn't bring herself to, for a multitude of reasons. There was a certain shame in how she'd conducted herself, but there was also that simmering anger over how her father had endangered his family. And then her mother's involvement in securing their betrothal. She swallowed, not meeting Edmund's gaze.

His attention was calm, patient, even. A far cry from the first man she'd met at a ball months ago. How would he react if he found out the truth regarding the contract?

She looked at the plethora of flowers surrounding her, dancing in undesigned abandon, flowering where they chose instead of being snipped and prodded into place. Despite herself, she smiled.

"This is truly lovely."

"I meant it when I said this garden is for you." The husky tone of his voice whispered awareness through her. She searched his face, seeing the truth reflected in the darkness of his gaze. A pirate loitering in a garden of roses. She grinned.

"This shall be my happy place." She reached out and put her hand on his, where it lay on the stone table. "Edmund, I must know something."

"Now it is know? Before it was confess. Confessions tend to be juicier. I am to be disappointed, am I?"

Her smile wobbled. "That has been precisely my fear, and what I wish to speak to you of."

"Speak, sweet Duchess."

His endearment caught her off guard. Biting her lip, she tightened her hold on his hand. "I have feared that my outburst a week ago may have been off-putting for you. That perhaps I may not be the duchess you expected to have. And so I must apologize—"

He opened his mouth to interrupt, but she placed a finger against his lips. When his mouth closed, she moved her finger. How dark he looked at this moment, how uncommonly dangerous, and a shiver whispered down her spine.

"I must apologize," she continued, "for behavior unbecoming of a lady."

He laughed, low and husky. "You were in a family setting and there was nothing unladylike about you."

"Unchecked, then."

"More beautiful than I have ever seen."

His words soothed, but more than that, they curried a deep and intense response that she felt powerless to control. "But I did not act how I should."

"And how is that? A cold and aloof porcelain doll who shows no feelings? That is not what I want." He grasped her shoulders, leaning forward so that his face was inches from hers. "Who told you that you had to be this way? Why?"

"I… I had to secure a good marriage." A dry laugh. "Though I did not."

"You have a good marriage now." There was a fierceness to his touch, a strength in his grip, that almost made her believe him.

She wet her lips, seeing his eyes follow the movement. "So, you are happy with the marriage?"

"I am most happy."

"Though I am far from perfect."

"Perfection is for a diamond."

Sophia's heart stuttered at the words. Hadn't her Charles said something similar? How was it that two men so completely different could hold the exact sentiment? Her pulse picked up, her cheeks heated. There was a synchrony to this moment, to the warm afternoon and the fragrance of flowers, that muddled her thoughts.

And Edmund, so close she could see the stubble upon his cheeks, the delineation between iris and pupil, and feel the heat of his breath.

"You are who I needed, Sophia, and you are who I want."

He leaned forward, closing the gap, bringing with him the scent of fresh soap and sandalwood. His lips claimed hers, and the kiss changed, deepening in a way it hadn't before. All of the worry drained from Sophia. She kissed her husband, unrepentant, her hand circling around his neck to draw him closer.

Her fingers traced his cheek, wanting him to know that she admired him. That he was like this niche of wild flowers, beautifully untamed by society. She did not want him to ever stop kissing her.

Edmund had to stop kissing her.

The thought, a pesky fly, buzzed about his mind. He wanted to swat it away, to revel in this moment of shared intimacy, of closeness. Sophia's lips were warm beneath his. Her fingers rested hesitantly upon his neck like fragile ivy, and all he wanted was to draw her close and make the moment last.

But your secrets will ruin her.

The thought lanced deeper, striking his most vulnerable places. He pulled away, too abruptly. She blinked in confusion, her eyes the color of a stormy ocean, her face soft and yielding.

He sucked in a deep breath, willing his pulse to stop crashing through him. He brushed his hair back, leaning into his seat, away from Sophia. What an idiot he was. Absolute imbecile.

He felt Sophia's stare but did not risk looking at her. Not while he indulged in mental self-flagellation. He had let things get too far. He had convinced himself that he could care for her as a friend but his masculine instincts had taken over.

Had it been the same for his father and his brother? Had they started out caring for someone and then slowly over time been unable to control their emotions? Had they intended good but instead poisoned all who they touched? He could not bear to do the same. His heart squeezed in painful pulses, and his hands fisted.

"Edmund." Sophia's voice filtered through the cacophony of thoughts overtaking his mind. "Please look at me."

"I do not want to," he said darkly, avoiding her.

"Why?"

His throat constricted and he was not sure he could answer her. This meeting of emotions had grown too painful. This was not what he intended when he married her. He waited for anger to rise, hoped for it, but instead all that filled him was a deep assurance that he had made a muck of things. He stood, his back to Sophia, hating the bone-deep certainty that any happiness he might have grasped was now out of reach.

Because of a kiss. Could they even still develop a friendship? He kneaded his neck, turning toward the house. He could walk away right now. Once the Season ended, leave for his estate and not look back.

Behind him, Sophia cleared her throat. "Will you leave me in the middle of a conversation?"

His mouth reluctantly quirked. Cheeky woman, to throw his own words back at him. "I am tempted to."

"Would it not be better to sit with me and explain your sudden anger?"

"I am not angry." He faced her, noting the heightened color to her cheeks. "I am, however, upset. There is no reason to speak of why."

"But there is a reason." She leaned forward and patted the stone chair. "I will be quite mournful if you leave in this state. I will be happy if you stay and explain your mood."

He eyed the chair.

"Come now, emotions do not bite and neither do I. Unless, of course, I am duly provoked." She winked at him, the minx.

His heartbeat settled back into a normal rhythm. Perhaps there was wisdom to her words. He took the chair. Smug satisfaction lightened her gaze.

"Now you are happy," he said.

"Yes. And I must say, you are a very good kisser."

Heat rose up his neck. "You do not want to alter the trajectory of your life."

She did not answer, as he thought she would. Which left him to direct the focus of the conversation. Sighing heavily, he rested back in his chair. His left arm found the table and his fingers drummed its surface.

"I have failed to keep my attraction at bay," he finally said. "Though it is something I need to do. For reasons that I cannot explain."

"You can explain, and you should." Her voice was gentle. "I found it odd that a duke would marry in name only. But because it suited my purposes—" her shoulders lifted in a delicate way "—I believed it to be fine. Now I ask myself why you would not want heirs. Why you would be so eager to marry a stranger."

"I do not wish for children. I do not like women hankering after me. I only want to be left alone."

"Were you not active in society before you became a duke?"

He cringed, the stone table scraping his fingertips. "Yes."

"What changed? Help me understand. I…have thoroughly enjoyed your kisses and your company. If you wish to stop, I shall certainly heed that. Perhaps it is for the best."

"It is for the best," he rasped, for memories rained down upon him, squatting upon his shoulders like dark and heavy clouds.

"Why?" she insisted, and there was that tender concern upon her features which had so many times grabbed at his heart. It did not fail to do so this time either. Could he tell her?

The secrets he had kept for so long. They had rotted within him, the acid of their decomposition corroding his hopes and dreams. And now they loosened his tongue, for who better to share the sorrows of his past with than his own wife? A woman he trusted, whom he had seen put the good of others before herself.

She would not betray him and God Himself knew that Edmund needed someone to trust. Sophia watched him with such openness, such vulnerable compassion. He longed to unburden himself. He swallowed the stone that seemed embedded within his throat. Above them, a cloud moved across the sky, throwing their little flower corner into shadow.

"My brother killed his wife," he said.

Sophia did not even gasp, though her eyes flickered. It certainly could not be what she'd expected to hear, yet even still, Edmund could not stop the avalanche of history that began to pour out of his mouth.

"My father had a temper." He paused, hardly seeing Sophia for the memories suppressing him. "I was a great deal younger than my brother. William. That was his name. My nanny shielded me, I think, from the brunt of Father's rages. She was old. She had nannied my father, and then my brother, and finally me. I think I told you that William was twenty years my senior?"

"Yes." She tilted her head, thoughtful. "And Naomi was closer to your age."

"About so. My nanny had seen a good bit. She had been around enough to know when Father was angry and could spirit me away. Sometimes she failed."

"Did your father hit you?"

The word *hit* did not adequately describe how it felt for a boy to get broad-handed across the face by his father. He nodded.

"Nanny said his father, my grandfather, had been the same. Anger is a blight upon my bloodline. She raised my father, but could not curb his temper. And then he married my mother, who Nanny adored. She vowed to do whatever she must to keep her job so that she could keep us safe." Edmund hardened his voice. Now was not a time for emotion, but to help Sophia understand who exactly she had linked her life to. "For years the house was filled with violence when my father was home. My mother wasted away. Nanny could not protect William as well as she did me. She was younger when he was a child, more of a physical threat to my father, and terrified if she left that something dreadful might happen."

"And my father was friends with this man," she breathed.

"The *ton* was not aware. All who knew my father respected him. He was a sober-minded duke who took his responsibilities seriously. Do not fault your father."

She nodded, though he did not think she believed him.

"And so Nanny stayed. She raised William, and then I came along. By this time, she was getting older, and so was my father. William focused on learning his duties, and I was a boy who learned how to dodge when needed. William was different than my father. He had a tender side. A sensitivity that even I could see." Edmund frowned. "He liked to paint, which infuriated Father. He married Naomi, who had nothing to her name, and he was completely enamored of her. Hannah is not unlike her mother. Naomi loved to laugh and to play and to have fun. She spent his funds freely. She was kind to me."

That was a hard memory to recall. He'd had a disagreement with his father over some trivial thing and been rewarded with a black eye. Naomi had brought him a cold beefsteak to calm the swelling.

"Go on," said Sophia.

"Over time, Naomi and I became closer. Her relationship with my brother, however, disintegrated. I heard talk that she had been unfaithful. He married her for love, but it was said she married him for his money."

"Was it true?"

He nodded, his face hot with shame. "I asked her and she was honest. She admitted that she had no prospects and she had done what any smart girl would do. She was not smart enough, though."

"Because she could not escape your brother?" The words were stilted, as though even saying them brought Sophia grief.

Edmund nodded woodenly. "I graduated Eton and discovered that even though it was the Season, Naomi was convalescing in the country. Hannah was visiting an aunt. Naturally I assumed Naomi to be with another child. I was a brash, excitable young man. Quick to laugh, quick to temper. I rode to the estate and discovered that she was not pregnant."

"What was wrong?"

"Split lip. Bruised ribs. I thought William had caught her in an affair, but she told me that he no longer cared. Sometimes he'd just get angry at her and there was no escaping the beating. She was downtrodden, and not the Naomi he first married. She said that it was who he was, it was in his blood, and that mostly he treated her kindly."

Sadness washed across Sophia's face so heavily that Edmund's own chest clenched. His ribs felt too tight, as though he could not draw the proper amount of air.

"I tried to get her to leave, to get away from him, but she refused. And so I left," he continued. "I did not know what to think, what to do. Reputation was important in our family."

Sophia's eyes widened. "So no one truly knew?"

"Never. She hid her bruises." And Father and William were both the epitome of control. Nevertheless, I went back to London. A week or so later she returned. I saw her at several social events, always laughing gaily. Then she was to meet me at the opera house with some friends."

"Didn't your brother go?"

"No, he preferred to run the estates or to hole up within his house and paint. His collection is preserved at my estate." Edmund closed his eyes briefly, remembering. With a deep sigh, he opened his eyes to see his beautiful wife's kind expression. "Naomi did not make the opera. Afterward, I went to their townhome. I felt that something was amiss, and there was a dread in my gut that I could not explain. The butler did not wish to allow me in, but I forced my way through and ran up to her bedroom. I knocked but she did not answer. I went in and found her on the bed. Her face." He stopped, a sudden vise about his throat. After several deep breaths, he could breathe again. "She was clutching her ribs and stomach. She could barely speak. I told her she must leave, that I was taking her."

Edmund's hands hardened into fists. "My brother appeared. He no longer looked like the man I remembered. He had always been gentle with me. He never put a hand upon Nanny. But he had done this to Naomi. And I swear that I saw regret in the haunted emptiness of his eyes. He cried and said he would never hurt her again. He admitted to the evil reigning in him. Then he had me forcibly removed from the house."

His stomach ached. How patient Sophia was, to listen like this. He had to make her understand. "The next morning they were found dead. Both stabbed in the heart. Lying in their bed. He killed her and then himself and wiped the murder weapon clean with his last breaths, I imagine. Bow Street had their suspicions about a robbery gone wrong and I didn't disabuse them of that notion. Since I didn't push for answers, they lost interest, particularly as suspicion among the *ton* fell on me. Bow Street was only too happy to move on to other cases."

"But why not tell the truth?" breathed Sophia. "Was your family's reputation so important? And what of the servants? Surely they knew the true circumstances of the home."

"Have you ever heard gossip regarding my family and physical violence?"

"No."

He shrugged. "There are ways to be circumspect, and there are ways to buy silence. My father paid a handsome sum to his close servants. He was still alive, too. No doubt they did not dare breathe a word against him."

"And you suppressed the truth for Hannah's sake?" Understanding dawned in her eyes.

He nodded. "I adored my niece, though I rarely saw her, and I did not think she deserved to grow up with the shadow of gossip looming over her."

"People assumed you killed them to get the title."

"Yes. I didn't anticipate that kind of gossip. And so, Hannah was still affected. People knew my brother and I did not get along, you see. We had several public disagreements. I was brash. Foolish. A servant observed me leaving their house that night, and it was bandied about that William and I had argued. When the news of their deaths came out, I was given the cut direct."

He paused, remembering. "No one would look at me. I sometimes wonder if my father fanned the flames of that. For what reasons, I can't presume. That began my long retreat, and anger ate at my soul. Bitterness. I hadn't wanted the duchy. I still don't. Which leads me to something very important." He caught her hands in his, and brought them to his lips, kissing each delicate knuckle. "I care for you. I trust you. But I can never put you in the position where I might hurt you."

She blanched, pulling back. "Whatever are you talking about?"

"It's in my blood," he said patiently. "Violence. My brother, moody as he was, never lifted a hand against anyone until he was married. Friendship is all I can offer you, for your own safety."

"That's absurd."

He shook his head, resolute. "The fact is that you loved your husband. You had a once-in-a-lifetime kind

of love. And I will never be an even-tempered husband.
It's just not in my nature, and I cannot risk the happiness or safety of a woman who I respect and admire. I
can never take the light from your eyes the way William did to Naomi."

"Stop it." Sophia stomped one slipper-clad foot.
"This is the most ridiculous hogwash I've ever heard."

He pulled his hands from hers, stung. She immediately grabbed his hands back. "Not what happened,
Edmund. But that some evil runs in your blood. I refuse to believe it. You have a temper. That doesn't mean
you'd ever harm me."

"You haven't seen what I've seen," he said stubbornly. Hadn't William loved Naomi? And even his
own father had been gentle at times. Teaching him to
ride, to hunt.

"I see a strong, loyal man who would do anything
to protect his family. Even live with a secret that alien-
ated him from his friends and community." She stood
abruptly, coming over and plopping unexpectedly in his
lap. "You are not a beast. You are a kind and wonderful
human who I am proud to call my husband."

She pressed her lips against his cheek, and the sweetness of the kiss brought a sting to the corner of his eyes.
Blinking, he lifted her off his lap and deposited her on
the ground.

He strode away, hearing her call out that she would
prove him wrong. He left her standing there, in the garden he had made for her, knowing she could not.

He had been born into a family of beasts, and a beast
he would always be.

Chapter Nineteen

Why were men so stubborn?

Sophia tapped her foot impatiently. She had accompanied Hannah to a soiree and apparently Mr. Aimsley had also decided to go. They were dancing at the moment, while Sophia was wishing Edmund wasn't so pigheaded. Hannah and Mr. Aimsley were in love. One could see it in the way they looked at each other.

Even if it was enthrallment, that often led to love and commitment. Nevertheless, Edmund would not be happy if he found out Mr. Aimsley had attended this soiree. She must get Hannah away, but how? Suddenly the job of chaperone seemed a bit too arduous.

She crossed her arms, then uncrossed them. Edmund was rubbing off on her, she realized, as she felt a frown digging at her face. Her ability to keep a placid expression was waning. Though she respected his ability to emote, she herself preferred gentility to unabashed expressions.

There had been much to dwell on these past few days. She had barely seen Edmund since he'd produced his shocking confession. How her heart hurt for him, to carry those secrets, that shame, and then to put it on himself and live in fear. She'd had much time to think of him, and to even examine her own heart, and she had come to a worrisome conclusion.

It was very possible she might be falling in love with Edmund.

One shouldn't worry about such a thing, in average circumstances, but they did not have a normal arrangement. There had been specific parameters, boundaries. Now those were blurring, and Edmund had grown uncomfortable. Especially because of the secret he'd shared with her.

Why else would he be avoiding her?

"Sophia, darling." Her mother sauntered over, Father in tow. "It has been too long."

So formal, always proper. No wonder she had molded herself the way she had. She took in Father's svelte appearance. He had regained some health, it seemed. His cheeks were fuller. There was sadness in his eyes, though.

She leaned forward for an airy kiss against her mother's face. Then the same for her father. "Are you both well?"

"Indeed. We are greatly excited about the cottage. We went last week to have a look."

"Cottage?"

"Oh, did you not know?" Mother fanned herself, darting a quick glance to her husband as if asking permission. His head tipped in acceptance. "The duke, your fabulous husband, gave us a cottage for use when we are not in town. I call it a cottage but it is truly darling and spacious enough for all of us. And four servants." She held up four fingers. "*Four*. I am simply beside myself."

"I see that," murmured Sophia. Edmund's thoughtfulness knew no bounds. Why could he not see that?

"My lady," said Father to his wife, "might I have a moment alone with our daughter."

"Of course, my darling." Sparkling with happiness, her mother swept off to a different group of people.

Leaving Sophia with her father, whom she had not seen since her outburst.

All that had transpired came rushing back to her. Father stood beside her, watching the room as she did. There was the hint of tobacco to him, as always, and the scent recalled the days when she was young and he'd read the Bible to her as she worked on her sewing.

He cleared his throat. "I am ashamed of my behavior."

As you should be, she wanted to say, but could not bring herself to utter the condemning words. So she simply stood, waiting for him to continue.

"I taught you to be honest and humble, but I failed to live up to my own expectations. When one is a man of faith, and finds himself trapped in a web of greed and deceit, there is plenty of reason to hide."

Her eyes burned a little, for it was true, and it pained her.

"Gambling was fun, at first. But over the years, I relied on it more and more. Your mother was only slightly aware of…my problem." He stopped. Cleared his throat again. "I, myself, did not see the scope of the problem until you yelled at me. My gentle, proper Sophia, losing her temper."

She snuck a look and saw a bit of admiration on his face, humor in his tone.

"You certainly set me in my place. I looked at Eliza and Frederika, and I saw what I had done to my family. Then my wonderful Martha, trying so valiantly to hold her head up. Do not judge her too harshly for what she did. All turned out well."

Sophia let herself meet his pleading eyes. "What she did was unacceptable and brings dishonor. As for you, I cannot claim to understand what burdens you."

"I know." His chin dipped. "And I am so sorry. Please do not lay my weakness at God's door. He is my reason for being, and He knows the depths of my sins. I know you may not be able to forgive—"

"I do forgive you. Mother, too." The words rushed out, for seeing him like this caused her heart to ache. Holding bitterness against them was not worth the cost of her conscience, she had found. "Until you are well, Mother should not allow you access to funds. If this is indeed a sickness, then you must participate in your healing. I am praying for you, Father. My faith has been shaken, but it is not destroyed."

"My dear girl." Her father hugged her, his arms encircling her in a familiar and comfortable way. "You have always been such a blessing."

"Even when I married a poor third son?" she muttered against his shoulder.

He laughed and released her. "Even then."

The thought reminded her of her current predicament. *Hannah*. Sophia swiveled, searching the room for her charge's flaming red hair and not finding it. "Father, I must go."

She parted from him and rounded the room. It was smaller, and separated into other rooms. She popped her head into an alcove filled with tables for whist. Though it was full, Hannah definitely was not there.

Suppressing a groan, she checked the dining room,

as well. No Hannah. She wouldn't put it past the girl to do something foolish, like wandering out alone into the gardens with Mr. Aimsley. Then they'd have to marry to avoid ruination.

Edmund might truly die from apoplexy should that happen.

Sighing, she slowed her walk so there'd be no gossip about her frantic pacing about. A duchess, after all, was always on display. She made eye contact with several acquaintances, smiled serenely, exchanged nods and waves. There was an alcove ahead, potted plants partially covering its entrance. As she neared, she heard the words "Gretna Green," and froze.

Surely not. Surely the impulsive little hoyden would not spirit Mr. Aimsley off to Scotland to be married without Edmund's consent. Chewing her lower lip, Sophia moved closer to the plants.

Yes, that was Hannah's bright white dress lined with blue velvet, and the hideous shoes she'd insisted on wearing peeked out from beneath the sequined hem. The two were whispering now. Sophia shook her head. The foolishness of youth. Yes, there was only seven years difference between she and Hannah, yet it seemed a lifetime of experience.

Sophia moved to the front of the alcove. The pair looked up at her, guilt stamped across their faces. A hint of rebellion on Hannah's. Sophia recognized the telltale jut to her jaw.

"Making plans, are you?" Sophia asked them.

Hannah glanced past Sophia, possibly to ascertain if anyone else was listening to their little tête-à-tête. Satisfied they were alone, she glared at Sophia.

"You know very well that Uncle Edmund is opposed to our union."

"So you have proposed? Without speaking to her guardian?" Sophia gave Mr. Aimsley an intentional stare. He knew the proper etiquette.

He shuffled on his feet, embarrassed. Beads of sweat formed on his forehead. "I had planned to speak with him. I needed first to discover Hannah's thoughts on the matter." His face flushed with pleasure. "I'm happy to say she has accepted my proposal."

"A proposal offered in secret."

"The duke has banned me from his residence. I have tried to secure a meeting with him on several occasions."

That sounded like Edmund. Hadn't he ignored her own communications when she'd discovered the contract? She would have to speak with him about ignoring others. It was the height of rudeness, to be sure.

"He is being his usual bullheaded self," put in Hannah. "I won't stand for it. Paul has a small holding and once his brother marries, there will be funds to purchase a commission. We will not be rich but we will certainly not be paupers."

"You do realize that certain social doors and connections may be closed to you once you marry Mr. Aimsley. Especially if you two sneak off. Especially since he has no title, no funds of his own." Sophia gave him a conciliatory nod. "Not to speak ill of you, but I must make sure Hannah understands the full scope of her decision."

Hannah shrugged and hugged her rib cage. There was a suddenly vulnerable look to her stance. "Uncle Edmund will not cast us out."

Sophia wanted to agree, but she wasn't so sure.

There was always that side to him that she couldn't quite reach, an aloof side that might cause him to cut all ties with those who loved him. Hannah must have seen Sophia's indecision, for her bottom lip quivered.

"You are right, Your Grace. I will wait," said Mr. Aimsley in a resolute tone. He glanced at Hannah, his expression softening. "You are worth more than what I can give you. I shall gain my commission, and when I do so, if you are still unattached, I will propose again."

"But that could be years."

"Will you wait for me, my sweet?"

Sophia felt like an interloper, and she longed to leave them to their privacy of the moment. How this man with such a mild personality, with nothing to set him apart, had captured Hannah was now apparent. Intensity and honor vibrated within his words. It brought her back to her Charles and his sweet proposal. He had given her his treasured ring. It had belonged to a beloved grandmother before being passed down to him.

"I can help," she said.

Hannah's head shot up. The girl had tears rolling down her cheeks, and Sophia suppressed a smile. She supposed she would never be able to fully teach her to control her emotions in public. Behind Sophia, music played and people laughed and chatted. Mr. Aimsley looked confused.

"You remind me of my first husband," she said softly. "Hannah, do you feel that you will always be loyal to Mr. Aimsley? That you will give him as much as he gives you? That your union will be one of love and joy?"

Hannah's hands went to her hips and she scowled through her tears. "I cannot believe you would ask me that."

"If you marry Mr. Aimsley, and he is an officer, you

will travel to other parts of the world. You must be a devoted wife."

"I can and I will, Sophia." Her tone had turned sharp. "I declare, this is quite irritating."

Sophia grinned, because irritating Hannah felt a bit like recompense for all the times she'd made Sophia want to pull her own hair out. "Very well. My late husband believed deeply in romantic love, as do I. How much do you have for your commission, Mr. Aimsley?"

He named a sum.

Satisfied, Sophia continued, "My wedding ring is worth an exorbitant amount, an heirloom my late husband held on to until our marriage. It represents the value of the love Charles and I shared. I shall sell it and you shall have the funds you need for your commission."

"I can't let you do that," said Mr. Aimsley.

"You can and you shall. That time in my life has ended and it will give me immense pleasure to fund a union of love. In the meantime, you two must practice honesty. No more alcoves and secret plans."

Hannah nodded vigorously.

"Come, Hannah. You shall spend the rest of the night with me and I will contact Mr. Aimsley later for further planning."

"Goodbye, my love." Hannah strung her arm through Sophia's and they headed toward the dining room.

A shuddering wave of apprehension roared through Sophia. What had she done? Yet, it felt good and right. Edmund would not protest a commissioned officer. It was a great honor to serve in His Majesty's army. She took a deep breath to calm her quivering nerves. What were titles and wealth without love?

Nothing, she was learning.

Nothing at all.

"You are wearing a scowl, Duke."

Sophia smiled up at him, nonplussed by his irritation. Somehow she had managed to talk him into accompanying her to a rout tonight, and he was already regretting the decision. He hadn't been to a ball in at least a week, though she had gone to one it seemed every night. Couples waltzed about, their jewelry glittering beneath the lights. Sophia herself looked as delicate and priceless as the finest jewels.

His scowl deepened.

She put her hand upon his arm, a physical liberty that surprised him. "Come, do you not wish to waltz with your wife?"

"No." He glared at the dancers. Hannah was somewhere in the throng, searching for her future husband. Ever since he'd bared his soul to Sophia, he'd been unsettled. She did not seem to comprehend the depth of danger he represented to her, should he ever lose his temper.

He was in a foul mood. He was certain to lose Hannah, and he could not allow himself to let Sophia any closer than she'd already become. He would never forgive himself if he hurt her. Yet the woman kept needling him.

"You are a spoilsport," she said, a faux pout edging her lips.

"You can dance with someone else."

"But what if I only wish to dance with you?" She

touched his chin with her forefinger, her eyes a teasing cyan.

"What game are you playing? Stop."

"It's called Cheer Up the Duke."

"Well, touching my face is not going to help matters."

"Perhaps a kiss?"

"You are bold, lady." The thought of a kiss did have merit. Why was she doing this to him? He had explained very well, he thought, the reasons their relationship must stay distant.

"Do you see my parents?" She looped her arm through his, and he was uncomfortably aware of the tantalizing aroma of her hair. She'd pulled it into a chignon, with a few long curls trailing her face. He had always admired her hair. Having her this close boggled his thoughts.

She dug her elbow into his side. "I asked if you see my parents. Over there, near those brocaded curtains."

He followed the line of her vision. Yes, there they were. Smiling with each other and dancing. "Why aren't they on the dance floor?"

"Because they prefer one another. You said I am bold. You do not like my teasing. But I have learned from my mother that it is important to make your husband smile."

He grunted.

"And there are many games I shall play with you, until you allow that beautiful smile to show itself."

"Many games?" She was distracting him with her teasing talk. Beautiful smile? This was a different Sophia. She was grinning at him, her eyes alight, diamonds sparkling at her ears.

"Yes, until you smile. I do so miss your smile."

His brow lifted.

With her free hand, she had the audacity to touch his chin again. Then she put her finger at the corner of his mouth, right in the dip of his dimple, and pushed upward.

"This is how you smile, Edmund. Now lift the other side," she commanded.

"You are absurd." But a laugh popped out of him as he brushed her hand away. "Quit touching my face."

"If you insist," she said primly, and instead dropped her arm and laced her fingers through his. Her thumb caressed his hand.

Now he couldn't stop the smile. "Does anyone know how obstinate you are?"

"It shall be our little secret." She winked at him. *Winked.* His wife was flirting with him. Two could play that game. He pivoted so that they were face-to-face. He used the hand she wasn't holding to tilt her chin.

"A secret? That is not proper, Duchess."

A rosy hue washed across her porcelain features. "Do you wish me to always be proper?"

He felt his lips tilting even further upward. How had she made him smile? How had she teased him out of the pique that had bogged down his last few days?

A familiar, tinkling laugh cut his attention away. Only feet behind Sophia, Hannah swirled upon the dance floor, laughing, tossing her red hair in delight. Her partner was none other than the forbidden Mr. Aimsley.

Edmund dropped his hands from Sophia.

"What?" Her brows drew together. "Whatever is the matter?"

A slow, burning anger formed in the pit of his gut. He had expressly told Hannah that she was not to encourage Mr. Aimsley's attentions. She had disobeyed him. Outright, to his face, even. His jaw set, aching with the force of the clench. He started forward, but Sophia's hand against his chest stopped him.

"Please, Edmund." Her eyes were wide and troubled. "Wait until the dance is over. Do not humiliate her in front of everyone."

Every instinct told him to rush forward, to take Hannah away from that man who would spirit her halfway across the world should he become an officer.

"Fine," he gritted, letting Sophia take his hand, though it did little to ease the knot growing in his chest. "But there will be a reckoning at the end of this waltz. Your position as chaperone may have just ended."

Sophia's eyes widened.

Let her disapprove. He no longer cared, not when his niece went explicitly against his wishes. As soon as the waltz ended, he waylaid Hannah and they went home. Sophia was strangely silent, but perhaps that was due to Hannah's copious and loud tears.

They had barely entered the house before Hannah whirled on him.

"How dare you?"

He crossed his arms. "There is no dare, niece. There is only do, and do not. And you have gone against my word."

Hannah lost her temper at that, and as she began her ranting, as his own blood boiled, he was not unaware of Sophia slowly sliding out of the room, an incomparable sadness upon her face that brought a reciprocal emotion to his own heart.

It seemed that perhaps he was destroying everything, just as Hannah was accusing him of, and he did not know how to stop the ruination.

Chapter Twenty

They were going to be late, and not fashionably so.

Sophia paced the parlor, glancing at the grand clock in the corner of the room every few minutes. Perhaps she should send a maid to find Hannah? The duke's townhome was overflowing with them. Though she had grown up in a reasonably secure station, they'd not had the huge quantities of servants Edmund employed. Though it was not in style to know their names, Sophia had endeavored for days until she realized she just wouldn't be able to remember everyone.

"You are going to start a fire on that rug," remarked Betsy.

"Hannah is the one who begged to go to this tea. Perhaps she is sick."

"Did you check her room?" Betsy sat sewing in a small chair. She had elected to follow Sophia into Edmund's household, though Sophia had tried to get her to apply at a modiste's shop for a position.

"I knocked." Sophia walked to the parlor door and looked down the hall. Besides the discriminate movements of maids, there was no one.

"Send Mrs. Botts. She's a beast of a lady." Betsy employed a mock shudder.

Sophia studied Betsy, who sewed avidly as if her piece of cloth might disappear on her.

"Are you happy here?" she asked Betsy.

The woman shrugged. "I'm happy with you, Your Grace."

"Cut that out. I am Sophia to you." Thoughts of Hannah put to the side, Sophia sidled over to Betsy and sat on a small, decorative ottoman next to her. "Be truthful with me. Is there something I should know?"

Betsy looked up from her sewing, mouth twisted to one side. "Just trying to fit in with the snobberies of servants."

"Snobberies?"

"Oh, yes. They have their own classes, and mark my words, I ain't fit to be lady's maid to a duchess."

"Nonsense." Sophia reached out and rubbed Betsy's arm. "I have thoroughly enjoyed your company. I will keep you for as long as you will have me."

And it was true. A sudden swell of affection filled her for the brash Betsy. The woman was loyal and truthful and kind. She could not ask for someone better. They hugged, though Sophia knew it was not proper, and then she stood, mind on Hannah again.

"I will see what's keeping her." She left Betsy and strolled down the enormous hall. Edmund's home, though not as ostentatious as some ducal townhomes, could still hold its own amongst them. She found herself missing her little home, especially after the other night's debacle.

In the days since, she had attempted to speak to Edmund regarding his opinion of Mr. Aimsley.

All to no avail.

She frowned now, going up the curved staircase in search of Hannah. Would that be a theme in their relationship? She speaking, and he not listening? Though perhaps it was not an uncommon theme, she had still hoped for something similar to her parents' relationship.

Though to be fair, she reminded herself, her father had lost the family fortune right beneath her mother's nose. A sobering thought.

The sound of raised voices drew her down the second-floor hallway to the library, which was situated near Edmund's offices. Sometimes she thought she might get lost in this home. One day she had accidentally wandered down to the servants' quarters. They had been kind in assisting her back to her own domain, no doubt pitying her.

Overall the servants here had accepted her, unlikely as she was for the position. For that, she was thankful.

As she neared the library, she identified Edmund's low tones and Hannah's high-pitched cadence. She stopped at the open door. Edmund paced near the fireplace, his hair sprouting in all directions as though he'd repeatedly used his fingers as an ineffective comb. Hannah lounged on a couch. Not pouting, but there was something bright and indefinable in her expression that gave Sophia pause.

When Edmund saw her, his gaze grew hooded. "What do you want?"

"I see you've reverted to the manners of our original meeting." She glided into the room, determined to not allow his emotions to affect her. "Hannah, we are late for tea."

"I'm not going."

Sophia raised a brow at her, a gentle rebuke.

Hannah shifted on the couch, having the grace to look a tad mollified. "I apologize. I will send them a note."

"If you do not mind, I shall still attend."

Edmund's niece made a face. "I was hoping you might stay."

"Why?" Sophia looked between the two of them, Hannah pleading and Edmund glowering.

"It seems my niece has a surprise for me," he said in a rough voice.

Just then, Mr. Reed made an entrance. "Your Grace, a Mr. Aimsley calling for you."

Edmund's brows lowered more than any brow should lower. Sophia might laugh if she did not recognize the seriousness of the situation. Though she had tried multiple times to speak with Edmund about his approach to Hannah's romance, he was intractable and her words had fallen on unhearing ears. More than once she had retreated to the garden niche he'd designed for her so that she might remember he wasn't a completely stubborn oaf.

To her surprise, Edmund waved a hand. "Show him in."

Mr. Reed bowed and exited. A tense silence filled the room. Edmund's brooding pace filled Sophia with trepidation. Even still, how handsome he looked to her. Not the perfect handsome of the peerage, but a wild and untamed attractiveness that gave her the same feeling she had in her rose garden.

That she was in the presence of great beauty.

And he did not see it. She found that saddest of all. How could she show him? Especially when he was being unequivocally unbeautiful at the moment. A rueful smile played at her lips.

"Mr. Aimsley, Your Grace." The butler left the young and nervous man at the door.

"Your Grace." Mr. Aimsley walked in, bowed, but Edmund held up a hand.

"Shall we cut to the chase? You wish to marry my niece. The answer is no. Now leave."

How intimidating Edmund looked at this moment, his face carved in stone, his eyes forceful. The set of his mouth cut his cheekbones into sharp blades, giving him that edgy, dominant air that no doubt had caused Eliza to label him a pirate. Sophia could not help the frisson of admiration she felt at that moment, for though she could not agree with Edmund, there was no mistaking that he protected those he loved.

It was a most attractive quality.

Mr. Aimsley should be quivering in his boots. Instead, the man lifted his chin and met Edmund's glower with a respectful clarity.

"May I ask why, Your Grace?" The question, delivered in an amicable matter, gave Edmund pause. Sophia saw the change in the way his stance shifted. He folded his arms against his chest, planted his feet and skewered young Mr. Aimsley with a look so sharp anyone else might flinch.

Thankfully Hannah remained quiet on the sofa. Her interference might harm Aimsley's position, and the man was doing an impressive job of holding his own.

"You do not know why, Aimsley?" The duke cocked his head.

Mr. Aimsley shuffled on his feet. "I can hazard a

few guesses, but they are minor complications, easily resolved."

"And how do you plan to resolve your station in life? I do not forsee you inheriting an earldom anytime soon."

"No doubt you did not see yourself inheriting a dukedom."

Sophia resisted the urge to gasp at the bold truth. Well done, Mr. Aimsley. Well done.

"That is fair. Nevertheless, the question remains. How will you support my niece?"

Mr. Aimsley opened his mouth to speak, but Edmund cut him off.

"And I do not mean financially, per se. Hannah means a great deal to me. I will always see to it that she is adequately cared for. Can you support her socially?" Edmund began a slow arc around Mr. Aimsley, much like a wolf circling its prey. "I've made inquiries. Your family, though not impoverished, is not well-off. The estates haven't brought in as much income as in years past. There are five grown children your father supports. And…you cannot even afford to buy a commission. Do you plan to whisk Hannah to one of your failing estates and expect her to play country wife?"

Sophia cringed.

"I like the country," put in Hannah, apparently no longer able to keep silent. She jumped off the couch and ran to Mr. Aimsley's side. Grabbing his hand, she proffered a glare to Edmund that was so similar to his own that Sophia almost smiled.

"Furthermore," Hannah continued in a shrill voice, "Paul is not without a commission."

Mr. Aimsley grimaced as Edmund swung his glare from Hannah to her would-be fiancé.

"Is that so?" Edmund asked softly.

"I have my papers. I shall be serving in His Majesty's army as an officer." The man visibly gulped.

Sophia felt like an interloper. But she had helped them. She had sold her wedding ring and it had been enough to allow Mr. Aimsley's future betterment. To encourage their love. She moistened her lips, only feeling a small pang of loss, and in her heart, she knew Charles would have applauded the move. He had been a romantic soul.

Unlike Edmund, who looked even more angry at this turn of events.

"An officer, you say." Edmund's arms had not uncrossed. He towered over Aimsley like an avenging father. "Congratulations, and thank you for your service. There's the door."

"But he has a future," blurted Hannah, casting a desperate look to Sophia.

"Not with you," said Edmund. His hand swept out toward the door. "Now leave."

"No." Hannah pushed between them, panic flashing across her face. "I love Paul. We wish to marry, and Sophia did not make her sacrifice just for you to deny us our commitment to each other."

In a slow way that scuttled goose bumps up Sophia's arms, Edmund turned to look at her. "Sophia?"

The way Sophia's lovely eyes widened told Edmund at once that she had meddled where she should not have meddled. He advanced toward her, intent on getting to the bottom of things, but then he remembered the young buck standing behind him. Trying to take Hannah.

Growling, he pivoted. "Go."

His instruction finally knocked sense into the man. Aimsley almost tripped in his haste to leave. Once the man was gone, he focused on Hannah. "What happens now is between me and my wife. You are to go to your room and stay there until I call for you. Do not think to disobey, or I assure you that you will no longer be participating in this Season."

Hannah's lips pressed into a straight line. "You are being unreasonable."

"You went behind my back," he countered.

"Paul is a good man." Her notes cracked, and he recognized that his niece was close to a wail. She was holding it in, which was just as well. If she wanted to be an adult, ready for marriage, it was time she behaved like a lady.

Like Sophia, who stood quietly behind him. Always the lady, his Sophia. He rubbed at his chest, in the vicinity of his heart. The ache did not subside.

He sighed, taking in the hurt in Hannah's eyes. "I know that he is a good man," he said quietly. "It does not mean he is the best man for you. Should you decide to sneak away, do not think Aimsley will help you. He has done everything in good order, and properly. I do not believe he will risk the ire of a duke for a young woman's impetuous actions."

Hannah sniffed, and he saw traces of tears beginning in her eyes.

Edmund wanted to hug her, but he knew from experience it would only release a floodgate of emotion and right now, he had another woman to deal with. "Go to your room," he said in a more gentle tone.

Hannah's face crumpled. She fled, her footsteps pattering up the next flight of steps. Swiping his hands down his face, he slowly rotated and found Sophia sitting quietly on the couch, her hands clasped in front of her.

The very picture of meekness. He scowled. No doubt a storm raged within her, but unlike him, she had mastered control over her emotions. Yes, she appeared to be a delicate porcelain lady perched on the edge of a couch, acting as though she hadn't conspired with his niece to go completely against his wishes.

A steady anger flared within. Clasping his hands behind his back, he stalked to the far wall. He felt her eyes on him. Good. Let her feel nervous. Let her understand that he was in charge. Not she.

But when he turned to check the status of her docility, he found her smiling. The flare shot into flames. He marched to the couch, glaring.

"There is nothing to smile about. Cease, at once."

"Do not order me about, Your Grace. You forget, we are equals." She stood, matching his ire with a peaceful solidity that gave him a moment's pause. "You shall not control my smile any more than you are attempting to control Hannah's heart."

She moved closer to him, and Edmund had the foreign urge to back away. Her perfume congested his brain. His jaw tightened. She had gone behind his back.

"You undermined me." He refused to step back, even though she had moved close enough that he could almost feel the warmth of her skin. She was a head shorter than him, precipitating the need for him to look down, and that was a mistake.

His heart beat hard and erratically, pumping annoyance throughout him. He wanted to argue with her, but staring into her lovely sea-green eyes was quickly cooling the simmer of his anger.

"I thought you disapproved because he didn't have his papers. Because he wasn't financially set," she said.

"And so you bought him a subscription?" He swiveled, stepping quickly away from her intoxicating fragrance and sincere expression. If he wanted to be able to think, he needed distance.

"I contributed to the funding he already had." Her tone was level.

"It's unacceptable. My own wife."

"Yes, your own wife with her own thoughts and her own opinion."

"But not her own money." He glared at her, recognizing that it was a jab, and not one he was proud of. Still. "Perhaps you forget the nature of our arrangement."

"Do you mean our contract," she said coolly, betraying nothing.

"Yes." He paced again, his pulse quickening. "You were to help her find a suitable husband. Not encourage a second son who cannot even afford papers. And he's bland. The man should have come to me sooner if he wanted my niece."

"Have heart, Edmund. He is young and perhaps a little terrified of one such as yourself."

"Do you mean, one such as the Beast of London?" A roaring filled his ears as all of his feelings found power in his anger.

"No." She regarded him in a way that made him

want to shake some emotion out of her. How could she show nothing? Nothing at all? His teeth grit so hard his jaw hurt.

"I meant," she said slowly, "one who is a duke of great wealth. But you do not see yourself that way. You wallow in the pit you have carved for yourself."

"I told you what happened." He paced the room, needing a way to release the energy within.

"Yes. You did." Finally a hint of sympathy in her voice, though that was almost more annoying. "And ten years later, you are using your pain as a reason to hide. You are letting a ridiculous, gossipy label define your entire existence."

"I married you for one reason, Sophia. To guide Hannah." He stopped pacing abruptly, standing directly in front of the woman who had upset his plans in every way. "My life was perfectly fine."

"Hiding at your Rennington estate?" she asked in a flippant manner that both made him want to kiss her and to toss his hands in complete annoyance.

"I like Rennington. It is my home. But now I am stuck in London—"

"Because you lovingly raised an amazing young woman who wanted a Season to secure her future."

His hands dropped to his sides as he regarded the woman in front of him. Portrait worthy, perfection, and yet he knew she felt life as deeply as he. Behind those composed features lay thoughts and feelings one might never know if one didn't dig for them.

"Do not try to change the subject. Do not try to paint me as someone I'm not."

She laughed, but it was without humor. "I did not make you raise an orphan. I did not make you donate a home for women wishing to leave prostitution. I did not make you give your time and energy to Lord Windley's causes." Her mouth pursed into a lovely, disapproving bow. "I did not make you act like a big bully when Hannah found a man to love."

"A bully?" He glared down at her, and she met his glare with an unflinching, sad smile.

"Yes. Things have not gone as expected and now you wish to order us all about. Try to intimidate us into bowing to your great, ducal power. I won't have it, Edmund. You have overstepped your bounds."

"My bounds?" His hands found her arms, drawing her close to him, so that their lips almost touched. "You are mistaken, Duchess."

"Am I?"

The way she looked at him created warring emotions so strong he had to release her, else he might kiss her. "You've complicated my life," he said, voice tight. "This was a contract between us. I did not marry you to mother Hannah nor to tell me how to raise her."

"Raise her? She is grown, Edmund. She is no longer a child. She is a woman who is ready to live her life in the way she deems best. What did you expect?" For the first time, a hint of frustration filled her voice. "Your life shall never go back to what it was. And do you truly want it to? Don't you want Hannah to find love and happiness? To have a family? Mr. Aimsley is a reputable, good man. They were thinking of running off to Gretna Green in Scotland to get married, I'll have you know."

Surprise rushed through Edmund, and it must have shown on his face, for Sophia continued a little more sternly.

"They are young and impulsive, but they know what they want. Unlike some people."

Was that last comment directed at him? He knew what he wanted, didn't he? Flexing his fingers, he watched as Sophia marched to the door, her head held impossibly high, her stride as regal as he'd ever seen.

"I am going to visit my parents." She tossed that over her shoulder and disappeared from view.

Edmund stayed where he was, dumbfounded. She had called him a bully. Said he didn't know what he wanted. But he did. He was protecting Hannah. If they had been planning to run off, and he fully realized Hannah was capable of such a thing, then maybe he was misguided as to how to control the situation.

Maybe there was some truth to Sophia's words. But how much? He stared at the doorway, realizing that her departure left more than the doorway empty.

Chapter Twenty-One

Apologies required humility.

A trait Edmund realized he did not possess in abundance. When the evening meal came around and Sophia still had not returned, it became clear that if he wanted a happy duchess, he had some groveling to do. He'd had all afternoon to think about the situation, too.

He had attempted to meet with Mr. Reed regarding the household budget and morale, but found himself frustrated by repeated thoughts of Sophia. He dismissed the butler, who no doubt was relieved. Then he went up to see Hannah, but she refused to open her door. When he threatened to crash the thing down, she dared him to do so.

Which caused extreme consternation. Of course he wouldn't crash a door down, and how like her to call his bluff. He took his bay for a vigorous ride in Hyde Park, instead. Even still, when he returned, his consternation remained.

He remembered the days when all he felt was anger or affection. Two simple emotions. Easy to handle. And now…he growled from his place at the long dining table. Sophia had disrupted more than his life.

And he missed her already.

"Reed!"

"Your Grace?" His butler must have been hovering in the hall, for he appeared promptly. Edmund quelled the bit of liking he had for the timid if not efficient butler, and held out a note he'd written.

"Have this delivered to Bow Street. Bring round my carriage. I shall be going out for the evening. I do not know how long I'll be, but keep supper warm. See that Hannah is served."

Reed nodded, took the missive and left. Edmund stood, smoothing out his waistcoat. A ridiculous movement. Sophia cared not how he looked. Of that he was certain.

No, she cared that he wouldn't let his ward, his niece, the girl he thought of as a daughter, marry a man of no standing and no fortune.

And wasn't that what had made him feel so deeply for Sophia? That moral code of hers that took marriage to be so much more than a grasping for wealth and title? More than a business contract? He had determined to make Sophia utterly happy, as happy as she deserved, and he had failed.

Her words echoed in his mind as he mounted his carriage. It clattered through the streets toward her parents' home, just as memories clattered through his mind. What had upset Sophia the most? If he could narrow it down, then he had a better chance of getting back into her good graces.

A worthwhile goal, in his opinion. Smiling ruefully, he looked out the carriage window. His apology must be acceptable and then surely she would return home. He was stubborn. He knew that. But he and Sophia would work through this miscommunication.

The carriage pulled up to the townhome, and without waiting for assistance, he jumped down and strode up to the house. He did not bother knocking. He simply opened the door. He owned the place, after all. The hall was empty, but voices could be heard drifting from a small parlor to his right.

"No. The duke must never know."

The words, clear and crisp, were unmistakably Lady Worland's. His head tilted. A butler appeared from a different door, but he held his finger to his mouth. He did not normally eavesdrop. He preferred to face conflicts headfirst, but her pitch raised an internal alarm.

Something was amiss.

He edged closer and Lord Worland's low tones became clearer. "He deserves to know, Martha."

"Why? It makes no matter now. It changes nothing."

"But I am tired of deceit."

"Just because you almost ruined us does not mean that I regret anything I did."

Edmund had enough. He stepped into the room and cleared his throat. Five very surprised-looking faces turned his way. So this was a family affair? Frederika began to stand, but he halted her with a simple look.

Sophia sat at an opposite couch, a book lying on her lap, her expression reserved. A pit opened in his stomach. Behind her, in a chair, Eliza sat with fear on her face. Lord Worland dipped his head, unable to even look Edmund in the eyes.

He turned to Lady Worland. An unnatural flush suffused her cheeks, but she met his stare with determination and a firm chin.

"I feel that I have interrupted something." He moved to where Sophia sat, and lowered himself beside her. He heard her intake of breath, and there was a flutter in the elegant surface of her neck. Her pulse must be racing. He frowned, turning to where Sophia's parents sat across from him. "Would anyone care to enlighten me?"

"Humph." Lady Worland returned to a pile of knitting nearby, making little smacking noises with her lips that might have been amusing if there wasn't such a grim silence to the room.

Lord Worland was shaking his head back and forth. Obviously the man did not approve of whatever had transpired, which meant he had not participated. Edmund felt a dark dread deepening within him. He turned to Sophia, whose coloring had paled to alabaster.

"Sophia? I came here to apologize, to beg forgiveness, but I now find that perhaps I should know whatever it is that you do not wish me to know." He raised his brow at her, noting the tiny, delicate flare of her nostrils. Her hands were twisting in her lap.

He had heard of deafening silences before. He had not actually sat in one.

"Did you all murder someone?" He raised a brow, scanning each face. They all looked so guilty, but surely there had been no crime. He leaned back into the couch, enjoying that the tiny cushions forced him closer to his always pleasant-smelling wife. He stretched out his legs. Folded his hands against his abdomen. "Come now, speak."

"Your Grace," said Lord Worland. "There was a foolish decision made and it really has no consequence to you, therefore I beg you to not insist we tell you…" His words faltered spectacularly.

The wife took up for him. "It was all in my family's best interest. And yours, too, I might add."

"Is that so."

She nodded emphatically, and beside him, Sophia shifted away. More elbow room for him. He spread his arms a little farther so that one elbow touched her leg. It was truly impressive how quiet the three sisters were.

"I take that to mean Lord Worland has not gambled away the allowance I've given your family?"

"Oh, no, Your Grace." Lady Worland shook her head just as vigorously in the other direction. "I have retained full control of those funds and my husband is both repentant and understanding."

"Excellent. But," he said, and leaned forward, resting his elbows on his knees and giving her a serious look, "I did not come here to play guessing games. So, do tell me, Lady Worland. What must I not know?"

Her gaze skittered to Sophia. There was regret on her face now. "I do not wish to harm the relationship you've built with my daughter. I never guessed…well, I simply did not expect that you two would develop feelings for each other. I mean, she has been mourning her late husband for seven years, and you…you were—"

"The Beast," he supplied. How he hated that moniker.

"You were known for not caring about anything or anyone."

"Was I known for that, or was it simply gossip?"

A flush suffused her face.

"You see," Edmund said softly, "gambling is not the only vice one can indulge."

Lady Worland looked deeply worried now. The knitting in her hand crumpled beneath the twisting of her fingers. "I hope you can understand." She cast another look at Sophia, and Edmund held up a finger.

"Quit looking at my wife," he said. "Look at me."

She did, tears pooling in her eyes. Edmund felt a pang for distressing her so, but there were also his own feelings and those of Sophia's to consider. Had her family ever protected her? He felt now as though he must do so.

Or perhaps he was protecting himself.

He did not know.

"You see, I was desperate." Lady Worland dabbed at the corners of her eyes. "My husband was missing, but I could tell no one."

"Because of your position in society."

"Exactly." She flashed him a grateful, quivering smile, little comprehending that while he understood her motives, he did not approve of them. "I was searching through Lord Worland's office for any help, any money, and I came across the betrothal contract that I had saved many years ago."

"Complete honesty, Martha," murmured Lord Worland. The man had become haggard and Edmund wondered briefly if he should let this go. But no. He could not.

"I—I knew it was not valid."

Edmund straightened. "Not valid?" That was news.

"My husband and your father had made it while gambling, and in their cups, in a moment of fraternal camaraderie. Later they decided to null the agreement, as neither believed in choosing their child's spouse. Your father disposed of his somehow. I can only assume, as I've not heard of another copy being discovered. But when Lord Worland threw his away—" now her hands fluttered "—I retrieved it from the trash."

No one gasped.

Had the entire family known that the agreement was not valid? His jaw hardened. "Go on."

"I had it added to our family financial papers where I knew our solicitor would find it at the right time, thanks to a note sent to check all our papers for any assets. You know the rest."

"All of it, Mother," said Sophia. Her voice was hoarse, and Edmund dared not look at her.

"Yes." Lady Worland looked down at her lap, then lifted her chin. "We were in a true bind. No more money."

"I had an aunt." Lord Worland sounded resigned.

"A faraway aunt," snipped Lady Worland. "We've daughters to come out still."

Sighing, Edmund waved a hand for her to continue and out came the rest of the sordid tale. How Sophia's mother couldn't believe they wouldn't honor the contract, and induced her cousin to relinquish her role as Hannah's guardian. And then she spread a few rumors so that others would not help him. It was so quintessentially what he expected from the *haut monde* Edmund couldn't even feel surprised.

He simply felt a hollow betrayal.

"Edmund—" began Sophia, but he silenced her with a look.

Sophia had known, as had her sisters.

He stood, tugging at his cravat, which had decided to start choking him. "I find that I am in need of fresh air." Without looking at his wife, he said in general, "Sophia should probably stay here for a few days. I'll be bogged down this week with parliament matters and charitable affairs."

He pivoted, leaving the scheming lot behind him.

He needed to breathe, to go out and think things through. He could expect this of her family, perhaps. But Sophia?

Suddenly, he felt as though he did not know his duchess at all.

Sophia could not sleep.

Donning her wrapper, she tiptoed her way down to the little garden area behind her parents'—no, Edmund's, she corrected herself—townhome. The last few days had been restless and difficult. Though she'd chaperoned Hannah to several events, Edmund remained home.

The place she wanted to be.

The rest of the house was sleeping. Not the servants, of course, but her family. Last night had been a late one. First they'd gone to the opera, and then they'd attended a rout. Sophia had been miserable the entire time.

She plopped into a chair that faced a neat hedgerow of trimmed and deliberately placed flowers. Morning sun had barely risen into the sky, casting its golden threads across waves of smoky, undulating fog. God's mercies, new every morning. She shivered, pulling her shawl more tightly about her shoulders.

Did she deserve such mercy?

Perhaps not. How quickly she had judged her father for hiding his shameful secret, but hadn't she done the very same? Instead of telling Edmund what her family had done, she had brushed the information under the proverbial rug in hopes he'd never know.

Because she hadn't wanted him to think badly of her. She swallowed, regret a lump in her windpipe, shame a burn in her soul. She could admit she hadn't wanted him to look down on her family either.

And perhaps she should have talked to him about Mr. Aimsley. She could have told him that she would use her own money to buy him papers. Perhaps if they had spoken privately, communicated, then a better solution may have been reached.

Instead, he now thought her dishonest in not one, but two instances. Would he ever trust her again? She blinked, not allowing any tears to slide out, and watched as the sky grew pink with the swelling sunrise.

How very frozen she had felt on that couch. Everything within had wanted to beg him to understand, to explain that she hadn't known about her mother's duplicity until after their marriage. She would have never gone along with such a plan. She was not greedy nor desperate.

Edmund had not seemed shocked by what he heard, but he had left so quickly after her mother's confession, that Sophia didn't know how he truly felt. Hannah reported that he paced about the house like an angry bear. She didn't think Sophia should return yet, that he needed time to calm down.

Sophia disagreed. Perhaps she would go today. Insist he see her. This entire fiasco had taught her something. She wanted Edmund in her life. She had grown to love him, somehow. The way he smelled, how he dove into charities, his loyalty to Hannah. And she adored that he laughed during plays.

So many things.

Yes. She loved him. A lighthearted feeling spread

through her, fluttering like a bird in the morning, headed toward the bright new day. In some ways, it was different from how she'd loved Charles. More mature, edged with fear, because mortality was always near. But this love felt deeper in different ways. She knew the risks of loving someone, and she was ready to take those risks.

Could Edmund, though? Did he even love her? She thought surely he must like her. And his reasons for avoiding a loving marriage were preposterous, even if he didn't think so.

Drawing a deep lungful of fresh morning air, she went back in the house and found Betsy in her bedroom, straightening the bed.

"Good morning, Betsy," she said, laying her shawl across a chair.

"Good morning, my lady."

"Your Grace," Sophia corrected her pertly.

"Eh, it's all too difficult to remember."

"You'll do fine. Why are you making my bed? A housemaid should be doing that."

"I take care of the duchess." Betsy shot her a crooked grin. "That's far better than working at a modiste's."

"Are you certain?"

"Quite." Betsy straightened. "Now, now, that's a plucky smile on yer face."

"Is it?" Sophia touched her cheeks, realizing they were bunched. She simply could not stop smiling. "I am returning to Edmund's today. You may pack my things."

She would go back, whether he liked it or not.

"Very well. I daresay you saw today's paper, then?"

Sophia dropped her hands from her face, perplexed. "No, I have not. There is good news?"

"In a manner of sorts." Betsy grabbed the paper and handed it to Sophia. "Third or fourth page. I suppose it answers some of the questions you 'ad about the duke before you married 'im. You'll be happy to hear 'e's no murderer."

Sophia blinked, then flipped through the pages. "What do you mean?"

"Look. Right 'ere."

"Try to pronounce the letter *h*."

"Here." Betsy tapped a spot in the middle of the paper with triumph. "Just goes to show, gossip is a terrible, terrible thing. I wonder if they'll keep calling him a beast?"

"Oh, no. No." Sophia's heart fell like a stone. She read the words, then reread them, hardly believing what she saw. "This can't be. How?" Panic flooded her, racing so quickly through her veins that her vision wavered. What must Hannah feel? And Edmund?

"Sit," ordered Betsy, grabbing her by the arm and guiding her to a nearby chair.

"No, I can't." Sophia pulled away. "Get me dressed at once."

But as Betsy worked, there was a growing certainty that nothing she said would make Edmund believe in her now.

She wanted him to love her, but if she couldn't convince him of her innocence, he would hate her instead.

Chapter Twenty-Two

Truth was an obsequious little beast.

Edmund sifted through papers on his desk, taking the mail when Mr. Reed brought it in and setting it to the side. He longed to speak with Sophia, to get her version of the events. Perhaps it was like with Mr. Aimsley.

She had understood that he didn't want the man for Hannah because he had no prospects. So she had helped Aimsley get prospects. Using Edmund's money, which bothered him, too. He groaned. Everything bothered him lately.

Why couldn't Sophia be who he wanted her to be? *Perfect?* The sarcastic thought pricked his conscience.

If he tried, he could almost see why she'd be party to such machinations by her mother. Even with her declared faith, perhaps she had felt the pressure to protect her sisters at any cost. Though her father had said something about an aunt. Nevertheless, he must have misunderstood something about Sophia or her moral code. At some point he'd need to face her again. Forgive her.

She was only human, and though her actions gave

him pause, they did not entirely reflect the Sophia he had come to know. He did not want to stay angry any longer. He would give her space to explain herself.

He tapped his fingers on his desk, and then reached for the mail. Invitations, a letter from his solicitor, something from Bow Street. And a letter from Hannah's aunt. She communicated monthly with Hannah, but strangely, the envelope was addressed to him.

Bow Street first.

He took a fortifying breath and opened the note. His detective had written that Mr. Aimsley appeared to be a man of upright character, with no gambling debts nor other apparent character flaws, and was indeed an officer in His Majesty's army.

Edmund dropped the letter. That was it, then. Sophia had been right that Aimsley was an acceptable choice. Though he wanted more for Hannah, he had grown weary of arguing with her. What did he know of matters of the heart? She would be well cared for as an officer's wife.

And if she had been willing to run away for the man... He sighed and rang for Mr. Reed.

Once the butler had been instructed to send for Hannah, Edmund stood and stretched. He'd been busy for days. Trying to avoid thinking of Sophia. What was she doing? Who was she with? Did she miss him as he missed her?

The thought pulled him up short, and a snag in his breath caused a short coughing fit. He grabbed his morning tea and gulped, as the horrifying realization dawned on him. He cared for Sophia. Enough to miss her. Enough to want her back.

"Uncle Edmund?" Hannah's small voice intruded.

She stood in the doorway, her hair mussed, her eyes sorrowful.

"What's wrong?" He crossed the floor in two short strides, and then grabbed her hands within his. They were icy cold. "Hannah?"

"You called for me?"

"Yes." He led her to the settee he kept at the side of the room. He rang for tea and then sat next to her. "I wasn't sure if you'd be awake yet."

"I've had trouble sleeping lately. I miss Paul."

"You should be calling him Mr. Aimsley."

Hannah wrinkled her nose. "You sound like Sophia."

Edmund grimaced, and Hannah patted his shoulder.

"All is well," she said. "I believe she's been a good influence on you and it is time for her to return."

He grunted.

"I want to marry Aimsley." Hannah patted his shoulder, harder. "I have been miffed with you for very good reasons. Surely you see that I am meant to be with him."

"Meant?" Edmund coughed out a laugh. "No, I do not see that. Tell me, why should I allow him to marry my wonderful, unique niece."

Hannah sat taller, a small smile beginning to curve her lips. "Because I deserve a man like him, Uncle Edmund. He is kind, patient, and he is quietly entertaining."

"What will you offer him?"

"Unadulterated adoration."

Edmund eyed her.

"Oh, fine." She let out an overdone sigh. "I will be faithful to him because I am completely loyal to those I love. I will also keep him on his toes lest he fade away into some kind of boring monotony."

Edmund closed his eyes and leaned back against the wall. "I didn't want to lose you, Hannah."

"I know." Sadness softened her tone. "But you will have Sophia. Especially now. All has worked out as it should."

"What has?" Exhaustion seeped through him. He had not been sleeping well. His muscles quivered with tiredness and his eyelids felt too heavy to lift.

"Life. Do you remember anything good about my father?"

Her father? He forced his eyes opened and sat up. She wore a frown, and on Hannah, frowns were heartbreaking masterpieces. Her green eyes glittered.

"I'm trying to remember anything good at all. To hold on to," she said.

He shook his head, trying to clear out the exhaustion so that he could follow her train of words. "He was a man of many moods. An artist. I have his paintings stored. You've never asked to see them."

"I snuck in," she whispered. "He was not very good."

"Hannah, why are we speaking of your father?"

"Haven't you seen the paper?" She tilted her head, her red eyebrows bright against her skin.

Churning began. Had it ever stopped? For days he'd felt like his stomach was in upheaval, his chest tight with nerves, restless. "No," he said sharply. "I have not."

Hannah popped up, walked to his desk and retrieved the day's post. She handed it to him, and then settled beside him. "I cried at first. To read such a thing, to have the scandal reopened." Her voice quavered.

He flipped quickly through until he spotted his brother's name. The story was in the gossip columns, but it was completely true. Every last detail.

Things he had only told to Sophia.

A wintry frost descended, so cold and numbing that for a moment, it almost felt as though his heart stopped beating. It simply iced over. He set the paper to the side. Focus on Hannah first. She deserved his attention on the subject of her parents. And his love.

"What do you think?" he asked Hannah through stiff lips.

She peered up at him, looking for a moment like the bright-eyed little girl who had turned his world upside down and made everything right. "I believe it to be true."

He nodded, every movement slow and labored. "Do you have any questions?"

"Do you know if the accounting is correct?" Her hands moved to clasp his, and he had the oddest feeling that she was trying to protect him.

He released a heavy sigh. "I wanted to shield you."

"I know." She gave him a tiny smile. "And you did, marvelously so. I could not have asked for a more loving or kind guardian."

"Even with my temper?"

She waved a hand. "Please, Edmund. I saw my father go off in rages."

Shock pierced the cold void, engulfing him. "You've never said anything."

"They are muted memories. I wasn't sure if they were real or not, and I had no reason to dwell on them. Not when I had to focus on irritating my aunt, and then you, and then my headmistresses. So many goals, Edmund, and not enough time." She shrugged, but her gaze still looked so sad.

He leaned forward and pulled her into his arms. "I'm

sorry, Hannah. It wasn't what I wanted you to know about your parents. It's not a burden any child should carry."

"And I didn't. You made sure of that. You offered a haven, and no matter how much I bothered you, no matter what I did, I never feared that I might feel your fists. I never feared your anger." She pulled away, giving him a quick peck on the cheek. "I'm no longer a child, and while it grieves me that my father and mother had such a tumultuous relationship, it is not a surprise." She put the flat of her palm against his cheek. "Love can be complicated. Now, if you don't mind, I must run and see Eliza. She will be so thrilled about my betrothal."

"Shouldn't you talk with Mr. Aimsley first?"

Hannah grinned, which thawed a fraction of his heart for a brief moment. "I'm sure you know me better by now. Do you really believe I'd tell him to quit courting me? Absolutely not. He is to standby and wait for instruction."

Edmund cracked a smile. "Very well. Keep me apprised of your pending nuptials."

Hannah gasped. "You are certain?"

"Yes. I've been assured that he is the good man you—and Sophia—believe him to be. Perhaps I should have had more faith in your judgment."

"Thank you, Uncle Edmund." She planted one more kiss on his cheek, accepting his change of heart with grace. Then she flounced from the room, her lilting gait still so young. She would always be a daughter to him.

The tender moment did not last long.

Hannah might always be a daughter, but Sophia would not always be a wife.

Not to him.

* * *

The duke's townhome was most intimidating. Sophia stood outside of it, drumming up the backbone to enter. Though the morning had been lovely, the pink sky held warning, for clouds hid the sun and an uncharacteristically cool breeze snuck beneath her shawl and chilled her skin. The scent of coming rain lingered in the air.

She rubbed at her arms, praying for courage. What God had joined together, let no man tear apart. Perhaps their marriage had not started out as anything special, but they were still married. They had made vows before God and witnesses. That had to mean something.

She drew her shawl tighter, praying for a moment, begging for wisdom. Then she ascended the stairs. She entered without knocking, and the front hall was brighter than the quickly dimming outdoors. Mr. Reed saw her and smiled. She smiled back and went toward the stairs.

There was a stillness to the place, and the front entryway gleamed with freshly polished floors. Edmund was probably in his office. She would check there first.

Her throat felt tight and scratchy as she slowly made her way upstairs. Her dress rustled quietly, its pale blue fabric sliding as she took each step. Betsy hadn't given her jewelry and had left her hair down. Perhaps it was silly, but Sophia had the sinking feeling that if Edmund could not believe her, then she would be forever cast from his home.

She needed to look as plain and unadorned as possible, for he expected subterfuge. He expected artifice. She would not give him that.

She reached the top step and walked slowly to his office. The door was open. Light spilled in a rectangle across the hall floor. When she reached the doorway, she paused. Edmund did not hear her, and so she took time to drink in the sight of his black hair falling forward as he bent over his desk.

His broad shoulders, spectacularly encased in blue superfine, were a little hunched. Scribbling sounded quietly in the room. Perhaps he had not seen the papers yet. Perhaps she had a chance to explain everything.

She stepped into the room, and his head lifted. Those dark eyes, hard and unyielding, did not even blink. He straightened to his full posture, an imposing figure that brought a curling, knotty churning to her stomach. She clutched the small purse she carried against her abdomen, forcing herself to walk to the chair across from him.

His face was a rough-hewn rock, all craggy shadows and sharp edges. His hands rested on the top of the desk, motionless. He did not smile as she neared.

"Edmund." She moistened her lips, for they felt unbearably dry. Shrunken even, just as her confidence was withering from within. "I must speak to you."

"Presumably that is why you are standing in my office."

His gravelly tones, deep and masculine, caused her eyes to sting with sorrow. How she had missed his voice. She stood near the chair, but could not bring herself to sit.

"There are many things to discuss." What first, though? What could she say to soften the cruel impenetrable stare he wore? "I am sorry about Mr. Aimsley. I only meant to help."

"I think there are other, more pressing matters we could discuss." His fingers folded loosely together. His lips were an unyielding line.

"Yes. Perhaps so."

"Perhaps?" At last, a break in his stony demeanor. Temper lit his eyes. "Why are you really here? What else can I possibly give to you? Congratulations. You married a duke. You've now an exceptional purse. And you've betrayed any trust I might ever have in you. You're nothing but exactly what I believed you originally to be. A superficial product of an immoral society. Manipulative." He spit out the last word, and his fingers moved restlessly.

"Are you finished?" she asked faintly, her heart thudding precariously against her ribs.

"I am finished with you."

"But I am not finished with you, Edmund." She blinked, because those terrible tears were threatening again, and she did not wish to cry. "Were you planning to hear my side, or will you assume the worst?"

"Assume?" He held up the paper, which she had not noticed lying on his desk, and waved it about in angry swipes. "This is not assumption. This is what I told you, word for word. What could you have possibly gained by revealing these details? Were you worried I'd take your pin money and so looked for payment another way? By selling my life to a gossip rag?" He ran his hands through his hair, his expression racked with torment. "And if you thought telling the truth of the past could better our lives, you are greatly mistaken. It will only increase the gossip and reopen old wounds."

His words pained her. They were tiny daggers slicing through her heart, but she willed herself to stay calm. He was used to betrayal. He chose to be angry and when she married him, she knew of his reputation. This was the Edmund she had married, and this part of him was merely a piece of the whole man she had come to love.

She squared her shoulders and eyed him with calmness. "I did not know that my mother had any part in our betrothal. I found out after the marriage."

"You did not tell me," he growled, rising from his seat.

"No. Why would I?" And she waited for him to think things through, to understand.

He rounded the desk, advancing so quickly she almost backed up. Through self-control, she locked her legs and stood her ground. He stopped inches away. "Perhaps because you are supposed to be an honest person."

"I am honest, Edmund. But I had no reason to tell you something that would only serve to degrade your view of my family and make you angry. Our marriage had already been accomplished." She lifted her hands, palms up. "Do not think I don't regret not telling you. I do, because then we would not be in the place we are right now."

His face twisted. "Oh, wouldn't we? You are saying you did not reveal the darkest part of my life to gossip rags?"

"Of course I didn't," she said, primly.

"You deny it?" His voice was a roar. He pivoted, clearly caught in his temper, and strode across the room. To the curtains, where he faced away from her, shoulders heaving.

Sophia bit her lip. If she could not handle this, then she would never be able to get through to him. Gathering her pluck, she joined him at the window and touched his back. She felt his ripple of surprise before he jerked away.

As though her touch was fire.

Did she have any chance at all?

"I did not tell anyone of your history, Edmund," she said quietly. "I do not know how the papers obtained the information, but it was not through me."

And she waited, her breath caught in her lungs and her heart barely beating, for his response determined her future.

No, not merely hers.

But their future. Together.

Chapter Twenty-Three

Was it possible to know when a woman lied?

Sophia's insistence that she had not told the papers tempted Edmund to believe her. He looked down at her, noting her flushed cheeks and trembling lip. She had already fooled him, though. Could he really believe she had not been in cahoots with her mother?

The entire family, suckering him into a marriage. He glowered at Sophia but she did not move away from him. She shifted closer, trying to take his hand, but he snatched it away and stepped back.

"You must have had a good laugh," he said coldly. "Not only did you acquire a rich husband, but he paid your father's debts and set you up nicely. I commend your acting abilities, Sophia."

She bit her lip, and then stepped closer to him again. Panic lodged against his sternum, icy and sharp.

"Why do you leap to the worst conclusion?" She peered up at him, her lashes sweeping across her fine brow. And her hair was down. He'd noticed something different but hadn't realized what, at first. But her hair…

it draped across her shoulders, straight and heavy, the white blond interspersed with caramel-colored strands.

Indeed, her entire outfit was simple and authentic. He lowered his brows, scanning her, thinking. Had she come here trying to look as young as a debutante? Because she did, but she wasn't young. She was a widow who had snagged a rich husband through fakery and lies.

Guilt pinched him. Surely her work with the ladies of the night was not contrived. And she seemed to truly care about Hannah. What could possibly explain why she'd revealed his secrets?

His jaw hardening, he crossed his arms. "Very well. I assume the worst because within the space of a week, I find out that you snuck behind my back, lied and then ironically told the truth that I did not expect you to reveal."

She had the character to at least wince. "I didn't sneak behind your back. You said Mr. Aimsley was not appropriate because he could not provide. I fixed that."

"I am willing to let that go for the other flaws in your character. Mainly, your avarice."

"*My* avarice." Her mouth dropped. Snapping it closed, she returned his glare. "I have repeatedly told you I had nothing to do with my mother's deceits. I can only humbly apologize, but I doubt you'll accept it because you're stubborn and convinced of your own self-righteousness."

"At least I am real. One never knows who the true Sophia is because she is too busy pandering to everyone around her."

She gasped. A deep flush mounted her cheekbones. Good. She should feel as upset as he did. Although a bit of conscience prodded him, he ignored it and instead welcomed the vexation that was so familiar.

He turned away, battling an internal confusion that threatened to rip him apart. The event that had caused him so much pain his entire life, that he had guarded so carefully, why would she expose that?

Summoning steely self-control, he faced her again. Her hands were bunched at her sides. Her lashes fringed with angry tears. He could not let her tears phase him.

"Just tell me why," he said hoarsely. "It hurt Hannah, you know."

"You do not listen, so why should I tell you anything?"

"As I figured." He moved to go around her, but she grabbed at his shirt, snagging it and not letting go, though he shrugged violently.

"You figure too much." She took advantage of his impeded path to step in front of him. Both her hands had him now, and though he could easily fling her away, he did not wish to hurt her. Her nails dug into his biceps.

"Sophia."

"No." She shook her head wildly. "I did not come here to explain why someone wrote about you. I came because—" She blinked hard, and a tear trailed down her cheek. "Because I do not want to live my life without you in it. I have already lost so much. I love you, Edmund." Her voice dropped, cut short by a broken sob.

Edmund felt gutted to his core. Never had he expected her to say she loved him. And yes, in some dark, recessed corner of his soul, he rejoiced. The words snuck past walls and defenses, they slipped into the secret hollows of his pain, and for the slightest of seconds, they soothed.

But then he remembered the article. The wan smile of his niece. And there was no other possible answer as to why or how the information had gotten out, except that Sophia had revealed it. They'd had a row and she, for whatever reason that she refused to admit to, gossiped. He wanted so badly to believe her, though.

The need smoldered within him, an excruciating ache that begged for relief.

He lifted his hands to encircle each of Sophia's arms, which still clung to him. Her small frame fit neatly within his, as though they were meant for each other. Hannah's words flowed back to him. *Meant for each other.*

He did not believe in that nonsense.

Gently, and though it took some force, he removed her fingers from his sleeves.

"You do not love me," he told her in a tight voice.

She wilted before his eyes.

"You said it yourself," and though he heard his brutish tone, he did not stop himself. "You fell in love with your Charles in the space of a month. Love comes quickly to you. It will depart just as easily."

He went around her, stalking to the doorway, and then stopped to face her one last time. "I am going to stay with Boxing. I expect you gone at the end of the Season. I will not annul our marriage. I realize now that my family's sins are not my own. Hannah pointed out that she has never feared me. And though the girl has tried my temper in numerous ways throughout the years, I have never struck her. I shall not cast you and your family into poverty. When the Season is over, you may stay in the cottage I have supplied for them. Rest assured—" and he set his gaze on her beautiful, deceptive face "—that I do not ever want to see you again."

Somehow Sophia made it up the stairs to her room. The master room. Betsy had not yet arrived, and shadows stretched along the floor in creeping silhouettes. The darkness in the room welcomed her, for her heart had been ruthlessly squashed by Edmund's insistence on believing the lie he had told himself.

There was no way to prove the truth. She lay on her bed and fingered the locket around her neck. She had already lost her wedding ring. It was gone, nestled in some pawnshop to be sold to some other soul in love. What reason was there to keep this locket? It no longer brought her peace. Charles was gone and looking at his portrait would never make her feel better. And now Edmund…gone in a different way.

For whatever purpose, God wished her to be alone.

She pressed her face against the pillows, willing tears to release the pressure, but they did not come. What was she doing here? Edmund did not want her. Would not believe her.

At least Mr. Aimsley had his commission. Lord Windley had his mastiffs to protect the charity homes. And her family had their security back. Eliza would debut next Season and all would be well. Sophia sat up and perused the room. Large, ornate, fit for a duke. Far removed from the tiny town house she had called home for so long.

She didn't belong here anymore.

She never had. She had been an unlikely duchess.

Resolute, she stood and unhooked her locket. She placed it in her jewelry box and then went downstairs.

Mr. Reed met her at the front door, a crease lining the space between his eyebrows.

"Mr. Reed, I shall need transportation, please." She paused, seeing his concern. "The Season has worn me out. Give me strong horses and a comfortable carriage suitable for a journey. I hope to see you again."

And she did. She hoped the man would not let Edmund's irascibility scare him off.

Once comfortable in the carriage, she instructed the driver to take her to her parents'. They were still abed when she arrived. So was Eliza, but Frederika sat at the kitchen table, a newspaper in her hands.

"Sister, you are up early." Frederika sipped black coffee. A terrible habit that Sophia did not understand, yet it engendered a fervent admiration for the strong woman her youngest sister was becoming.

"I am tired of the Season," said Sophia, grabbing a tart from the breakfast tray. Nibbling it, she sat across from Frederika. "What do you know of the cottage Edmund gifted our family?"

"Not much, and it is in Mother's name." Frederika lifted her gaze from her paper. "You never know what Father might gamble away."

Sad enough, and it had been wise of Edmund to see that.

"Is this gossip true?" Frederika pointed to the terrible page which had ruined the life Sophia had dared hope for.

"Yes."

"He deserves to be freed from that lie."

"It cast a shadow, certainly." Sophia gave Frederika a hug. She wished she knew who had released the truth, though. "I am going to retire early from the Season. Let the rest of the family know, please."

"Of course."

"Where is the cottage?"

"Outside of his Rennington estate, near Devonshire."

"Excellent." Sophia blew out a breath, feeling unladylike as she did so.

Frederika looked up with uncharacteristic concern. "Are you well? Should I go with you?"

"I shall be well enough." Sophia patted her shoulder. "Do you not have some symposium to attend?"

"Yes. But it has been dreadfully hard finding a maid to attend with me," she grumbled.

Though Sophia had not thought it possible, a little laugh escaped her. She had gone with Frederika once and almost perished of boredom. The poor maids. They probably hid whenever her sister called for them.

She left the kitchen and found Betsy in her room, still packing. Within an hour, they were on their way. The afternoon was as forbidding as Edmund's behavior, as bleak as the state of Sophia's heart. The trip would take days. She sent a note ahead to warn the servants of their pending arrival.

They stopped for the night at a small inn that looked clean, and that the driver assured them was safe.

"You should eat." Betsy slurped stew with gusto.

Sophia stirred her own idly. "I will."

"I haven't seen you eat at all."

Sighing, she took a sip of the stew. It was hearty and rich. She would try to finish the bowl, though her stomach protested. They had made good time today. What would the cottage look like? She needed somewhere quiet. Peaceful.

Like her old library, which had still smelled of Edmund's sandalwood the day she left. Her heart squeezed and she pushed the soup away.

"Are you sick?" Betsy's bright eyes probed, and Sophia looked away.

"Ah." Betsy clapped her hands, startling Sophia and causing her to look at her. "You're 'eartsick, aren't you?"

"Edmund does not love me," she said through numb lips. Saying it made it ever so real. "I did not expect him to, but I suppose I thought he might have some tender feeling toward me."

Betsy waved a hand. "Women always 'ope for more than a man will give—'tis the way of the world."

"That is not comforting." Sophia eyed Betsy darkly.

"You can give me that look all you want, but I've been around scores more women than you whose 'earts were dying piece by piece. Abandoned by their fathers when young, abandoned by their benefactors when old. It's a hard world." Betsy shook her head, a faraway look entering her eye as though remembering her own trials.

Sophia reached across the table and grabbed her maid's hand. "We are escaping that world for a while. Edmund mentioned the Celtic Sea. I have great hopes we shall see it and walk its salty shores."

"Aye, but you can't escape heartbreak no matter where you go." Betsy patted her hand.

"It is just galling that, knowing how much it hurt to lose Charles, I still let myself fall in love with Edmund."

"Well, he can be a charming gent. That dark hair and unexpected smile, and all." Betsy stuffed a piece of crusty, buttery bread into her mouth with enthusiasm.

Sophia tried another bite of soup, but it tasted like sludge. Her stomach hurt, her eyes burned.

"He'll probably be around," continued Betsy, chewing happily. "It's not the end of the world. There's plenty of other fish in the sea." She waggled her eyebrows, obviously trying to cheer Sophia up.

She managed a tiny smile, though it felt forced. Edmund had called out her inauthenticity. Said she pandered. Perhaps there was truth to his words, to a certain extent. "I do not believe in committing adultery, Betsy."

Her maid shrugged. "Me neither. That Lord Windley has us going to church, you know. I 'eard some sermons I've never heard before. Really makes a girl think."

They finished their meal and took a room for the night. In the morning, they continued their journey. It was slow and boring, though Betsy taught her a few card games she'd never heard of, ones of which her mother would highly disapprove.

After many long days, they passed Devonshire and turned toward the Rennington estate. The driver had told them it was close to the sea. Sophia drew in a deep breath, hoping for a hint of salty air. She hadn't ever visited the south of England before.

She admired the craggy horizon and the verdant land cushioning the hilly base of the rocky hills. This would be her new home. A place to rest and heal. To try to forget that she was married to a man who stirred her blood and inspired her mind and who would never care for her again.

Memories flooded her. Waltzing, his kisses, the way he laughed. The fatherly affection he displayed toward Hannah, so at odds with his usual countenance. Her stomach wrenched, and she placed her palm against it.

She felt Betsy's worried look but ignored it, searching the horizon for a hint of cyan. Edmund had said her eyes looked like the sea.

The carriage finally turned down a dusty lane edged

with colorful wildflowers and green grasses. When it stopped, Sophia ventured out slowly, her limbs stiff from the days of riding. Sunlight spilled across the earth in warm, golden tones. The carriage had stopped in front of a cottage decorated by climbing ivy.

The place certainly looked large enough for her family and multiple servants. Betsy gasped behind her, just as struck by its beauty.

"This is to be our home?" asked Betsy, her voice filled with wonderment.

"Yes." Sophia smiled. The driver and footman who had accompanied them began carrying their bags to the cottage door. It opened, and an elderly lady stepped out. She was about medium height, the same as Sophia.

Surprised, Sophia started forward, meeting her halfway.

"So you are Edmund's bride," said the woman, her voice comforting, her accent thick. "I've come to welcome ye."

Bride. Such a lovely sounding name for something that had not been lovely. Just a contract. Just a way to save her family.

She nodded to the woman, whom she had not expected to meet. Her eyes, a pale gray, crinkled into well-used wrinkles as she smiled. "I am Nelly Smith, but you may call me Nanny."

"It is an honor to meet you, Nanny." Sophia's voice broke.

Nanny pulled her into a hug, and then the tears that had eluded her for days leaked out and turned into weeping.

Chapter Twenty-Four

"You're an idiot." Boxing slapped his hand of cards on the table, annoyingly exultant.

Edmund glanced at his pocket watch. "I lost on purpose. I have somewhere to be."

"You lost because you're mooning over Sophia. Admit it." Boxing sat back with such a satisfied look that Edmund briefly entertained the thought of knocking it off his face.

Instead, he stood. "Come with me. The charity needs more benefactors. Your support would be welcomed."

Boxing laughed and followed Edmund out of White's. They hopped into his curricle and Edmund flicked the reins. As they rode through London's crowded streets, the summer sun beating upon their heads, Edmund rubbed the ever-present stitch beneath his breastbone.

Boxing, irritating dandy, noticed. "Feeling some heartbreak, are you?"

"Heartburn," muttered Edmund.

"As well it should." Boxing's voice took on a serious note. "Sophia is one of the finest women I know. Whatever you're arguing about needs to be resolved."

Edmund shook his head, wanting to call her a superficial, dishonest duchess, but unable to make himself say such a thing. Did he even really believe that? The more time went by that he didn't see her, the harder it became to hold on to his anger.

"How long has it been?" asked Boxing as Edmund turned the curricle toward a poorer section of London.

"Since what?" he asked irritably.

"Since you've spoken to Sophia."

"A fortnight." And a long, miserable fortnight it had been. He missed smelling the scent of her perfume. He missed the sound of her laugh and the way she teased. He even missed her disapproval when he deliberately slighted societal manners. "Hannah won't leave me alone about it. She keeps begging me to come home."

"My house does feel darker with your presence. The servants tiptoe about."

"I'm not that bad." He pulled the curricle up to the modest home he had let out to Lord Windley at a cheap rate. "Here we are."

"What is this?"

"It is charity, Boxing. Perhaps you've never heard of such a thing." He leaped out and together they strode inside. Lord Windley met them, as did two giant mastiffs and a mastiff puppy.

After introductions and some vigorous dog petting, Edmund left Boxing with Windley to discuss business. As much as he hated to do so, he needed to stop at his own home to check the post and consult with his butler and head housekeeper. On the ride over, he focused on guiding the horses through the busy streets and tried not to think of what he would do if he saw Sophia.

She had claimed to love him. He couldn't shake the memory of the earnest appeal in her eyes, the sincerity in her voice. If she loved him, though, why had she shared his deepest secret with the entire *ton*?

In the last two weeks he had fended off questions from the nosier of his peers, shook hands with those who pretended they had never doubted him and endured hugs from compassionate acquaintances. It had been a whirlwind.

Hannah seemed to be faring well through it all. He had hardly seen her since he'd given permission for her to marry Aimsley. She had sent word that the banns would be read this weekend, so he supposed he ought to prepare to attend a wedding soon.

When he reached his town house, he wrapped the reins around the post and then ascended the stairs. He had made peace with Hannah's marriage. He would miss her, though, and that ache added to the ache of missing Sophia so that his entire chest oftentimes felt as if an unforgiving vise encircled his ribs.

He went up to his office and took care of a few pressing matters. Mr. Reed dropped off the post, looking less fearful than usual. Was that a tiny hint of disapproval in his eyes?

Frowning, Edmund took the mail and bestowed a simmering glare upon his recalcitrant servant. The man scurried away. Shaking his head, he thumbed through the mail, stopping on a letter from Hannah's aunt, addressed to her.

Wait. Hadn't she written already? He flipped through the papers on his desk, finding not only the earlier letter he'd forgotten to open, but also the newspaper which had changed the way he thought of Sophia.

He set the letters to the side and then opened the paper. Teeth clenching, he reread the article, every word piercing him with memories. It was hard to believe Naomi was gone. His brother, too. He'd almost forgotten about Naomi's strawberry blond hair. When Hannah had been born and been what his father called a carrottop, there'd been laughter because his brother had brown hair with shades of auburn, and no one would have guessed he'd have a redheaded child.

There had been good times, he could admit, even amidst the bad. And wasn't that the crux of humanity; the joy interspersed with the misery? He scanned the article again, something niggling at him. It was that line about Naomi's strawberry blond hair not covering the swelling on her face. Had he told Sophia the color of Naomi's hair?

Deep in thought, he startled when a thud sounded on the ceiling. It was followed by giggles and more thuds. He set the paper and the newest letter to the side, but tucked the earlier letter from Hannah's aunt within his jacket.

He found Hannah and Eliza wrestling a trunk in the master bedroom. As soon as he entered, he could smell Sophia's perfume.

"What are you two doing?" he asked a bit too brusquely.

Eliza's blue eyes widened but Hannah gave him a jaunty smile. "We are collecting Sophia's things for her."

Something like a rock plummeted within his chest. Surely not his heart. "Whatever for?"

"For the cottage, silly." Hannah bent to push the trunk again.

"Stop," said Edmund.

With an overdrawn sigh, she straightened, as did Eliza. "You cannot expect her to keep wearing the same clothing, Edmund. Truly, sometimes I think you are daft, but then I realize you are simply a man."

"I'm confused."

Hannah placed her hands on her hips. "Do you mean to tell me you don't know?"

He scowled.

Hannah looked at Eliza, an overdone, dramatic shock upon her features. "He truly doesn't know."

Eliza winced, seemingly sympathetic to his plight.

"Spit it out, Hannah." He could feel a cramp beginning at his jaw.

"Very well. Your wife is at the cottage near Rennington."

"What?" Edmund knew he was yelling and didn't care. "Why?"

"Because you have broken her heart, you ninny. Look. We found this." She held up a gold chain with a locket dangling at the bottom.

"But I told her to finish the Season."

"Why would she?" Hannah held out the locket and he reached to take it. "I've been trying to get you home, but you've been avoiding someone who is not even here. I've seen how she looks at you. Even more, I've seen how you look at her."

He tucked the locket in his jacket pocket, next to the letter.

"You've correspondence from your aunt on my desk," he said. "Sophia isn't trustworthy. I told her something in confidence and the moment we had a fight, she ran to the papers."

"Sophia does not engage in gossip," Eliza spoke up firmly.

"Then she told someone who thought it important enough to get printed."

Hannah looked at him like he had just sprouted horns from his temples. "That's pure balderdash. I don't know how it ended up in print, but Sophia would never do that. You should have seen the chilly glares she gave me whenever I tried to share a juicy tidbit with her."

The girls exchanged looks and giggled.

Edmund glowered and gestured toward the door. "Go. I will see to the trunk being delivered."

"Oh, and can you do one more thing?"

"What," he barked, and Hannah laughed.

"If you are personally taking the trunk to her, then will you let her know our plan worked?"

He was getting tired of repeating what she said whenever she didn't make sense. He raised a brow and she continued.

"Sophia believed in Paul and me so much that she sold her first wedding ring to help him buy his conscription papers."

A giant overflowing of wretchedness swept through Edmund. Her wedding ring? She wouldn't. But, with a sinking feeling, he knew she would.

"Shocking, isn't it? That a woman you accused of avarice would sell her most meaningful item for love?"

"You were listening."

"I like to know what's happening in my own home." Hannah shot him a smug look, paired with a strong side of censure. "Come along, Eliza. We shall let Edmund handle things. *Everything*," she enunciated as they slid past him.

Life always continued, even when one's heart felt quite dead.

Sophia sat back on her heels, admiring the mounds of dirt where she'd just finished planting chard and flat-leaved parsley. The hazy scent of sunlight and fresh-

turned soil brought a refreshing peace to the afternoon.
At the other side of the garden, Betsy pulled weeds. She
seemed at peace.

Nanny had gone home to rest.

Brushing off her skirts, Sophia stood and shaded her
face to look out past the garden. The view behind the
cottage was magnificent. From here, she could see the
foaming waves of the sea, rising and falling in white-
crested glory. There was a steep trail she and Betsy
had taken to walking in the afternoons. It led down to
a rocky beach where they'd had picnics and even braved
sticking their toes in the cold surf.

She dropped her hands, noting the calluses form-
ing on her palms and the soil staining her fingertips.
She certainly did not look the part of a duchess now.
Digging in the dirt. Carrying water in heavy buckets.

She headed toward the gate, ready for a break. Perhaps she'd wander to the cliffs, overlook the ocean, ab-
sorb sun and salt. It had been a month, she thought, at
least a month, since she'd seen Edmund. She'd written
Eliza and asked her to send clothes and personal items.
The trunks should arrive any day now.

After all, even if she lived in the country, it did not
mean she eschewed society. She had found the neigh-
bors to be lovely, friendly people. They all liked the
duke, and when they heard she was his wife, they ex-
tended the greatest of courtesies. No one had dared ask
why she wasn't staying at Rennington.

She picked her way across the grass, toward an ir-
regular cliff. As she neared the ocean, the sound of
waves breaking grew stronger. The breeze filled her
senses with the bouquet of salt and sand.

Hopefully her trunks arrived today. There was

a country dance at an assembly hall nearby that she wished to attend. Just because she was not in London did not mean she wanted to be a hermit. One must stay busy in order to avoid the pungent potency of sorrow.

She was almost to the cliffs when the faint crunch of a carriage pulling up to the cottage filtered to her. She turned and with relief saw several men unloading trunks. Perfect.

Tonight she would dance late into the night, so that when she came home, she fell asleep promptly. She would not have to battle memories this evening, for she would be making new ones.

Nevertheless, her soul felt heavy. Just as King David's had. She had been looking over the big, heavy Bible Nanny kept in the library. This morning Psalms caught her eye.

Have mercy upon me, O Lord, for I am in trouble: mine eye is consumed with grief, yea, my soul and my belly.

She mouthed the words, repeating them until they carved themselves into her heart.

"Sophia."

Her name rode the breeze, faint. She blinked.

"Sophia."

She turned. A man strode toward her, tall and broad, purposeful. His overly long black hair whipped about his head, and as he neared, his dear features became clearer. Her breath hitched in her throat.

What did he want?

Edmund stopped a foot away, as though seeking words. His gaze probed, searching in that way he had, as though he was looking for the true Sophia. She hugged her body, the wind flogging her skirts against her legs.

He came closer, and now she could see the intensity tightening his features. "You have lost weight," he said.

She shrugged but did not respond.

"And you have not been wearing a hat." His finger reached out and touched her nose, where she knew a sprinkling of freckles had sprouted up. Her mother would be horrified. Edmund merely looked curious.

His hand dropped and he looked beyond her, to the sea. His expression was pensive.

"Why are you here?" she asked, no longer able to contain her fear. Was he going to exile her somewhere else? Surely he had other properties, bigger homes than a cottage, to which he could stow a wife. No one would even think it odd if they resided at different residences. It was the way of the peerage.

"Do you remember when I told you your eyes looked like the Celtic Sea?"

Every day. But she only said, "Yes."

"This place has been home to me for a long time." He faced her, his hair flying around his face, his eyes serious. "I wasn't raised here, you know. There are no terrible memories. Only the peace I felt when I ran to Rennington for refuge, and then I raised Hannah there with the help of Nanny. For her retirement, I gave her a cottage nearby."

"I've met Nanny." Sophia wanted to reach out and touch Edmund. She wanted his hug. His forgiveness. But she still couldn't tell what he was getting at, or why he had come. Surely not only to deliver her trunks. A message, perhaps? "Is my family well? Is that why you are here?"

The corner of his lip unexpectedly quirked. "Yes and no. I am here for you, Sophia."

Her heart twisted, and she pressed her palm against her bodice as if that would quell the pain.

"I am here because I have been miserable without

you. Do you know why I love that your eyes look like the sea?" he asked.

She shook her head mutely, though her heart had begun an erratic drumming.

"Because this sea is home to me." His hand lifted and touched her cheek, the pads of his fingers warm and endearing. "And when I look into your eyes, I feel home."

"But—" His hand moved to cover her lips, and how she wanted to kiss him. To pull him to her and show him that she would never betray him. But his words, those biting, awful words, still clawed at her mind. And so instead, she took his hand in hers and regarded him soberly. "You called me fake."

"I am deeply sorry, Sophia. What I failed to understand is that you are a woman of many layers, and that your society face is a part of who you are. You accused me once of bombarding others with my fickle emotions." His hands tightened around hers, comforting in their strength. "You were right. I was selfish, in a sense. And you are unselfish because you care for others' feelings and will withhold your own to spare them."

"I admire your frankness, though." She had to make sure he understood. "There is an honor in bluntness, and an authenticity in being true to oneself."

"Perhaps we complement each other."

She swallowed because every nerve ending was afire, and her emotions astir, and she did not know what to make of him standing before her like this.

"To get on with things…" And he smiled. "Your character attested to so much that I found it difficult to think you gossiped about the truth of my brother's death. As angry as I was, I struggled to believe it. Then

I realized the paper mentioned Naomi's hair color. And I had never told you that detail."

Hope blossomed as she began to understand his true reasons for coming to the cottage.

"Distrust has been my armor, and I too readily used it to ward off the very thing I want most—you. Though I tried to convince myself of your perfidy, I failed. You are not the kind of woman to air secrets."

Sophia stared at him.

"Then I happened upon Hannah and Eliza packing your trunks. I decided to bring your trunks myself, to apologize for how I've treated you, to try to explain all this. On my way, I read a recent letter from Hannah's aunt." His eyes flickered then, and a regretful look passed over his swarthy features. "To boil it down, my father was being blackmailed by a servant who knew the true circumstances of my brother's and Naomi's deaths. Father set the man up with a small fortune, but when he spent the last of it, he tried to blackmail Hannah's aunt, little realizing Hannah has been with me for the past years. Her aunt and uncle refused to pay and he sold the story to the paper. I have had him arrested."

Sophia sighed. "I am so sorry."

"No, it is I who must beg forgiveness. And I do hope you will extend it to me, for I have been lost without you. My anger has taken from me a most precious soul, and I want you back." He released her hands to dig into his coat pocket. To her surprise, he brought out a closed fist. "These are yours. Hannah shall marry Aimsley, but you will not sacrifice for that."

He dropped to his knees and opened his hand. Within his palm glistened both her locket and her old wedding ring. "I know that I am not Charles. I am not retiring nor intellectual. I do not have a tender countenance. And I know that the love you held for Charles was uniquely for him. But…" His gaze met hers, causing her heart to race with hope. "I love you, Sophia, my duchess. With every part of my being, I adore you and want to be your husband in every way, until death do us part."

Her eyes filled with hot tears and they spilled over, traveling down her cheeks in rivulets. She pulled him up and drew him close. Taking his hand, she placed it on the neckline of her dress, to the place where her wedding ring hung near her heart. "Do you feel that?" she asked.

His gaze turned quizzical. "A ring?"

"Our wedding ring, next to my heart. Because that is where you are, Edmund. I love you, deeply and truly. I should not have hid the unsavory parts of my life, of myself, from you." She wrapped her arms around his neck and brought her face close to his.

"I shall endeavor to kiss you and hold you close until I die, if you will have me," he said huskily, his breath a warm whisper against her lips.

And then he pressed his mouth against hers and tightened his hold until there was only the roar of the sea crashing in her ears, and the beautiful certainty that they would love each other until the end of their days.

* * * * *

LOVE INSPIRED

Stories to uplift and inspire

Fall in love with Love Inspired—
inspirational and uplifting stories of faith
and hope. Find strength and comfort in
the bonds of friendship and community.
Revel in the warmth of possibility and the
promise of new beginnings.

Sign up for the Love Inspired newsletter
at **LoveInspired.com** to be the first
to find out about upcoming titles,
special promotions and exclusive content.

CONNECT WITH US AT:

f Facebook.com/LoveInspiredBooks

🐦 Twitter.com/LoveInspiredBks

IF YOU ENJOYED THIS BOOK, DON'T MISS NEW EXTENDED-LENGTH NOVELS FROM LOVE INSPIRED!

In addition to the Love Inspired books you know and love, we're excited to introduce even more uplifting stories in a longer format, with more inspiring fresh starts and page-turning thrills!

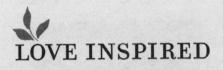

Stories to uplift and inspire.

Fall in love with Love Inspired—inspirational and uplifting stories of faith and hope. Find strength and comfort in the bonds of friendship and community. Revel in the warmth of possibility, and the promise of new beginnings.

LOOK FOR THESE LOVE INSPIRED TITLES ONLINE AND IN THE BOOK DEPARTMENT OF YOUR FAVORITE RETAILER!

**With her family's legacy on the line,
a woman with everything to lose must rely
on a man hiding from his past...**

Don't miss this thrilling and uplifting page-turner from
New York Times bestselling author

LINDA GOODNIGHT

"Linda Goodnight has a true knack for writing historical Western
fiction, with characters who come off the pages with life."
—**Jodi Thomas**, *New York Times* and *USA TODAY* bestselling author

Coming soon from Love Inspired!

LOVE INSPIRED
LoveInspired.com

LI41876BPA